Published by The Head & The Hand Press, 2015

Printed in the United States of America

Original cover design by Claire Margheim

ISBN: 978-0-9893125-8-5

PUBLISHER'S NOTE
This is a work of fiction. Names, characters, places, and incidents are
either the product of the author's imagination or are used fictitiously, and
any resemblance to actual persons living or dead, business establishments,
events, or locales is entirely coincidental.

The Head & The Hand Press
Philadelphia, Pennsylvania
www.theheadandthehand.com

10 9 8 7 6 5 4 3 2 1

Thanks for your support!

WAVE
LAND

A NOVEL BY **SIMONE ZELITCH**

Simone Zelitch
April 2015

For Jane.
I used to tell you stories.

TELL
THE
STORY

1

ONCE THERE WAS A GIRL who did everything wrong. Take the time in 1963 when she took part in a wade-in to desegregate a public pool in Chester, Pennsylvania. She almost drowned. She had been the only white girl in the demonstration. When the crowd took the pool by storm, she flailed and sank, and she was pulled out by a lifeguard who forcibly detained her as her Negro comrades were loaded into vans. The police refused to arrest her. They said she should go home and learn to swim.

"Did she?" Tamara asked. She was sitting in the bathtub, with her knees drawn under her chin. The tub was ancient, and the faucet leaked enough to draw a dull brown line across the porcelain.

"Eventually," Beth said. "Your daddy taught her."

So Beth had done it. She'd mentioned Ron. It was the third time that week, and though Tamara let it pass without much comment, that girl noticed. Tamara was the sort of girl who noticed everything. And if Beth was going to bring him up, these stories were as good a way as any.

Beth couldn't remember when the stories started. It might have been the time she'd dropped a book in the bathtub. It might have been after a day of teaching French to sullen engineering students, when she could no longer contain her angst and let it weigh down the first line about the girl who did everything wrong which fell, like a lead sinker, into the cozy hour before she put her daughter to bed.

Those were hard years. Beth was teaching part-time at two colleges and starting her dissertation, and she and her daughter occupied the top floor of a house full of graduate students who considered Beth bourgeois because she kept her own refrigerator. But the stories were a success. Tamara couldn't get enough of them. Beth rationed her to one a day, at bath time. Tamara wanted to hear about the time the girl crossed the wrong street searching for an open store where she could buy a mop, or drove down the wrong Mississippi highway and hit a cow, destroyed her car, and was picked up by two elderly and terrified Negroes who hitched that car to the back of their pick-up truck and drove her as far as they dared. This

time, Beth did end up in jail. The old men were arrested for running a
towing service without a license.

"Was daddy arrested too?" Tamara asked. Her voice was tentative.

"Not that time," Beth replied. "No, then I was on my own."

But that was not quite true. She'd shared the cell with a local prostitute
who slept with her skirt hiked well above her waist, and a foul-mouthed
teenaged girl who exchanged banter with the matron, mainly about Beth,
hardly the cellmates Beth expected when she'd volunteered for Freedom
Summer. Of course, Beth had been charged with prostitution. Also, the
words "on my own" implied self-pity, and Beth had been too busy to feel
anything like that at the time. No, that came later. Feeling came later.

NOT IN 1964. BACK THEN, Beth Fine, age twenty, was
always, relentlessly occupied. It was as though if she let herself stop moving,
something terrible would happen. Everything about her in those days was
marked by acute anxiety: buggy hazel eyes, frizzy red hair, a chin wrinkly
with concentration. She would storm into rooms, or back into furniture.
There wasn't a door she wouldn't slam. In those days, if a gesture wasn't
emphatic, it seemed, to her, half-hearted, and force was a form of honesty.

Such was her state of mind the spring she met Ron Beauchamp. Ron
had come to Swarthmore to recruit students for the Mississippi Summer
Project. His photograph had been in *Life Magazine* the previous fall when
he had handed out copies of the U.S. Constitution to high school students
in the Delta and then marched them to a courthouse by the Yazoo River
where he'd fallen to his knees and led them in prayer until he was struck
across the head and shoulders with a two-by-four. In the photograph, his
features were distorted with agony and the caption below read: *The Face of
Freedom. Ronald Beauchamp of the Student Non-Violent Coordinating Committee
(SNCC) cradles a copy of the Constitution on the Courthouse Steps.*

In that photograph, he'd looked about sixteen. In person, his age
wasn't easy to determine. He was slight and angular, and he wore dark
glasses that made him look as inaccessible as a movie star, but his voice was
gentle with fatigue as he said, "You kids got the prettiest college I've seen
yet. We sure appreciated those blankets you all sent down last winter. That
was you, wasn't it? Sorry if I seem a little unsteady on my feet, but I been
on all these Greyhound buses for two weeks now." He was well known in
the Movement for his cowboy driving, tearing across cotton fields at ninety
miles an hour to evade the Klan. He'd gone by bus, because the Greenwood project couldn't spare a car.

"You got to understand, in Mississippi, we Negroes got these old cars, right? Maybe twenty-five years old, but on the road. Because when a Negro has a car, it is a way to keep his dignity. Your car's your kingdom. And when you travel from Greenwood down to the Gulf Coast, you don't stop at some restaurant where they won't serve you. You make yourself a picnic on the side of the road and nobody can tell you where to sit, or what to say."

It was, he said, his first time out of Mississippi. He was a country boy, born in the Delta. The people in the Delta were a little slow, but they would all have to get used to that if they went to Mississippi. They would have to get used to a lot of things—outhouses, baths in tin tubs, people who didn't answer right away

"You all got watches? Don't bring them along. You all got patience? Bring that. Bring us books and school supplies. Bring typewriters. We got an office in Greenwood, got three typewriters working full-time typing affidavits, and two of them typewriters skip the letters *e* and *i*. Both of them letters are in *license*, as in the license plate of the car that keeps circling the Freedom House that belongs to a man we've been unable to identi-fy. Those letters are in the name of Corrine Saunders, a Negro girl who was strip-searched and beaten for taking her momma to our Citizenship School to learn to register to vote."

And then he told them about those Citizenship Schools, about the trips to the courthouse, and the Mississippi Freedom Democratic Party. He told them there would be danger. He told them there would be frus-tration. And maybe they'd know a little of the danger and frustration that Mississippi Negroes faced every day, and they could take that home with them and tell the story.

"Bring the goodwill of your families. We'll need you to tell them ev-erything you see—and I mean everything. And when the white and Negro Freedom delegates show up in Atlantic City at the Democratic conven-tion, come August, we need the support of everyone you know. We are David facing Goliath. We are Gideon's army, outnumbered, and you all have to be our trumpet. We may not have watches, but we know what time it is. That's why we all say Freedom Now. Not someday. *Now!* Hear me, brothers. *Freedom!*"

Beth rose to her feet to chant "*Now!*" along with the other Swarth-more students who filled the compact auditorium. She was in the third row, having arrived early to see if she'd run into anyone she knew from the demonstrations. But Ron Beauchamp had attracted a different crowd; well-dressed young men in ties, girls wearing ironed blouses, none of the Chester people. She felt conspicuous, unwashed, unbuttoned, a different class of person altogether.

A couple of kids from the Northern Friends of SNCC passed out the applications and brochures, and Beth took one of each just as the professor who'd introduced Ron came back to the microphone and announced that, regrettably, the speaker could not stay for questions. He would be expected at a fund-raiser at Carnegie Hall that night and had to catch a bus. Could anyone volunteer to take him to the Greyhound Station in Philadelphia?

That was when Beth called out, "I can take you all the way."

Ron turned then. So did everybody else.

Exposed, blushing to the roots of her hair, Beth clarified in a voice so high and trembling that she might have been singing opera. "All the way to New York. I can drive you."

And when Beth looked back on the girl she had been then, she found the next turn of events incredible. Ron Beauchamp, who'd been looking at the bus schedule, lowered it. He took a step forward. Then, he asked, "What kind of car you got?"

IT WAS A 1962 CORVAIR two-door, powder blue. The upholstery was white and very clean. Ron seemed to wake up a little at the sight of it, and when Beth opened the door, he checked the odometer and shook his head. "This ain't even broken in."

The same professor who had tried to find Ron a ride to the bus station followed him to Beth's car and made a final attempt to dissuade him from what seemed like an unnecessary adventure. "Aren't your people expecting you at the Greyhound station? What am I supposed to tell them?"

"That I'll meet them in Manhattan. Isn't that another name for New York, baby?" he asked Beth. His voice gave a little lilt when he said "baby."

The professor asked Ron, "And what am I supposed to say if you don't show up in Manhattan?"

Ron turned to him. Those dark glasses made his face unreadable. "You tell them I've been kidnapped."

BETH'S FATHER MAX ONCE TOLD her that if she wanted to make the world a better place, she could start by being a better driver. Like most of what her father said, it couldn't be dismissed entirely. Beth made a point of keeping her eyes on the road. Still, how could she help but let them slip sideways occasionally to look at Ron, the same Ron Beauchamp who'd brought those students to their feet, and there he was, sitting in her car, playing with some knobs and dials Beth had never even noticed. The windows were open and the late afternoon sun pulsed through. "Are you comfortable?" Beth asked Ron. "You can adjust the seat."

Ron said, "I like it just the way it is." He leaned back and seemed to listen to the engine. "You got a cigarette?"

Beth's former boyfriend was a smoker. She still had a pack in the glove compartment. "This is pretty old. I hope they're not stale."

Ron lit up. "Beautiful. Now, where do they hide the ashtray in this vehicle?"

Beth showed him. Then, she asked, "Do you know a boy named Marty Weinglass? He went to Greenwood last year. He was one of the ones who brought you blankets, and I gave him two sweaters. Did someone take them? The sweaters, I mean. They were brand new. My aunt gave them to me, but I never wore them."

"Why not?" Ron asked.

"They made my skin itch," said Beth. Then she blushed again. "I guess they probably itched the same for a Negro girl. But then maybe one person can throw something away and it ends up being just what someone else would want, you know, so you can't make assumptions."

"Baby," Ron said, "we take what we can get."

Something in the way Ron said that brought on silence. Beth risked another sidelong glance in his direction. He was looking straight ahead, with the sun beating on his dark glasses and after a while, he asked, "You joining us in Mississippi this summer?"

"I can't," said Beth. "I've got an obligation. I always work in the public library during the summer."

"Is that so?"

"I believe in fulfilling obligations. I'm an existentialist," Beth said.

Ron drew the cigarette to his lips, inhaled, and asked, "What's that?"

"That means I don't believe that good intentions are enough. We need to take responsibility for the results of our own actions, even if they have consequences we can't foresee. So, I guess not going to Mississippi is the consequence, right?"

Ron didn't reply. He seemed to be holding a thought.

Beth could guess it. Here was Ron Beauchamp, beaten to unconsciousness in front of the Leflore County courthouse, and she was talking about her summer job. In his silence, she read judgment. No, he wouldn't judge her. He would have more patience. No, for all his talk of patience, he would not suffer fools. Yet he had suffered that beating, on his knees and praying. Did he believe in God? Given the evil that he saw around him, was that core faith shaken? She wanted to ask question after question, but now she had squandered all the good will he could give her.

Ron didn't use the ashtray. He flicked his ashes out the window, gazed ahead, and turned the cigarette between his fingertips. "Where are we now?"

"Camden," Beth said. "We're taking the turnpike."

After some silence gathered, Ron said, "So you don't do much driving. Don't use the car much at all."

Beth said, "Don't worry. I'll get you to New York in one piece." Her voice shook a little, but she tried to smile.

Ron said, "The Movement got two Corvairs signed over to us last year."

"Oh," said Beth. "That's interesting."

"Yeah," said Ron. "A lot of what we do in Mississippi is just driving down back roads, picking up people and taking them to meetings, to the courthouse. We wear those cars into the ground. We got a new Triumph this spring, named him Tonto. Now, he's nothing but a piece of junk. Must have put around 200,000 miles on him."

Beth's own odometer was all the more diminished by comparison. "Poor Tonto," Beth said, just to say something.

"Well," said Ron, "we got a nice little graveyard of cars that gave their lives for freedom. We use them for parts. Of course, we couldn't get along without donations. See, you sign over the car to what we called the Sojourner Motor Fleet. We buy it for a dollar, get some Mississippi plates, and we're in business."

Beth didn't answer.

"We go through a car a month," said Ron. "That's why I'm so shameless about asking for them."

He turned towards Beth now, and laid one arm across the back of her seat. Beth kept on driving. It was hard not to look at him. Then, after a while, she forced herself to say, "I can't give you the car."

"You wouldn't be giving it to me," Ron said. "You'd be giving it to the Movement."

"I'm sorry," Beth said. "I can't."

"Yeah, sure. No sweat, baby. I'm sure you're sorry. If you can't, you can't." Ron tossed his cigarette out the window, and looked after it. Then, he sat back and stopped talking.

Soon, his breathing became audible. He was asleep. He'd turned his cheek against the seat, and Beth could watch his jaw move subtly under the skin. One of the things that Ron had said when he was interviewed in *Life Magazine* was that he could sleep anywhere, in an office that had just been vandalized, on the floor in Parchman Penitentiary, under a porch while vigilantes searched a house. It was his way of showing he was larger and more lasting than his circumstance. Just then, Beth was the circumstance, and he wanted her to know it.

She pulled off the turnpike onto an old state highway, a familiar route that took her as far as her father's house in Princeton. The highway skirted a pine forest and passed through farmlands and orchards. What if she *was* kidnapping Ron Beauchamp? What if she demanded that he take off those sunglasses and look at her? Sometimes a car would approach, and Beth slowed to let it pass, and it was like life passing, over and over again. There was a long stretch of winding road between two meadows. A white pick-up waiting to pass her moved in close enough for Beth to read contempt and anger on the driver's face. As far as Beth could tell, it was the world's contempt. How could she help but take it personally?

Then, Ron sat up. "Where are we?"

Beth said, "New Jersey."

"No. What road is this?"

"Route 206. What difference does it make?"

"This isn't a U.S. Highway."

"It's just as direct. Besides, this way we won't get caught in rush-hour traffic."

"Oh, man," said Ron. He was fully awake now, and he eyed the rear-view mirror. "How long has that truck been on our tail?"

"He'll pass us in a minute."

"Speed up. Get us on a main road!"

The truck filled the rearview mirror. Beth said, "I know what I'm doing."

But Ron shouted, "Come on—you've got to floor it!" Then, he lurched over and stomped on the gas and Beth's foot. The Corvair leaped and flew, and Beth gripped the wheel but couldn't keep the car from tearing off the road and into a plowed field where it rattled over furrows and spun to a stop when Ron finally pulled the brake.

"My God!" Beth said. Her heart was in her throat. She could barely get the words out. "You're crazy."

Ron didn't reply. He opened the passenger door and walked to Beth's side of the car. Then he said, "Get out. I'm driving."

"You'll kill us," said Beth.

"You were the one who almost killed us," Ron said. "Get out."

"It's my car," said Beth.

There was a silence just long enough for Beth to feel a throb of animosity. Then, Ron said, "Turn off the engine."

Beth hadn't even noticed that the car was still running. She took the keys out of the ignition.

"Now give me the keys," Ron said.

Beth passed the keys through the open window, opened the door, and, with legs like twine, passed him and started through the loose dirt to the passenger side.

"You're sitting in the back," said Ron.

"Why?" Beth asked him.

"Because," said Ron, "we're not sitting together."

Beth didn't have much fight left in her, and Ron's direct hostility turned it rancid. She did say, "The sun's going down. How are you going to drive with those sunglasses on?"

"That's my business," said Ron. Beth wedged herself into the back, tucked her trembling legs against her chest, and hugged them hard. She wanted to tell him to slow down. She was afraid to look at the speedometer, but she didn't think he looked at it either, and, more than once, she heard a siren and made up her mind to say something, but then he reached a cloverleaf with signs pointing towards the turnpike. There was a toll. When Beth handed him a dollar bill, he took it without a word and left the change on the dashboard. It rattled there for the next hour as they drove in silence.

Somewhere in there, Beth said, "I didn't mean it."

Ron didn't answer. Beth thought he hadn't heard, so she spoke again. "I didn't mean it about this being my car."

Ron spoke then. "Why shouldn't you mean it? It *is* your car."

"No it's not," said Beth. "It belongs to my father. It's in his name. I'm going to Paris in September and he'll want it back, but he says he'll give it to me when I graduate if I get honors."

"Oh, you'll get honors," Ron said in a neutral sort of way. He was trying to see past the truck in front of him. The traffic had stopped dead, no great surprise at five o'clock on a Friday evening not so far from the Lincoln Tunnel. Ron let go of the wheel and leaned back into the seat. Without looking at Beth, he said, "I know you think I shouldn't have done what I did. It's just, where I come from, a colored man and white girl don't get on a back road. Anything can happen there, and nobody would know until they found the bodies."

Beth said, "You mean, in Mississippi."

"I know what I know,' said Ron. "The man in the truck behind us didn't care what state we were in. He didn't like what he was seeing. If I'd known you were going down a road like that, I'd never have us both up front."

"But isn't that segregation?" Beth asked.

"It's common sense," Ron said. His tone had softened, though there remained a slight edge of exasperation. "Look, I can't make you understand. You haven't been there."

Beth said, "Does that mean I can't have an opinion?"

Ron sat back, and stretched out the joints of his neck. Then he said, "Baby, you can have all the opinions you want."

"Don't talk to me like that, please.'

"Like what, baby?"

"Like I'm some snooty white girl," Beth said. "I can't help being white and I can't help being a girl. And I can't stand it that you're up there like you're my driver or something. We're not in Mississippi. We're in New Jersey. We're about to go into a tunnel and if you keep those sunglasses on, we're going to get into an accident."

"And there goes your daddy's car."

Beth said, "Shut up!"

"I thought you said this was his car."

"I don't know! I don't know!" Beth was close to crying now. "I can't help whose car this is or who my father is and I can't help who I am. I can't help that you know things I don't know. Sometimes I can't even help what comes out of my mouth!"

Around them, cars and trucks soaked in their own exhaust, and the blistering landscape wavered like a reflection. Ron didn't respond for a while. Then, he turned in his seat and, for the first time, faced her. "Why don't you kiss me?"

Beth said, "What?"

He leaned over and laid an arm across the seat. He put his chin on it. "Seems we're stuck here," he said. "Seems you think you can't know what I know. That's right. You can't. But one thing we both know is that talking isn't getting us much of anywhere."

He moved in close. Now Beth could make out an indentation, a scar from his old beating at the courthouse that traveled up his temple and lost itself in his hair. The dark glasses made him inscrutable, giving the proposition a serious and academic feel. A lump of something lodged in her throat, and it took effort to swallow. Her heart pounded. Her red hair was electric with sweat, and Ron reached a hand to move it back. That hand stayed there.

Years later, Beth would remember little more than the awkwardness of the thick seat between them, awareness that in such still traffic they were on display, and almost from nowhere, horns honking like the ghostly calls of geese, which might have meant that they were being observed but also somehow implied that, somehow, traffic was once again in motion.

Then, Beth said, "I'll kiss you if you take off those sunglasses."

After a pause, Ron did. That's when Beth saw that he was terrified.

WHEN BETH TOLD THAT STORY, Tamara said, "She should kiss wrong."

"Who should?" Beth asked. Her mind had been elsewhere. She had been combing out Tamara's hair. It was a little gummy. When left to herself, Tamara never got out all of the shampoo, and she could never be persuaded to go back into the tub again.

"You know. The girl." Tamara scowled in a way that made her look as though she'd been practicing in the mirror. "Like she misses. And then she gets really embarrassed and runs away."

"You know better than that," Beth said. "The Girl Who Does Everything Wrong never runs away."

"She's weird," said Tamara.

"That's right," said Beth.

By now, Tamara's hair was braided, and she'd tossed her towel onto the floor and was halfway into her nightgown. She wandered to the kitchen table with her head still underneath the nightgown's collar, which was her way of letting Beth know that her statement was ridiculous. She had a nine-year-old's conviction that there was a right way and a wrong way to do everything, including kissing. She wanted this confirmed. Beth could not oblige.

Beth pulled a bedtime snack out of the freezer compartment. It was a Dixie cup. They always had the same thing every night after Tamara's hair was braided and before she could read in bed. Tamara always ate the vanilla side, and Beth ate the chocolate. "You expect to eat your snack with your nightgown buttoned over your head?' Beth asked her.

Wordlessly, Tamara undid a button. She managed to navigate a spoonful of vanilla ice cream into her mouth.

"You plan to sleep like that too?"

She nodded her head, or what would have been her head if Beth could see it through the nightgown. Stubborn girl.

"You're acting like your daddy."

So, again, Beth brought Ron up. She was making the effort. She'd just gotten a letter, the first in a long time, and in that letter, Ron had suggested that Tamara might want to spend the summer with him in Tanzania.

Beth had been startled by the request. After all, Ron hadn't seen his daughter in six years. Still, she put the best face on it. He had written, after all. He remembered that he had a daughter. The trip itself, of course, was out of the question. It was one thing for Tamara to spend summers with Ron's aunt and uncle in Mississippi, but did he really expect Beth to pack up her pink plaid suitcase and put her on an airplane to Tanzania?

Tamara managed to keep her head inside her nightgown all the way to the bathroom in the hallway, and then Beth said, "Enough already," and pulled it down so she could brush her teeth. Tamara's face was flushed, which made her look even more beautiful, and she bared her teeth in a grimace that revealed a little lint caught in the place where her last front tooth was growing in. She spat the lint into the sink and said, "I guess she couldn't run away. I mean, if she kissed wrong. Not if they were driving. Then she'd have to get all the way home by herself."

"Brush," said Beth.

Fiercely, Tamara brushed her teeth, catching her own eye in the mirror and turning her head, first one way and then another, looking at herself with suspicion. She rinsed her mouth and let Beth tuck her in, something she sometimes didn't want her to do these days. Then she asked, "Was it a long tunnel they went through?"

"No more," Beth said. "You can read in bed for ten minutes."

"Was it the tunnel of love?" Tamara looked sly. She knew where this could lead.

"Sweetie," said Beth, "just read in bed. I can't start another story now. You know the rules. Besides," she added under her breath, "It's impossible."

Tamara caught that, as Beth knew she would. "What is?"

"You can't kiss wrong."

"What?"

"You heard me," said Beth. "You can't kiss wrong. Sometimes the wrong person, but not the wrong kiss. Now do you want to read in bed or should I turn out the light?"

But these were deep waters. Tamara looked cross and showed no sign of picking up a book. "Why do you always do that, Mom?" she asked Beth. "Why do you always say things that don't make sense?"

2

IN 1971, BETH CAME BACK to Philadelphia determined to complete her unfinished undergraduate degree and to move, with an unearthly swiftness, though a doctoral program in French literature. At the time, it didn't strike her as a hard thing to do, not nearly as hard as what she'd been trying to do since 1964.

She had two weeks before her daughter would arrive from Mississippi, where she had been staying with Ron's aunt and uncle. She had to find them a place to live, register her at the local nursery school, and generally settle into a routine. She discovered that her transcript from Swarthmore had never managed to make it to Temple University in time for her credits to be accepted, and she sat in the office, surrounded by bored and cranky young people in a similar position. She felt some passing interest in what else her record might contain.

She was still skinny then. She wore black jeans and a black sweater, and her hair was pulled away from her face with a dirty white band. While she waited for an underling to fish out her records, she picked at the skin around her fingers, a habit she'd had when she was a little girl and which had resurfaced only recently. She sensed, and somehow hoped, that she was scaring the students around her. Not to scare them felt a little like she was giving up something valuable.

A clerk appeared and said, "I'm afraid that even if we had that transcript, the credits won't be acceptable."

"Of course they're acceptable," said Beth. She stood up, conscious that whatever she'd been holding on her lap fell to the floor.

"It's been more than seven years."

"And what? Education was worth less seven years ago?" She took a step forward and tried to keep her temper. "Look, I spoke to Professor Mercer on the phone, and he didn't say anything about expired credits. He said there would be no problem."

"He was misinformed," the clerk said, gently. She was probably no older than Beth, but dressed in a manner appropriate to her age, in a skirt and blouse. "You can matriculate as a freshman, of course."

"I don't have time for this," Beth said. "Look, I'll just call Professor Mercer in the French Department. He'll explain." She felt a little short of breath but fought the urge to sit down. "Give me the phone."

"I'll give you an application," the clerk said, and she turned, but Beth reached across the little fence of the divider and grabbed the woman's shoulder.

"Give me the fucking phone."

Her hand was cold. She could feel the impact of her own grip all the way down her arm. The woman gave Beth a long look and said, "Excuse me?"

"Give me the phone. I have to call Professor Mercy."

She freed herself and said to Beth, "Ma'am, I have to ask you to leave until you calm down. There are other people waiting."

"Waiting for what? This school's a piece of shit!" Beth was only slightly aware that she was shouting. Her head swam, and she backed into her seat and, without realizing she had done so, put her head between her knees and kept it there for a long time. People made space for her, but no one came to cart her away. When she thought about it later, she realized that they'd assumed she was a junkie.

Beth walked through that first week feeling as though, at any moment, she would just stop walking, sit on a curb, and put her head back between those knees, which seemed to be the right place for it. Yet aside from the incident in the office, she didn't step over the line. She managed to return, find another clerk, and get most of her transfer credits accepted. She took the first available apartment, in a basement where the furnace and hot water heater gurgled night and day. She pulled herself together, almost literally. Buttoning her shirt, working a belt into the loops of her jeans, tying her shoes, were acts of will, and also acts of faith. She had to be okay by the time that Ron's Aunt Theresa arrived from Mississippi with Tamara.

She was okay. Beth had learned that if she pretended something for long enough, it would become true. She could pretend that she could take her daughter's hand at the bus station, lead her away from a tearful lady she called Grandma Risa, whom she clearly loved, and that somehow, it was appropriate that she should do so. She could pretend that she was capable of doing two semesters' work in one, taking classes through the summer, and completing her Masters Degree before she turned thirty. She could find daycare, could get by on a two thousand dollar a year stipend, could even wake up one morning smiling, as though a day were something she looked forward to. She started to dress a little less like a nihilist and a little more like a graduate student, and her eyes emerged from raccoon depths and gave off a mild, steady glow of interest in the world.

Still, there were evenings when she would sit at her desk after she'd put Tamara to bed, and she'd feel a stupor overtake her. It was a luxury. In the circle of light thrown by the goose-necked lamp, she'd sit, looking at nothing, sometimes all night.

Once, she was sitting that way when she felt fingers on her cheeks. It was Tamara, in her nightgown, who stood right in front of her, pulling the corners of her mouth up. She said, "Be merry."

"All right," said Beth. "I'll be merry." She put her arms around Tamara, hoisted her up, and carried her to bed, and she intended to leave her there, but Tamara wouldn't let her go.

"Sleep," Beth said.

Tamara said, "Stay with me."

Beth did stay with her, first sitting on the edge of the bed and finally stretching out beside her, something she didn't like to do because it seemed as though it might become a habit. Sometimes, she'd think of something Larry Walsh had said to her during the Waveland conference. She had, he'd claimed, inherent buoyancy. She would outlast her own mistakes, outlive her friends. She'd been insulted at the time: It seemed to be another way of calling her a floater, someone who drifted from project to project, drunk on personal freedom. Now, however, she knew that it meant she wasn't free at all. She would be the one who would surface and survive, who had to go on with the business of living.

WHEN BETH FINE JUMPED INTO that public pool in Chester, she knew she couldn't swim, but what was she supposed to do? She had to jump. It was too late to back out. She had already pulled off her wrap-around skirt and laid it with the other clothing by the side of the pool, and there seemed to be so many people that she managed to convince herself they'd hold her up. They didn't. It was all far too chaotic, and she had confused the deep and shallow end, and then there was the throbbing light at the pool's bottom, the limbs dangling and passing, a foot in her jaw, and finally a wrenched arm, rough, pulling, and the surface. She shivered on concrete. "I'm alright," she said to the Negro girl who threw a towel over her. "Really, don't worry about me."

By then, she'd been going out with Marty Weinglass for a while. She'd met him in a seminar the spring of her freshman year, where they were expected to read texts in the French original. Marty had an unapologetically atrocious accent, but he also sat next to a Senegalese student who spoke such beautiful French that Beth tried to engage that student in a conversation after class. Marty broke right in and said, in English, "I've seen you in Chester. What's a girl like you doing in Chester?" When she said she'd never been to Chester, he said, "Oh, guess I met your *doppelgänger*," in a tone that made Beth blush clear from her neck to her hairline. When he heard she was going to Paris, he asked, "Why? Camus is dead." Then, he gave her a look from underneath his curly hair and smiled enough to show some canines. The student from Senegal said to Beth, in French, "*He likes you. I can tell.*"

That winter, when Marty came back from a trip to Greenwood, Mississippi where he dropped off donations of clothing and blankets, he went straight to Beth's dorm room and collapsed in her arms. He slept for twenty-seven hours. Beth lay beside him with eyes open, watching his chest rise and fall. She was so proud he was her boyfriend that she didn't even bother to hide the evidence. His cigarettes were all over her windowsill. His black hairs were in the little sink she shared with suitemates. His presence made her a partner in what had done, and after he retreated to his own apartment, she went with him and cooked him a French meal from a cookbook, and they sat naked on his mattress and shared the cutlet and escalloped potatoes until his roommate came in, and then she scrambled into one of his T-shirts and wore it home.

Then, Marty went to a demonstration in Cambridge, Maryland and got a face full of tear gas. He was treated at a Negro hospital and returned half-blind. Beth put compresses on his eyes and tried to keep his friends away, but it wasn't long before she realized that he didn't much want her there either.

By March, Marty had moved to Chester with a group of organizers. He mentioned one girl in particular, Missy, who'd driven in from Michigan and who, Beth gathered, had started a very successful group for unwed mothers in Detroit. If it was so damned successful, what was she doing in Chester, Pennsylvania? Marty said, "Come on. You ought to know by now that the point is to make yourself obsolete."

Beth went cold when he said that. She just stared.

"Obsolete," Marty repeated. He obviously liked the word. "It's nothing personal. We've grown apart politically. You're still a liberal who wants to help Negroes."

There was a knot in Beth's throat, and she tried to loosen it with something like a laugh. "What do you want to do? Hurt Negroes?"

"Liberal paternalism does hurt Negroes," said Marty.

"Tell me," said Beth. "Did those blankets hurt the Negroes in Greenwood? If they did, why did they ask for them?"

Marty just smiled. "They wanted white kids down there to deliver them. Just like they're asking white kids to go to Mississippi this summer.

Because that's the only way people pay attention."

"Do you realize how much you sound like my father?" Beth asked him.

It was the lowest blow she could manage, but Marty just said, "I could do worse."

In fact, Beth suspected that Marty had a secret respect for her father, who had met him only once and treated him dismissively. Marty wasn't used to being dismissed, and at the time, it had made him sulky. Now, Beth realized that a little dismissiveness on her own part might not have hurt.

MAX FINE WAS A PROFESSOR of Mathematics at the Institute for Advanced Studies in Princeton, and his sole comment on meeting Marty Weinglass was, "Is that boy French?" That seemed to be the only way he could fathom Beth's interest in him. As for Beth's own involvement in anti-segregation demonstrations, he said, "Why are you wasting your time in that dismal charity work?"

Beth had been surprised. "I didn't think you'd mind. Segregation's an irrational system."

"And it's not your business," her father said. "Your participation is not only futile, Bitsy. It's condescending."

"We're all human beings," Beth said.

"Nor," said her father, "do you share the risks involved."

"That's just why I go. To share the risks."

Her father paused and finally said, "Now you've lost me, Bitsy. I was attempting to explicate a process and you've leapt into what I can only call ethical arrogance."

Those were the sorts of conversations Beth had with her father. He had been against her choosing Swarthmore on the grounds that it was a Quaker college and Quakers were the most ethically arrogant people on earth. He had initially been against her year in Paris too, and had relented only when it was clear that the program would concentrate on linguistics, rather than what he called "garbage philosophy," his general word for the range of thought that fell under the heading of existentialism.

"You don't even read French," said Beth. "How would you know?"

"I've read Pascal in translation," said Max. "There's a French Philosopher for you! At least he understood numbers." Then, he pulled out a copy of *The Pensées*, and said, "Add it to your list, Bitsy. I wish you'd change your major from French to philosophy. Your mind lacks discipline."

"And yours lacks imagination." Beth said.

Max Fine just laughed. "Another name for that, daughter, is humility. I know my limitations. I do not yet think you have discovered yours."

A FEW DAYS AFTER SHE'D DROPPED Ron Beauchamp in New York, Beth showed her father the application for the Mississippi Summer Project. She'd brought the brochure as well, a flier folded in four, with an arresting photograph on the cover of a young Negro boy looking over his shoulder, the cheeks, nose and chin liquid with sunlight, lips parted and eyes hooded.

"I'll need five hundred dollars for expenses," Beth said.

"Expenses?" Max Fine put the brochure down. "You mean I'm supposed to pay for you to be used?"

Beth kept her cool. "Who do you think is using me?"

"Bitsy," Max said, "I'm sorry. Here I draw the line."

"Don't you even care what happens in Mississippi?"

"I care, if I may be so bold, what happens to my daughter," he said. "You have your own work to do. They're expecting you at the library."

"The library can do without me. There's such a thing as a higher obligation. And I've been doing stuff like this all year, dad. You know about those bus trips down to Maryland."

"This is no extracurricular activity. This is enlisting in a war."

Beth bristled. "Those people in Mississippi are non-violent."

"All the people, Bitsy? Have you spoken with them, individually? Particularly the white ones. I'm sure they would welcome a consultation."

There was something in his tone that caught Beth short. Also in his face, which had broken into a sweat. He seemed about to reach for a book, and Beth forestalled him.

"This is useless," she said. She rose from her chair. "I can always get Aunt Bea to sponsor me. You know she will."

"What your Aunt Beatrice does or doesn't do," her father said, "is a mystery to me. I know I can't forbid you. But I can tell you as clearly as I can that you're making a mistake. What is the wisdom of asking a girl like you to go to Mississippi?"

The question stung. Beth took the application and brochure and started for the door.

"Reason it out, Bitsy. Ask yourself why you need to go all the way to Mississippi to find Negroes. There are plenty of Negroes in Princeton, not half a mile away, up Witherspoon Street. If you'd like, I would be happy to draw you a detailed map, and you could drive there this afternoon. Try knocking at their doors sometime. Ask them if they could use a little help."

Had HER FATHER REALLY THOUGHT she was in danger? It seemed unlikely. After all, surely Princeton, as well as Swarthmore, was full of students heading down to Mississippi for the summer. There would be federal protection. They'd be registering voters, not organizing sharecroppers. Then Beth understood. This was something her mother would have done.

Beth was nine when she had been told her mother died. She said, "You mean she's not coming back?" Her mother had been away quite a bit that year, but she'd always returned after a month or two. Aunt Beatrice had come in from New York where she worked for Eleanor Roosevelt, and she said, "Any time you want to come live with me, all you have to do is show up on my doorstep." Later, she formally approached Beth's father and said she had called her lawyer and intended to make Beth her legal ward.

Although Beth loved Aunt Beatrice, when she heard this, she became terrified and cried out, "I want to stay with daddy!"

Max Fine, never quick to show affection, looked a little shaken. He knelt down to stroke the back of her head. "Bitsy, I want you to stay with me too. But you must know your mother's not coming back."

"I know," said Beth.

"I can't be mother and father to you both," he said. "I can only be myself. Is that okay?"

"Don't speak to her that way," said Aunt Beatrice. "You're asking her to agree to something she can't possibly understand."

"I do so understand!" Beth said. Her voice was fierce.

Did she understand? Her father's face, so close to her own, looked unfamiliar, florid, tragic. His hand felt rough and strange on the back of her head. As years passed, slowly, Beth would know what her aunt meant, but she never regretted her decision. What could Aunt Beatrice give her but a second-rate version of what she had lost?

WHAT HAD BETH FINE LOST? She couldn't put it into words. When Beth told her Aunt Bea about the Summer Project, she hesitated. "Honey, it's admirable. It's right up your alley. But aren't you a little young?"

"I'm twenty," Beth said. "I'll be twenty-one in August." They had met for lunch at a smart restaurant with a view of the U.N. building, not so far from the office where Aunt Bea still worked for the Eleanor Roosevelt Foundation. Beth had brought along the brochure. It was worn from frequent handling, and Beth had spent so long looking at the picture of that soulful Negro boy that he had started looking back. Aunt Beatrice flipped it over and opened it like an accordion.

"Well, voter registration, freedom schools, community centers. Sounds perfectly legitimate."

"It is legitimate," Beth said.

"Aren't these the people who are forming some kind of rump party— the Freedom Democrats?" Aunt Beatrice asked. "I think they've called our office. They want to unseat the regular Mississippi delegates at the convention. It's certainly a long shot. But admirable. Just the sort of thing *she* would have approved of." Aunt Bea meant Eleanor Roosevelt, but for a strange, dizzying moment, Beth thought she was talking about her mother. "I suppose you'll need references. And press contacts. Let me get you the names of some people who can help."

She drew out a business card from a small fold in the front of a gray purse that matched her gloves.

"You'll have to write me," Aunt Beatrice said. "Every week."

"I'll be fine," Beth said.

"You can't know that," said Aunt Bea.

There'd been some stories about Vivian's year in Los Alamos, where Max Fine was posted during the war. She'd volunteered at a clinic in a Navajo reservation, though Beth was never clear about just what she did there. Then there was the time she got into trouble when she took a short-cut through a section of the compound that was quarantined. That might have been what got Max Fine exiled to Princeton where he was lucky to find work as a research assistant. Vivian Fine had a habit of —what was the word she was looking for? A habit of trespassing. Then, she died.

Beth was still not sure how her mother died. There had been absences. Absences implied illness. She'd lie down a lot. The same couch was still in the living room in Princeton, long and hard, with scrubby green upholstery. Beth had sometimes laid a cool towel on her mother's forehead. Vivian Fine as Beth had known her was already a diminished version of the woman she had been. Beth would see photographs of her mother as a girl, laughing with Aunt Bea beside Lake Michigan, her big hat almost flying off her head.

In September, Beth would go to Paris. She knew enough French to join in conversations with interesting strangers. Yet she would have nothing interesting to say to them. She would always be on the outside, looking in. Her father always told her that distance was the better part of wisdom, and like much of what her father said, it couldn't be dismissed entirely.

Yet that afternoon in the Corvair, when she and Ron had kissed with the wedge of the seat between them, she'd felt a flutter in her heart. Every time he had called her "baby," he had stepped across a line, and gone somewhere forbidden. She knew that now. The open panic on Ron Beauchamp's face had been a dare.

W HEN BETH AND RON FINALLY arrived in New York, Beth was sitting in the front seat, and Ron drove the wide streets with one arm around her and the other on the wheel. There was still hay and mud stuck to the side of the car, and what had happened on the way felt as though it had taken place in another lifetime.

Suddenly, Ron gave the horn a honk, slammed on the brake, jumped out, and ran straight for a skinny white boy who shouted: "You asshole! How was I supposed to know you weren't at the station?"

He'd opened his arms, and Ron threw himself into them as though they had been drowning until they found each other. They held on for so long that they seemed to have forgotten where they were. That was the first time Beth saw the SNCC hug. It was the way two Movement people met. They knew they'd only gotten that far through sheer luck and the grace of God, so they held on and held on, and when they let go, it was like letting go of luck and grace and not being sure when they would see it again.

The white boy was Frank Court. He was the son of a Mississippi sharecropper, a Freedom Rider, and just now Beth hated him from the heart because Ron Beauchamp had stepped back into the pages of *Life Magazine*, into someone she couldn't touch, who had nothing to do with her at all. "Man," Frank Court said. "You can't just do that. You can't not show up at the bus station. Even in New York. I'm not kidding. Who's this?" he asked, referring to Beth.

"Oh," said Ron. "That's Beth Fine. She's coming to Mississippi this summer, and she's giving us her car." He put his hand on the hood of the Corvair. "Isn't she cute? I named her Bluebell."

3

LARRY WALSH SPECIFICALLY ASKED FOR no white summer volunteers in
Melody. That meant that he might get no volunteers at all, and that
was fine with him. He'd come to Melody with nothing more than a couple of names on an index card and now he had a nice little project going.
"I don't want a bunch of over-privileged fools keeping my people down."

"They're not *your people*, Larry," said Frank Court.

"Oh, shut up. You know what I mean," Larry said. The two were
sitting on the floor of a workroom in the Greenwood Freedom House,
which was in the midst of preparing for the Summer Project. The room
was stuffed with stacks of registration forms for the Mississippi Freedom
Democratic Party, and assorted sleeping bags.

Ron was hunched over the Speed-O-Print machine they called the
Liberator. The model was too old and the new pad was too short, but as
the official SNCC mechanic, Ron was supposed to be able to fix anything,
and they still had five thousand ballots to duplicate and get out to the area
projects before the volunteers returned from the Ohio training. It wouldn't
have surprised Ron if Frank and Larry had gone at it all night. There were
a lot of all-night meeting in weeks before the Summer Project, though this
must have been what they called a rump session—just people mouthing off
until their rumps fell asleep.

Larry said that Frank could never understand his feelings about the
white volunteers. Mind you, Frank shouldn't take it personally. He knew
better than that. They'd been in too many tight spots together. But, Larry argued, some of those spots had been tight precisely because Frank
was white. Larry had ridden on the Greyhound bus into Montgomery at
Frank's side in '61, the day that Frank almost got his ear torn off by the mob
at the station.

"Really," said Larry, "you're wasted in the black community."

"Fuck you. You think I could organize white folks in my hometown?
I'd be dead in a week!"

What Ron really could not get used to was the language. The SNCC staff knew some local people didn't like it either, and they usually they toned it down when they knew Christians were in the room. What would Pastor Holden think if he heard the garbage coming out of their mouths?

When Ron had first heard about the Freedom House, he'd asked, "Is that a church?" The door had been opened by a pajama-bottomed Frank Q. Court, who'd handed Ron an RC Cola. Somewhere upstairs, in the room they were using as a library, the radio was playing, and a colored and a white girl were doing the twist. Ron had held his RC with such a grip it was a wonder it hadn't popped out of his hand.

His first impulse was to run away. What he saw seemed like it wasn't even possible. He knew the colored girl—Jackie Gordon. Her father owned the funeral parlor in Tutwiler, and she'd gone off to college in Memphis. He'd always been a little sweet on Jackie G., and maybe that's even why he'd shown up at the Freedom House in the first place. But the white girl gave him a soft, open smile as she danced, and pushed her soft brownish hair off her round face, and after the song ended, extended a soft, rosy-white hand. He shook it. The ground did not roll out from under him. The girl was Helen Forest, who was presently downstairs sorting through Summer Project applications. She was from Texas. Ron still avoided being alone in a room with her.

Oh, but they had a good time in the Freedom House. There were always new people showing up, just out of jail, books and clothes coming in, the telephone was always ringing, and at night, there'd be those meetings. They'd be on their feet, arguing and testifying. Sometimes, close to daybreak, Ron would have to slip back home to Tutwiler like a tomcat, which he wasn't, but he'd feel a little like a tomcat, like he had no master, or like a hero from a Bible story who could stand up to a giant, or like the stone the builders cast away.

This was the Lord's truth. He was a soldier in Gideon's army. So were they all, prostrate, ready to meet what God would give them. Your brother or sister could be dead tomorrow, shot through the neck or burned in the basement of a church. Ron always taped a hair to the hood of Movement cars to make sure no one had tampered with the engine. Sylvester's teeth were knocked out on the gearshift of a car Ron drove at ninety miles an hour when the two of them were chased across a field in Sunflower County. It was a miracle they hadn't ended up at the bottom of some river.

Yet at the thought of the Summer Project, the same terror he'd felt during his first trip out of Mississippi overcame him, and that terror brought on shame. There was no sense to it. Jackie Gordon always said that she could never judge anyone. She could only know herself. But what if he lost a grip on himself altogether? He wouldn't have time to turn things over and over in his mind once the summer began. That was the trouble. He thought things, sometimes, that he couldn't bring himself to say, at least not in front of Larry and the others. That's why he wandered downstairs, where he would find Sylvester.

Since the night Sylvester got his teeth knocked out, he and Ron spent a lot of time together. The theory was that Ron was trying to get Sylvester to go to church, but actually, most of the time Ron was cooking for him, something soft, with plenty of pepper. Not much cooking was done in the Freedom House, and what was in the refrigerator tended to be unrecognizable, but Ron had learned to cook from his Aunt Risa, and he was proud of it, and did the best he could. That night, they had the kitchen to themselves.

Ron spoke before he could lose his nerve. "I got to ask you something. And don't take it the wrong way. Larry and Frank and them, don't you ever get frustrated when they go on talking? Like, they think we got all the time in the world?"

"Don't we?" asked Sylvester. He opened the refrigerator. "Anything you can cook here, Ronny? You know I love your cooking."

"No," Ron said. "I mean, yes. I mean, I'll cook for you in a minute, but what I'm getting at is don't you sometimes just get angry?"

What Ron really wanted to talk about was that recruiting tour. Sylvester had been on it too. He'd gone to California to give half-whistling speeches through those missing teeth, and wrote a series of amusing postcards which were tacked to the refrigerator, featuring Homes of the Stars, and on one he wrote, in bold letters: *Colored Man Discovered in Beverly Hills. Harry Belafonte Insists Not Blood Relative. Police on High Alert.*

"I mean," Ron said, "there were these times. I was up there, and I was supposed to—you know—tell the story about that time at the courthouse, and how they all have to come on down and help us. But no one seemed to hear me. And then I started to think all the sudden that what they really wanted to do was see my scars."

"Your what?" Sylvester burst out laughing. But Ron was serious.

"Scars. You know. From that beating. Like, they'd start wondering if there was something wrong with my face, like I was paralyzed. Or maybe my head has a dent in it. You know I got a funny shape to my head. That's what they want to see. I could feel their eyes all over me like ants. They wanted me on my knees like in *Life Magazine*."

"So get on your knees," said Sylvester. "You a prayerful cat. Oblige them. And tell them you praying for dem. Lord knows those crackersh need it." As Sylvester spoke, he'd already dug around and found a box of macaroni. "Shpeaking of crackers, I tink dere's a little cheesh left." He opened the refrigerator and pulled out something hard to identify. "Now milk, we don got."

"I kissed a white girl," Ron said.

Sylvester didn't take his head out of the refrigerator, so Ron was inclined to say more.

"I called her 'baby.' I don't know what happened. It's just something about where I was got me all mixed up, somehow."

"Well, da's no shurprise," Sylvester said. He closed the refrigerator door and shook the macaroni box. "Jus' enough for two, or I'd ask Helen to join ush. You do know we're—well—you do know."

"I know," said Ron, though until then, he hadn't been sure. Helen and Sylvester always sat at opposite ends of the room during meetings, and there was something so open and self-effacing about Helen that it was hard to imagine her with anyone at all. Except she was.

Sylvester said, "I'll tell you something that Helen don't know. I got stories to tell abo' da little trip to California. I mean, what you was talking about—dat staring ting—you read it one way but it can be read another way, if you know what I mean. And then, dere are times when you get Charlie Fever."

So he explained it: Charlie Fever—the times when you got angry enough to lose yourself, when you began to forget who you were and what you wanted in the ferocity of your hatred of all white people—that was when it happened. How could Ron live with himself if he had to carry all that hatred? So Sylvester told Ron, as Ron obliged and tried to make a plate of macaroni and cheese without milk, which wasn't easy. So you had to make some connection, somehow. You had to just touch some white person. You had to know there was at least one you can love.

"Only," Sylvester added, "you got to keep it under control. Some of dese girls can get you' head turned real quick an' make you crazy so you hate them too. And that defeats the purposh."

"The purpose?" Ron did feel his head turned.

"Loving, Ronny baby," Sylvester said. "In case you don't remember. Loving. Not hating. Listhen to your older brother. What your momma tell you? You can't hate your fellow man, black or white, or you'll never get to see the face of God after you die."

Then Sylvester smiled. But somehow, Ron did not feel reassured. The gap in that smile turned it sinister as though you could see all the way down inside, into the dark. And Ron remembered all of that girl's strange red hair, the tense mouth, and the sun in his eyes as he pulled away from her and turned back to the road.

"So," Sylvester said. "Did you recruit her?"

"What?" Ron's mind had been somewhere else.

"I mean, is dis chick on her way to Mississippi? Did you sign her up?"

Ron put his head in his hands, and let it rest there.

"Good for you," Sylvester said. "I mean it, brother. Good for you."

4

ONCE THERE WAS A GIRL who did everything wrong. Take the time she was working in the Mississippi project office and taught three teen-aged girls some dirty words in French. The girls had somehow heard that Beth had plans to go to Paris in the fall, and they cornered her. "Come on, Miss Beth. What's the matter, Miss Beth? You don't want to tell us? You think we're all too ignorant?"

There was Sweetie, Bobbie and Freddie, cousins who favored tight blue jeans and halter-tops. Beth couldn't get their names straight, and they let her know it mattered.

"Now you ought to know I'm not Bobbie," said Sweetie. "Bobbie's twice my size. She's fat."

"I am not fat," Bobbie said.

"She's lazy too. She don't move unless she has to."

"I do so. I do move."

Freddie said, "Do you know who I am, Miss Beth?"

"You're Freddie."

"No. I'm Bobbie."

"That's not nice. You're being mean to Miss Beth. And then she won't teach us French."

All of this took place in the alcove just above the staircase from the pharmacy that served as the project office in Melody, Mississippi, in a cramped corner that was called the library, where Beth shelved books donated from a church in Boston. Those books were a strange assortment, old copies of James Fenimore Cooper novels, a set of Reader's Digest editions of books by Edna Ferber, and a surprising number of paperbacks by Camus as well as a complete, if dog-eared, set of the *World Book Encyclopedia*. The girls should have been in the Freedom School, but they'd wandered to the drug store where each got a Coca Cola, and now they sat sucking the necks of the bottles and looking at Beth with grim expressions.

Bobbie asked Beth, "Are there colored people in Paris, France?"

"Some," said Beth. "You know, the Algerians fought a long war against France and won, and they have dark skins."

"But we don't want to know Algerian," said Freddie. "We want to know French. Miss Beth, why are you holding out on us? Miss Beth, you think we're not good enough to know?"

How many times could they call her Miss Beth? And how long before, under the onslaught, she would give them what they wanted? She showed them *The Stranger* and *The Plague* and *The Myth of Sisyphus* and recited their French titles. Sweetie asked, "What about French kissing?" and that led to a wild fit of giggling and a demand for something *really* French. And so by dinnertime, the three girls were parading down Two Street, shouting what they'd learned at the top of their lungs.

Beth was called to Larry Walsh's desk, and he said to her, "What the hell do you think you're doing?"

Blushing hard, Beth said, "How was I supposed to know that you understood French."

Larry did not reply for some time. He sat back in his heavy, wooden chair and let the silence get lost in the rattle of the window fan.

Then, Beth said, "I never said I knew how to teach kids. I never said I wanted to work in the office. I didn't come to Mississippi to shelve books. I thought I'd be driving people to the courthouse."

"That's not your assignment."

"Why not?"

"If we put a white girl on that assignment, she'd make every house she visited a target. You want to have that on your conscience?"

Beth had heard it before, and what she had to say next had been said before as well. "If I could be reassigned to Greenwood, I could work in the office there. And I could drop off the car and donate it to the Movement."

"I don't have time for this conversation," Larry said.

He slipped on the half-glasses that made him look like a junior executive, even in his overalls. He was light tan, and had a small goatee.

"Listen, I have a project for you. The pharmacy downstairs could use a thorough cleaning. And I mean the floor, the shelves, the counter. Lift up those jars and wash under them."

"I suppose," said Beth, "that you'll want me to wash out those girls' mouths with soap."

Larry sighed. "Just watch yourself, alright? You're not going to be here in two months, but those girls are."

Beth walked through the office, past the piles of yet more donated books still in their boxes. She was supposed to sort through cartons as they came in and correspond with donors, communicate with the Greenwood project by WATS line, work—she was told at the training in Oxford,

Ohio—that was critical to the success of the Summer Project. But the office telephone broke down mysteriously the week that Beth arrived, and by the time Beth made it downstairs to the phone in the pharmacy, Mr. Davis had already answered it and was whispering something to Larry that she was wasn't considered seasoned or trustworthy enough to know.

Larry didn't even trust her enough to let her take that Corvair to Greenwood. "It's useless. It's too lightweight," he'd said, meaning the car, but also, Beth knew, meaning all the volunteers. And so she'd parked it under a tree, and, as he'd instructed her, put a paper bag over the license plate, and Ron wouldn't even know she'd come to Mississippi.

Then there was Sue Francis, a local Negro girl who was supposed to type affidavits. In the fall, Sue Francis was bound for a Negro college in Tupelo. Her mother had gone there and had joined a sorority, Gamma Nu, commonly known as the Honeybees. Sue Francis already wore her mother's Honeybee pin, a tiny black and yellow enamel badge that she stuck in the stiff, round, collar of her blouse. When Sue Francis was angry, which was most of the time, that badge would rise and fall with exasperation. She was angry now.

She said to Beth, "Do you plan on shelving those books?"

"Why?" Beth asked her. "Do you plan on reading them?"

"They're in the way," Sue Francis said, and then she turned up the fan, which made it impossible to continue the conversation.

BETH KNEW IT EARLY, AND confirmed it with Laurel. "That Sue girl's got something against me."

Laurel sat cross-legged on the bed they shared. Her glossy blonde hair was flipped over her shoulder, and she braided it while Beth spoke which, to Beth, implied a lack of serious attention. She said, "I get along with Sue Francis."

Of course Laurel would get along with Sue Francis. She was just Sue Francis's idea of a white girl, sunny and unconflicted, plink-plonking away on her guitar. Laurel had just returned from Ghana where she'd been a Peace Corps volunteer, and she maintained a level of distance from her circumstances that Beth couldn't fathom.

Laurel and Beth were living with Mrs. Claire Burgess and her grown son Po in one of the straight-line shotgun shacks that lined Monroe Street. The houses were set almost back-to-back, with no yards to speak of. Mrs. Burgess had planted some daylilies almost up against the front door, which Po watered in the mornings. Po was a hulking presence, light-skinned, with heavy eyebrows, and he held the watering can so close to his body that most of the water fell on him. They'd both been warned that he was "slow," but harmless, and if there was a Mr. Burgess, nobody seemed to know or care.

Mrs. Burgess was a laundress with white clientele she had managed to keep even after she had gone down to the courthouse to try to register, and opened her home to Summer Project volunteers. Beth had already fought a losing battle with her own laundry. The day she came, she and Laurel found their empty suitcases stowed underneath Mrs. Burgess's bed and everything from those suitcases hanging from the line.

Beth said, "Mrs. Burgess, I really wish you wouldn't do that. We can wash our own clothes."

Mrs. Burgess said, "Honey, do you know how to use this?" She presented her with a washboard.

Beth despaired. But Laurel wasn't disturbed by the clean clothes, or by the fact that they'd displaced Po to the couch and Mrs. Burgess's nephew George to a neighbor's house. Laurel had just said, "Isn't it wonderful, how much people have to give?"

"I think it's terrible," said Beth, and she meant it.

Beth tried to talk to Po, just asked him if he was comfortable on the couch, and if he really didn't mind if she and the other volunteer took his bedroom in the back of the house, and why he didn't eat with them at the table. Po, sullen and slack-mouthed, didn't reply.

"You'll only confuse him," said Mrs. Burgess, and she led Beth away, and from her endless reserve of patience, had the power to explain that Po really didn't much notice where he was. "He was born like that," she said. "He doesn't mean to look at you that way. You can't take it personally."

Beth never could get to sleep at night, thinking about Po on that couch, particularly as there wasn't a proper door between the bedroom and the sitting room and he never turned out the light. Mrs. Burgess said he was afraid of the dark. His eyebrows were heavy, his skin muddy-yellow, his jaw blue with stubble. Beth was repulsed by him, and also wanted to say she was sorry.

Laurel said, "You have to learn how to accept gifts."

"Why?" Beth asked.

"Because you insult people if you turn them down," Laurel said. Another case in point were the lunches put together for the volunteers at the Freedom School, a table over-laden with fried fish, macaroni salad, potato salad, pickles, chicken, ham, and a lot of heavily iced cakes. The platters were set out at noon and melted into a greasy mess before the white kids could get to them. Beth knew people couldn't afford to give them all that food. She would take a little bit of macaroni and pick at it. That was something else that Beth did wrong. Laurel said, "You've got to understand, they expect it of us."

"Why should we do what they expect?" Beth asked, angry at she did not know what.

But Laurel seemed impervious, or maybe she was just determined to like Beth because they had to share a bed. She wanted to show Beth her lesson plans, to trade outfits, to teach her how to run the printing press she'd brought from Indiana to duplicate a newspaper that the children named *Melody of Freedom*. She read Beth letters from her fiancé, a fellow Peace Corps volunteer who was still in Africa. The letters had magnificent stamps, great favorites of the kids in the Freedom School. The fiancé was digging wells.

"My boyfriend's in Chester, Pennsylvania," Beth said. "He's building an interracial movement of the poor."

Laurel said, "That's so beautiful."

If at any time Beth felt guilty about lying to Laurel, it was counterbalanced by the certainty that Laurel was lying to her. Those letters from Ghana were as colorless as press releases.

Beth hadn't written to her Aunt Beatrice yet, but she'd already sent two letters to Marty Weinglass. The first one began, *I have been sent not to the Delta, but to Melody, which is considered a safe project, which means we don't know what we are supposed to be afraid of. How are things in Chester?* The second one, sent a week later, said, *I can't help but notice that you have not responded to my last letter with news of the progress Missy is making with all of those unwed mothers. Write soon.* Another week had passed without a letter, colorless or otherwise.

The relative safety of the project was subject to debate. Cars without license plates would often pass by the office slowly, and threatening phone calls were commonplace. The male volunteers drove down back roads in a truck borrowed from J.B. Powder, who briefed them on the situation with his hands in the pockets of his clean denim jacket. He was far less forbidding than Larry, kind of smiling. His scrap-metal business had pretty much dried up since he joined the Movement, and he and his wife, Mae, got by on the SNCC salary of ten dollars a week.

"Thing is," he said, "the Negroes who own land won't deal with you at all, and the ones who don't will just say yes to anything a white man says, and then they'll happen to be out of town the day you pick them up to take them to the courthouse," and in fact the volunteers came back with cases of sunstroke and plenty of stories about ladies who'd say they'd sign up, only they couldn't find their reading glasses and old men who talked to them about pig farming, the price of feed, anything but Voter Registration. At mass meetings, they barely filled a third of the pews—and that was including the volunteers who all sat in the back, fanning themselves with Freedom Democratic Party registration forms.

Teaching had its own frustrations. Classes were held in a dim and airless room in the basement of the A.M.E. church. Judy, a high school teacher from Brooklyn, tried to interest the older girls in civics, but mostly, they'd rather be in the library, giving Beth a hard time.

The volunteers shared their troubles at a café across the street from the project office. Mrs. Burgess's nephew George and some local boys milled around, drinking wine, not very surreptitiously, from empty bottles of Coca Cola. George had been expelled from his school in Holly Springs for wearing a SNCC pin, less, as far as Beth could tell, a sign of commitment to the Movement than an excuse to get thrown out of school.

Laurel passed them by with a beer in either hand, and she swung her blonde braid over her shoulder. "When are you kids coming over to the Freedom School?"

"When you be the teacher, teacher," George replied. "What you gonna teach us?"

Beth looked on from her corner, sick at heart. She wasn't there to entertain the local people, just as she wasn't there to be thanked, or to accept gifts. She was there to give Ron Beauchamp her Corvair.

ONE YEAR LATER, RALPH NADER would make his name with a book entitled *Unsafe at Any Speed*, and that book would feature the Corvair. The car, Nader would write, had a faulty transmission, and on impact, the engine, located in the back, would have a tendency to fall through the floor.

Before Beth had left for the training in Ohio, she had a final audience with her father. She'd come into his study to say goodbye, and he'd said, "Sit down. You're making me nervous, Bitsy." It was clear he hadn't softened his position, but he seemed resigned. "Perhaps," he said, "this is inevitable. It is what young people do. But examine the circumstances. Don't act rashly. Don't suffer fools. Remember, you're my daughter."

"I know," said Beth. She felt a prickly warmth, which made it hard for her to get the words out. There was more she had to say, infinitely more, but then, Max Fine turned around and opened his desk drawer.

He pulled out his money-clip and said, "How much will you need?"

"Aunt Bea already sponsored me," Beth said.

"Bitsy, I'm not a scoundrel. Surely, things will come up. Fuel, incidentals."

Beth left with that strange square of money in her pocket. In the rush of the drive to Oxford, Ohio and the first day of training, she blessedly forgot it was there, and ran her blue jeans through the wash. As a result, the money bonded into a green wad. She managed to peel off a five, and stuffed the rest into the bottom of her suitcase.

Beth was heading into the unknown. She would take action and prepared to take responsibility for the consequences, even unintended consequences. Between the action and its consequences lay Greenwood, Mississippi, where she and the car would be profoundly changed.

BUT SHE HAD BEEN SENT to the wrong town. Melody had Larry Walsh for a project director, and he hated Beth. Those teenaged girls hated Beth too, and set her up to act like an imbecile. The worst part was, Beth would prove them right. When she was ordered to clean up the pharmacy below the office, she didn't even know where to find supplies. Of course, she could have asked Mrs. Burgess, but she knew what Mrs. Burgess would do, and that was all Beth needed: to have Larry or Sue Francis come downstairs and find Claire Burgess on her knees and scrubbing.

So Beth walked out into the gritty sunshine to use the five dollars she'd peeled off the wad of cash to buy cleaning supplies. What passed for the Negro business district was two blocks long, and lined on either side with shops so dim and windows so dirty that unless the door was propped open, it was impossible to tell if it was open or closed. If she followed Two Street uphill, she would reach the railroad tracks. The train from Chicago passed so close to Mrs. Burgess's house that it woke Beth at night. Across those tracks was the white part of Melody.

At the training in Ohio, Beth had been told several times that she was not to leave the Negro neighborhood. Beth scouted: what she saw looked more like no-man's land, a few warehouses, a patch of blighted grass, three oil tanks and what might have been a storefront. Mrs. Burgess sometimes sent Po to Third and Monroe for bleach. If she could see the store from here, it didn't really count. She crossed the tracks.

The store stood all by itself, covered with peeling stucco. There was a patch of light in the window, and a sign, in black block letters that had just about faded to green: COHEN DRY GOODS. Beth opened the door and a little bell rang.

"Miss, you need something?"

Beth's chest tightened. It was the first white Southern voice she'd heard in Melody. Maybe she could just back out the door before this could go further.

"You don't have to run away." A stocky, moon-faced boy in glasses emerged from a storage room and leaned against the register in a way that felt deliberately casual. He was maybe her age, but looked younger, with his big red ears and pimples and the Brylcreem in his hair.

"Um," Beth said, "I'm looking for a mop."

"They got you cleaning their houses now?"

She should just turn and go. That's what they would have told her to do in training. That was what Judy would have done or even Laurel. Instead, she stood there, under the intense scrutiny of the boy, who walked all the way around her like a dog marking its territory.

Then, he said, "You don't even know how to look for a mop. You're in a dry goods store, see? And it's a mop you want. That's hardware. You got to go to Greenfield's Department Store. He's got everything. But don't let him sell you a rag mop because they fall apart. You get yourself a sponge mop."

A little dizzy from the boy's proximity, Beth answered, "Thanks. I will."

"You know, you all have no idea how difficult you make it for us here."

He had raised an arm and blocked her way, and his eyes narrowed behind his glasses.

"Feel it."

"Excuse me?" said Beth.

"My arm," he said. "Charles Atlas. It really works. I used to weigh a hundred and twenty-three, and now I'm up to one-sixty. Seriously. Been working at it for two years. Feel it."

"No thanks," said Beth.

"Any of those colored boys got arms like that? I bet they don't," he said. "You better let me take you over to Greenfield's. He'll cheat you if I'm not there. Not everyone's like me."

"No really. I'll just go now," Beth said.

"You don't even know where the place is." He lowered his arm with some reluctance and let it hang at his side. "You don't even know what I'm talking about, do you? Don't even know who you're talking to. I own this store. That's just to say that I'd be happy to close up and take you over there myself."

Beth figured that she would find an excuse to break away once they got out of the shop, but the boy kept up a steady stream of conversation about his father who passed on last year and left the books a mess, about the accounting course he was taking by correspondence, and somehow, they ended up in front of a big, tan Packard that must have been twenty years old.

Beth hesitated. "I'd rather walk."

"What? You don't trust me?"

Beth said nothing.

He looked less angry than sheepish. "What? You think I'm gonna dump you in a river or something?" He looked crestfallen, and that somehow made it harder than ever for Beth to leave him. In the end, he started walking, and she followed him some distance, all the way to Sixth Avenue, a black-paved, two-lane tree-lined street where the shops had plate-glass windows and new awnings. Two white women walked out of a cafe, and one of them gave Beth a long look.

"Uh-oh," said the boy, grinning at her.

"How much farther?"

"What's the matter? You're in a nice part of town for once. You ought to see that Melody's more than Two Street and Monroe and colored boys drinking wine and smoking reefer. I'll bet I'm the first white person you've met since you showed up. I'm right, aren't I."

"You didn't answer my question."

"You didn't answer mine."

"Where are you taking me?"

"Greenfield's General Store. I told you. You really don't trust me, do you?" he said. "Look. We're right in front of it."

It looked too elegant, Beth thought, for a store where she would buy a mop. When the young man opened the door, the bell played a tune she could identify as the Winchester Chimes, and a burst of air conditioning made her sweat freeze. The young man seemed oblivious. He walked straight through neat aisles of ladies' handbags and umbrellas to the manager's office, and he called out, "Hey! Mr. Greenfield! I got a girl here, needs a good, sturdy sponge-mop to clean a colored home."

A dumpy, gray-faced fellow emerged. "I got mops." He had a heavy German accent. "You need a rag mop for that kind of a job."

"What'd I tell you?" the young man said to Beth. He gave her arm an abrupt squeeze. She flinched and knocked over a pile of hats. Nobody seemed to notice. "He figured you'll fall for that rag mop routine."

"A lot of people like a rag mop," Greenfield said, as he started walking them towards Housewares. "They don't like this replacing mop-heads, throwing them away. The colored think they save money."

"But they just end up getting a whole new mop," the young man said. "That's what certain people don't understand. It comes from slavery times. They don't look ahead. They just see what's in front of them. Don't know how to save, how to plan. Figure Master'll give it to them. Now, Mr. Greenfield, when you came here twenty years ago, did anyone give you a handout?"

"Thank God," said Mr. Greenfield, "I could take care of myself."

"See? That's the difference," the young man said to Beth. "You hear this man? This man survived Hitler. And did anyone come here from up north and say Mr. Greenfield, we're here to help?"

"The Temple helped me," said Mr. Greenfield. "Your father helped me get that loan."

"See?" He pounded the counter for emphasis. "We help each other. We always have. And that's what people like you can't understand."

Beth bore all of this in silence, as Mr. Greenfield laid on the counter a new plastic-covered sponge-mop and bucket full of cleaning supplies, but now she broke in. "How can you live with yourselves?"

The boy smiled with satisfaction, and Mr. Greenfield shook his head.

"Both of you—you sell to Negroes," Beth said. "You've gotten rich off of them."

"Who's rich?" Mr. Greenfield asked, mildly.

"Pardon me, Mr. Greenfield, I can't know what you've lived through, but you of all people should know better."

Mr. Greenfield shook his head again, a gesture of melancholy dismissal. Then he said something in Yiddish. The boy kept that slim, intimate smile on his face and gestured Beth towards the register, where she paid for the mop and the supplies. Then, she pushed through the door and walked at a fast clip down Monroe towards the tracks. The heat hit her like a dull club, but she kept going. She wasn't surprised to find that the young man stayed on her tail, and when she was forced to stop for a traffic light, he fell in next to her and said, "Nobody ever taught you manners?"

Beth said nothing. She willed the light to turn, gave up, and crossed against it, and he followed.

"What are you gonna do with that mop?"

"Things you can't even imagine," said Beth, turning, and her sweaty palm nearly lost its grip on the handle.

"Won't you let me carry that stuff?" he asked. "It's not right, you hauling it back down there."

"Do you plan to help me clean?" Beth asked him.

"What if I do?"

Beth knew he wasn't serious, but she wasn't sure what to do with what he said. He stood with his legs braced, and his heavy, over-bulky arms folded. It was a pose, one that he must have practiced in front of a mirror, intended to show off his new physique. But Charles Atlas couldn't do anything about his sheepish face, or those thick glasses, or the pink patches of acne on his cheeks and forehead.

He said to Beth, "You know what Sol Greenfield said about you?"

"No," said Beth.

"Well, you must know some Yiddish," he said. "You're Jewish, aren't you?"

"What difference does that make?" Beth asked. She felt her cheeks burn.

"It makes a difference. Just see if it doesn't," he said.

"What the hell are you talking about?" Beth began, but then she realized she had invited conversation, and she quickly hoisted the mop over her shoulder like a rifle and walked away, across the set of tracks towards Two Street.

Behind her, the young man called: "You want to help out oppressed people? I'm oppressed. Help me. You think it's easy living here? You think I don't have my share of trouble?"

That badly paved road felt as familiar as her own skin. A warmth, a gratitude for this place rose from her gut, and she lost herself in it to the point where she could barely hear him shout: "You and that blonde girl, staying with that yellow nigger, letting him drool all over you. You watch your step. Not everyone's like me."

5

I T WAS JUST CY COHEN'S luck that the only Jewish girl in Melody would be a beatnik. His mother was always after him to go to socials over at the temple in Oxford, and he wanted to tell her that he'd just had a little social of his own, but when he came back, she was in the middle of vacuuming behind the couch.

"Momma, didn't I tell you not to do that heavy work until I came home?"

"What? I'm an invalid, I should wait around all day and watch the dust pile up?"

Cy shrugged. "Okay, but if you strain your back again, you'll see a doctor right here. I'm not driving you to Memphis."

Was it in December that this bickering began? To someone listening through the door, Cy and his mother might have seemed like an old married couple. Sometimes, Cy wondered if he'd ever manage to have a real girlfriend. But when would he even have time for a girlfriend, what with working the register, ordering the inventory, and trying to balance those goddamned books?

The books were a disaster. His father had kept up with the accounting well beyond the point where his mind started to go. Until the end, Cy would let him use the adding machine and even work the register because the doctor said it was supposed to help. Maybe it would be a good day, one of the times he talked to the customers and told a few jokes. He was especially at ease with the colored customers. He had his favorites. He liked to show off the novelty pants intended for display. They were five feet wide. He held either end of that waist in his frail, shaking hands, and he grinned, and said, in his frail, shaking voice, "You think anybody's got an ass that big?"

"I sure don't know, Mr. Cohen," the man replied.

"I'd say an ass that big's gotta belong to a nigger. Nobody else could sit on his ass for that long. You bastard. Bastard. Fuck the bastard."

And the colored man would laugh would make noises of approval and confirmation, but Cy knew he seriously wanted to detach himself, pick up what he needed, and get out of the store.

Cᴙ HAD ALWAYS GOTTEN ALONG pretty well with colored people. Most of his father's customers were colored. As far as his father was concerned, a customer was a customer, and unlike some of the more high-toned shopkeepers on Sixth and Main, he made a point of stocking the sort of clothing working men needed, good quality dungarees and thick-seamed shirts that wouldn't fall apart the first time they went through a wringer. Of course, if he wanted to keep white customers, he had to make sure they knew their place. But no one ever asked to try on a pair of work-pants or overalls. What was the point? Later on, his father added a section of cotton dresses for their women, and drawers of shirts and undergarments all along a back wall. When he was a kid, the other boys always tried to get him to steal the bras and panties. Once, they could get him to do more or less anything they wanted because that was the only way he could get them to notice him at all, but by the time he was in High School, he knew that if somebody wanted to be his friend, it was because he wanted something, most of the time a fall-guy. He didn't have time for that shit.

He signed up for correspondence courses in bookkeeping and management. He liked getting the envelopes in the mail and studying by himself at night after his parents went to bed. He was good with numbers, quick, and as far as he was concerned, it would have been a waste of time for him to go to a regular college. His mother kept talking about colleges in up North in Philadelphia, but that was the way she was, homesick even after twenty-some years in Mississippi. Everything was better in Philadelphia, the stores, the beauty-shops, the weather. She'd grown up in a neighborhood with five synagogues, where her sister had married a dentist and had a second home in Margate, New Jersey, right on the beach; and if his father had seen a Philadelphia doctor, she was sure, his father would still be alive today.

Cy said to his mother, "One of the female volunteers is from Philadelphia."

"You keep away from those girls," his mother said.

"I figured I'd ask her to Temple on Friday," Cy said. Then, he said, "You're actually speechless. Never thought I'd see the day."

She crossed into the kitchen and turned on the tap. Her voice was obscured by the water. "You want to get us killed?"

"Momma, I wasn't serious."

"You shouldn't say that sort of thing. Not even in fun. The walls have ears in this town." It was characteristic that she still called Melody "this town," even after twenty-five years.

In fact, word did soon get out about Cy and the volunteer. Barney, who owned the gas station, said, "I hear you fucked one of them."

"What are you talking about?" Cy said. "I helped the girl get a mop."

"Well that's kind of cute," said Barney. He finished filling the Packard's tank and put the hose back on the pump. "Got her a mop. I guess you got her mop. Did you make her take a shower first? Or maybe you stink so much yourself you didn't notice, right Cohen?"

Cy didn't blink. He'd taken the Charles Atlas course precisely to avoid these situations. He was supposed to get out of the Packard now and show Barney his biceps, and that would be the end of the conversation. The trouble was, the attendant was such a skinny, sorry excuse for a man that Cy couldn't bring himself to do it. Somehow, getting those muscles didn't work the way it had been advertised. They didn't make him win fights. Instead, they made him just want to walk away from them. He took a dollar from his wallet to pay for the gas, and he held it out the open window.

"You fucking Jews all stick together." Barney said.

"You taking my money, Barney, or does it stink too much for you?"

Barney took the dollar, and said, "I'm not giving you change, or you'll hand it all to the N double-A Cee Pee."

"Now why would I go and do that?" Cy asked. "Don't you know I'm just a good old boy like you?"

TEMPLE BETH AMI WAS AN old Temple, older than many of the churches in town. It was built just after the War Between the States and untouched since the '20s. Some of the stucco had come off the front, and the roof of the activity room leaked, but the sanctuary was still in good shape, all things considered. There were maybe thirty families on the books—Cy kept those books—and they couldn't afford to have a rabbi of their own, but one came in from Memphis once a month, a young man who also performed circumcisions.

The Cohen family had lived in Melody for so long that Cy's father wasn't sure when they had lived anywhere else, and he told Cy that when he was a boy, the synagogue had two hundred families and included not only the present building, but the site next door. There had been a banquet hall. Although Cy's parents had married in Philadelphia, they'd had a lavish reception in Melody as well. The girls wore dresses that made the dresses in Philadelphia look like dishrags, and there were so many colored maids and butlers passing out trays of champagne that you couldn't turn around without knocking one over.

Now, the only colored boy at Temple was George from Holly Springs, the part-time janitor Cy had just hired as a favor to his Aunt Claire. George took care of odd jobs, like a clogged toilet, or putting buckets under the leaks in the activity room, but he didn't knock himself out. Most of the time, when Cy came in during off-hours, he'd find George sitting on one of the pews, reading a comic book. That's where he found him on Friday when he arrived to give him his pay.

George was a few years younger than Cy, and he had a quiet belligerence that made Cy reluctant to speak to him directly. Cy knew the type, both black and white. It was better just to leave the ten dollars in cash in an envelope by the door. But that day, Cy found himself walking up to George and saying, "Hey."

George looked up. The comic book was still open. He said, "Mister, you need something from me?"

"Just wondering what you were reading," said Cy. "Is that a new one?"

George didn't answer immediately. His eyes narrowed, and he clearly was trying to figure out what Cy wanted. Then he said, "I can't afford new ones on no ten dollars every two weeks."

It occurred to Cy that no colored boy in Melody would speak to a white man like that. He remembered that George had gotten into some kind of trouble in Holly Springs, and then he remembered why he'd chosen to speak to him in the first place. He said, "Look, boy, I met a friend of yours the other day. A white girl."

"I'm not friends with no white girls," said George.

"You've got a mouth on you," said Cy. "And if I were a different kind of fellow, you'd be in hot water."

George looked down at the comic book again and pointedly turned a page. His narrow, deep-brown face looked serious and triumphant, as though he were doing something important.

"But I'm not that kind of fellow," Cy said. "I might even be the kind of fellow who could help you out, give you a hand, you know?"

George mumbled something under his breath.

"What did you say?" Cy asked him.

George looked up then. "Mr. Cohen, I got nothing to say to you. I clean the bathroom. I sweep the hall. I empty out the papers from the trash. And if you don't got nothing else for me to do, I'd just as soon go home."

"You live on Monroe Street, don't you?"

"You got my pay, Mr. Cohen?"

"You live with Claire Burgess and that son of hers?"

"Not anymore. You got my pay?"

"Maybe I could pay you a little more," Cy said, "if you'd do a little more."

He wasn't even sure what he meant by that. There wasn't anything else for George to do. Years of indifferent upkeep and unfiltered light had turned Temple Beth Ami into a faded, threadbare place, and it was impossible to make it into something it was not.

George closed the comic book at last. He looked at Cy with a directness that was like a punch in the stomach. "What do you want?"

"I'm just making you an offer," said Cy.

"I don't need no kind of offer like that," said George. "I can take care of myself." He stood up. "Mr. Cohen, you got my ten dollars so I can go?"

"Yes, I do," said Cy. He walked to the office to get the petty cash box. George had, in fact, emptied the waste paper basket, but the desk was still covered with bills Cy hadn't filed, and the blotter was so fuzzy with wear that it looked like a piece of carpet. What did Cy want George to do for that extra money? Maybe just take everything in that office and shove it in a box, and throw that box in a ditch somewhere. He turned and was surprised to find that George had followed him into the office, and he stood with his comic book closed in one hand, waiting for his pay.

"I'd like it in ones," George said.

"I'll see what I can do." Cy felt his throat close, like a twitch, around those words. He counted out ten ones and added one more. "Have a good weekend."

George looked at him. "What's that for?"

"For a new comic book," said Cy, "Or for whatever you want. Just take it, okay?"

"Well, thanks," said George. He put it in his pocket and left in a hurry, as though he were afraid that Cy would think of something he had to do to earn that extra dollar. Cy lingered, to file bills and make sure the place was ready for services that night. He'd have to go, of course. But chances were, even with Sol Greenfield and his brother, Ike Mendelssohn, Moe Jacobs, and the Kornfelds, they wouldn't make a *minyan*.

For as long as he was able to go, Cy had to bring his father. Most of the time, he fell asleep in the pew, and then Cy would prop open a prayer book and try to keep the pages current. When they opened the ark, Cy would have to wake his father up, and he wouldn't know where he was and turn in a rage and shout "Fuck you, bastard!"

"Pop, everyone can hear you," Cy would say, though it would do no good.

His father knew that everyone could hear him. Cy understood. All of his life, in Melody, he'd kept his voice down, but not now. He'd rage and then he'd weep, and say "He won't let me sleep! Bastard treats me like a nigger!" but nobody at the Temple cared. For as long as he lived, he was their tenth man. For that, they would put up with anything.

6

WHEN LARRY WALSH ARRIVED IN Melody a year before, he had a single name on an index card: Harris Johnson, a chicken-farmer and church deacon who was a long-standing member of the NAACP. Johnson was stiff, and close-mouthed. He always wore a suit-jacket over his overalls and had a trace of childhood polio that only seemed to add to his dignity. He knew everyone in Melody: the A.M.E. deacons, the Tom minister of the Baptist church, the women who worked in white homes, the men who worked at the tire plant, small businessmen like J.B. Powder; and he knew who could be persuaded to break bread with a Freedom Rider. After a month of suppers, cups of cold tea on the porch, silent staring at the road, and slow, slow introductions, he said to Larry, "Let's take a drive." Out of those agonized efforts sprang the Citizenship school, where half a dozen local people studied copies of the Mississippi constitution and made trips to the courthouse in Holly Springs to register to vote.

When the need arose for an office, Harris Johnson used a toothache as an excuse to introduce Larry to Mr. Davis, the pharmacist who served as the town's Negro doctor. Mr. Davis offered the space upstairs and said, "I'm luckier than just about everyone else in this town. If I lose my business, I know I got my land."

Mr. Davis had two sons, Jack and Simon, who kept up the family farm. If they had an opinion about their father's new associates, they kept it to themselves. They would retrieve him at supper time and would wait outside beside the truck, or sometimes come in to help move some boxes. There was a stillness in them even more profound than Harris Johnson's, and so complete was their silence that the volunteers tended to shut up when they were present. They were darker than their father, and dressed identically in overalls, though Jack wore a hat.

The pharmacy had one of the few working phones in the Negro neighborhood, and it rang regularly. Sometimes, it would be a call from one of Mr. Davis's distributors and very occasionally from a customer, but nine times out of ten, Mr. Davis picked the receiver up and put it right back down again. One afternoon, Jack got to it first. Then, he said, "Shit."

"Just hang up. And watch your mouth," said Mr. Davis. "You're among civilized people in this store."

"Civilized. Shit," Jack said again. The calls were intended for the upstairs office.

They'd thought about disconnecting the pharmacy's phone and relying on the CB radio that J.B. had in his truck, but in the end, Mr. Davis calmly logged the time and nature of each call. There was the lady who called early in the morning and said, in a sweet voice, "You people are trash. We always got along well with the coloreds until you came." Then there was the man who said, "I want to talk to the girl who sleeps with the nigger."

The calls to the office seemed linked to the arrival of a small, battered, suspicious-looking package, which Sue Francis was in the process of opening when Larry caught sight of her from across the room and called out, "Stop right there!"

Sue Francis looked startled and dropped it. A small paperback book popped out: *The Beatnik Bride.*

On the cover was a disheveled blond girl in the arm of a swarthy, muscular man with a goatee. "Well," Larry said, "nice to see them donate to our library."

"The girl on the cover looks like that Laurel," said Sue Francis.

"You're right," said Larry. "By God, I think we've got a conspiracy at work here."

"You're making fun of me," said Sue Francis.

"Listen," said Larry, "don't go opening any more packages that don't have a return address." He took the book and gave Sue Francis a long look. "You're too young to read this thing."

THE BOOK SOMEHOW GOT FROM Larry's hands and into the hands of the volunteers, including Laurel, who started calling herself the Beatnik Bride. She struck a dramatic pose and read the jacket copy out loud to all of the volunteers at the café: "When Mary left her small town in Oklahoma to visit New York's notorious Greenwich Village, she never dreamed that a single marijuana cigarette would be her introduction to a world of jazz, sex, and race-mixing."

"Cut it out," said Judy. "You're reinforcing stereotypes."

"Miss Beth got a boyfriend." This came from George Burgess, who approached them unobserved. He leaned in confidently. "She's goin' with the Cohen boy. It's all over town."

The others turned to Beth, who blushed from the roots of her hair. George looked amused.

"Miss Beth, you all red. You so red, you not even a white girl anymore."

THE NEXT DAY, A HEADLINE appeared in the *Melody Sentinel*: "Unkempt Redhead Comes to Mississippi to Clean Colored Homes." The brief text below had mentioned her appearance on Sixth Avenue and highlighted the purchase of the sponge-mop at Greenfield's General. It wasn't long before another round of calls began: "I want to talk to the girl with the mop." Someone else asked, "Is her mop wet?" and someone else, "I gotta dirty job for that girl."

Come lunch-time, Beth couldn't bring herself to face the crowd around the picnic table, so she hunched upstairs, trying to figure out the best way to arrange the thirty assorted copies of Nietzsche, Sartre and Camus that didn't seem to belong anywhere on the shelves. She wrote to Marty Weinglass, *I should probably just stick them with the comic books. What would you do in my place? Make yourself obsolete, no doubt. How are things in Chester? You still haven't answered my first three letters. It's hotter than hell here. Where you can go, by the way. To hell.*

Sweetie, Freddie and Bobbie came up by late afternoon. Sweetie had brought Beth a piece of sweet-potato pie.

"You're too thin," said Sweetie. "How come you don't eat, Miss Beth. Don't you like our food?"

"That's a rude question," said Freddie. "How is she supposed to answer a question like that?"

"She like the food in Paris, France," said Bobbie.

"No. I like this food," said Beth. She accepted the pie, which had been crushed in transit, and she tried to eat it with her fingers. Most of it stuck to the plate.

Sweetie and Bobbie slumped down in the threadbare easy chairs that were wedged in the corner, and sullenly opened the *World Book Encyclopedia*, their general lunchtime reading. Freddie usually stuck to M/N because, as she said to Beth, she liked "Management, Math and Money." But that afternoon, she took down a paperback copy of *The Plague* from Beth's stack and didn't move to join the others. She sat at Beth's feet and opened the book to the first page. After a few minutes, she turned that page, feigning attention, Beth suspected.

Beth kept her voice low. "You don't want to read about money today?"

"I was just wondering," said Freddie, "why you brought that mop at Greenfield's."

Beth said, "I needed one. I guess I didn't know who to ask."

"You could have asked me," said Freddie. "I speak English, in case you haven't noticed." Then, she turned the book around and looked at the photograph of Camus. "So is this cat French?"

"Actually," said Beth, "the author's from Algeria."

Freddie shook her head. Camus was handsome in a froggy, glamorous way. In fact, he looked more than a little bit like Marty Weinglass. She frowned. "You said Algerians were colored. Now you got me all confused."

Downstairs, the telephone rang yet again.

WHEN LARRY WALSH RETURNED A few hours later, Beth heard him bounding up the stairs and steeled herself for confrontation. He passed her by.

Beth knew she shouldn't, but she trailed after him and said, "I'm sorry."

"For what?" Larry asked. He frowned. He had a piece of paper in his hand. "Is Sue Francis back yet?"

"It was stupid of me. I guess I wasn't thinking."

"What are *you* talking about?" Larry asked.

"When I went over the tracks," Beth said.

"Oh that. Yeah." Larry shrugged and spotted Sue Francis yanking a window open in the storage closet. He handed her a scrawled note. "So I need this typed. Are we out of carbons?"

Now Beth felt her head get hot, and she didn't even try to keep her voice under control. "What are you talking about? I knew it was dangerous."

There was some silence, filled only by the clack-a-clack of Sue Francis's fingers on the typewriter keys. Larry leaned over to check her accuracy and made a face he probably didn't intend for Beth to see, and his mouth twitched just a little underneath his goatee, as though he was thinking about whether this copy could possibly be legible. Then he turned to Beth.

"Listen," he said. "No one's going to kill you. You don't get it, and can't get it. In Mississippi, in the south, they kill black men."

Beth started to say something, but uncharacteristically, she couldn't put words together. Larry took the opportunity to go on.

"Black women are second on the list. And then, white men who stand with us like Goodman and Schwerner in Meridian. But you—you're safe."

"I—" Beth began through a clogged throat. "I didn't come to Mississippi to be safe."

"No, you're here for an adventure, obviously," said Larry. "I know white girls like you. Even the best of them—the ones who've been with us for years. They're floaters. They don't want to take orders. They want to find themselves. You white girls, you've been safe for so long, you want to stop being safe, so you float from project to project because you're privileged enough to think that discipline's the opposite of freedom."

Then, Larry turned back to Sue Francis, who had stopped typing to hear this little speech and who was clearly trying to decide how to show her approval. Her mouth turned up a little, quizzically. She smoothed down her hair. Then, because there was some silence, and because it was clear that Larry had no more to say, she showed him the page that had been sitting in the typewriter and asked, "Do I need to redo this?"

"It's perfect," said Larry.

SUE FRANCIS HAD BEEN TYPING an affidavit. Beth found this out not long after she went outside to clear her head. Preoccupied, she wandered up the road. She knew she ought to write the donors about books. She had a list of addresses. But her hand ached from all those letters to Marty Weinglass, and her heart ached because she never seemed to be walking in the right direction.

Then, the sun vanished. Storms came on quickly here, especially on hot days, when noon turned to midnight without warning. She headed back in the direction of the café.

No one was there. The owner sat behind the bar, counting the week's receipts. Beth asked, "What's going on? Did something happen?"

He looked up, startled. "Miss Beth, you ought to get yourself home."

She almost blurted out: Is this about the mop? Then, she caught herself in time and looked out the screen door. Two Street was empty, and there was a floodlight in the front of the Davis Pharmacy. Whiteness spilled onto the street like milk or glue. She made herself step outside, though the air smelled thick and sulfurous, and she stood just out of range. Inside, the phone rang. Would it be the one wanted to speak to the girl with the mop, or the one who asked for the white girl who slept with the nigger?

Someone opened the pharmacy door. Beth froze.

It was Ron Beauchamp. Unmistakably. Lean, dark, quick, in blue jeans and a work-shirt. He stood on the stoop of the pharmacy, lighting a cigarette.

Beth shouted out: "Hey!"

Ron didn't look up. He flicked a little bright ash.

Beth stepped out of the shadows and walked across the floodlit road.

"You know who I am, don't you?" Beth asked him. Then, she wished she hadn't.

He looked up at her, and she hadn't remembered how long his eyelashes were, and how they seemed to smother something underneath them. He started to answer, but then, Jack Davis stepped forward. He was holding a rifle.

Jack said to Beth, "Miss, there's been some trouble. You both need to get inside."

Ron cocked his head. "You guys are sharp. A fella can't even have a smoke."

Beth kept her voice steady. She said to Ron, "What are you doing here?"

"I'm the engine man," Ron said. "I fix all the cars."

Beth said, "I brought mine."

Jack broke in. "Miss Beth, I'll walk you to Mrs. Burgess's before this storm breaks." It wasn't a question. Beth found herself falling in beside him. Simon Davis stood next to Ron now, and Ron passed him another cigarette from the pack. Jack Davis held his rifle with a finger near the trigger as they walked, and he did not feel the need to say another word to Beth until he dropped her at the Burgess doorway.

Then he just said, "Don't go out again."

MRS. BURGESS WAS THE ONE who told Beth and Laurel about J.B. Powder's scrap metal truck. The volunteers had left it parked at a crossroads and separated to knock on doors. When they came back, the truck was gone. They walked back to the office and arrived at five o'clock, two hours later than expected, just as Larry was about to call the Greenwood office and report them missing. They were dehydrated, shaken, and not at all prepared for Larry's first question, which was why they had broken two rules: separating, and abandoning the truck. In their hands were fifteen Freedom Democratic Party registration forms, which were so stained with sweat and red dust as to be illegible. By seven, J.B. and Larry had found the truck. It was burnt to a cinder.

"Who did it? The Klan?" Laurel asked.

"The Ku Klux is not the only ones who set fires," said Claire Burgess. "You girls can't know how much evil there is in the world, and I hope you never do."

Mrs. Burgess, never an open book to Beth, seemed to be holding something back. She made a point of boiling fresh coffee for the girls and telling them they were her daughters for the summer.

"Nobody can say different than that," she said. "You're my daughters in Jesus. In heaven, they will recognize us as a family." Somehow, that wasn't reassuring. The rain pounded on the roof, and Po was unusually restless. He drank a lot of tepid coffee left over from that morning, and kept moving on the couch until the sound of the springs grated even on Mrs. Burgess. "Cut it out, baby," she said. She laid a hand on his shoulder, not so gently, and he stopped.

"I could play my guitar," said Laurel. "Sometimes, that calms him down."

"That's okay, honey," said Mrs. Burgess. "Something you got to know about my Po. When it rains like this, he gets all agitated, but then he wears himself out."

The three sat quietly for a while. Laurel was desperate to get out her guitar. Beth could tell. Silence didn't come easily to her. As for Beth, she wanted to ask Mrs. Burgess what she knew about Ron Beauchamp, if he'd been to Melody before, how long he usually stayed. Meanwhile, Mrs. Burgess seemed to be turning something over in her mind.

Suddenly, she rose and said, "Come with me, girls. I got something you need to see."

She took them to her bedroom. They had never been in that room before. It was an intimacy that made them both anxious.

She knelt beside her bed, slid her hand below the mattress, and pulled out a brown paper bag. "This is my gun," she said.

Beth asked, "Is it loaded?"

"Sure is," said Mrs. Burgess. She removed the gun from the bag. It was a revolver. "Now girls, if I'm not here, you know I keep it right under the mattress. You want to hold it?"

"No!" said Beth and Laurel together. Then, Mrs. Burgess showed them how to unlock the safety catch, and asked, once again, if they needed to try it for themselves. Again, they refused. She put the gun back in the bag.

Laurel hesitated. Then she said, "Mrs. Burgess, I'm sorry, but having that gun here doesn't make me feel safer. I mean, what if Po found it?"

"You ought to know better than that," said Mrs. Burgess. "Po may be slow, but he knows that if he so much as touched that thing, he'd get a beating he wouldn't soon forget."

Laurel moved closer and crouched a little. She was at least six inches taller than Claire Burgess, and it took some effort to be sure she'd meet her eyes. "Mrs. Burgess, we're a non-violent movement. Dr. King wouldn't want you to carry a gun. He'd want you to get rid of it."

Mrs. Burgess smiled and said, "That's why I'm so fond of you girls. You do have the most interesting ideas."

Beth found it hard to sleep that night. Laurel was restless too, but in the end, she always managed to adjust to any circumstances, and after a while, she curled up in her nightshirt, with her hand cupped under her cheek and her blond braid lying across Beth's side of the bed. Beth ended up on the stoop, and she sat there for some time. The rain had ended. She could see the floodlight by the pharmacy, and another across town, maybe at J.B.'s house.

She had *The Beatnik Bride* on hand, and because there was so much light out there, she read it. The chapters were brief and episodic. *Big Jim put down his saxophone. His hands were powerful. Mary shrank back. She knew that Big Jim would bring her an ecstasy greater than she had ever known before. He unzipped his trousers.*

After an hour of this, she put the book down. A note fluttered out.

We will burn you like the trash you are.

The springs on the couch gave a creak. Po was asleep at last.

7

YEARS LATER, BETH WOULD TRY, without success, to track down a copy of *The Beatnik Bride*. She would sort through the dollar bins at used bookstores, particularly the kind that specialized in kitsch. A new shop had opened at the corner of 12th and Pine called Camptastic that had a window display of paperbacks like *Lesbianism in the WACs*, *She Gave it Away for Nothing*, and *She-Men of the South Pacific*. It was a nasty store, dripping with self-important irony, and Beth always felt a little soiled if she spent too much time there.

In the end, Beth just gave up. If she brought *The Beatnik Bride* home, Tamara would take one look at the lurid cover and start reading it on the spot. One failing Beth Fine had as a mother was that it was hard for her to tell her daughter that a book or a drawer or the contents of her purse were off-limits. Sometimes, the policy had severe consequences. Soon after Tamara moved to Philadelphia, Beth took a nap and woke up when she heard glass shatter, and there was Tamara standing on the kitchen counter, having pulled jars of flour and sugar from the cabinet and laid them on the stove. She'd turned the burner on, and the sugar had exploded. Tamara was so terrified that all Beth could do was hold her, pick the glass out of her legs and arms, and let her cry.

The most attractive target was the medicine cabinet. There was a time when she was six when she found a diaphragm. She asked Beth, "Is this to plug the bathtub?"

Beth wanted to laugh. She'd actually forgotten that she owned it, and the rubber was probably corroded. "It's supposed to keep me from having babies," she said.

"Oh," said Tamara. "Don't you want more babies?"

"You're enough for me, sweetheart," said Beth. Of course, Tamara wasn't satisfied. When she first came to live with Beth, she used to ask why she didn't have a sister, as though Beth was holding out on her. Now, here was this rubber disk, stiff with disuse, which had some mysterious power to keep babies away. Tamara was still too young for that particular conversation, but fortunately, the girl had a gift for not asking questions when there were things she didn't want to know.

Take the time that she found Beth's lithium. "What are these for? Are you sick?"

"No. Not anymore."

Tamara just said, "You should throw it out." Then, she dropped the subject. Yet when she chose to, she could doggedly pursue a topic to the point where Beth felt bludgeoned. She was briefly taken with a box of memorabilia, old newspaper clippings and photographs that Beth kept in the closet.

That was when Tamara was twelve, the spring before she was going to take her first trip to Tanzania. She spent her allowance on a photograph album, and it was understood that she would fill it with family pictures, and when she went, the album would go with her. After she finished her homework, she laid the box on the kitchen table. At first, Beth graded quizzes from her Elementary French class in an adjoining room and kept the door open, but Tamara interrupted her so frequently with questions about the contents of the box that in the end, she had to either close the door, or do her work at the kitchen table too. Beth chose the kitchen.

"Who's this?" Tamara asked, holding up a Christmas card with a group photograph of one of the volunteers and his wife and children in their matching red sweaters. "Are they part of our family?"

"The father was with me in Mississippi," Beth said. "Now, he's a dentist in Los Angeles. He could fix your teeth."

Tamara frowned. She tossed the card aside and pulled out a number of copies of Laurel and Judy's old Summer Project newspaper, *Melody of Freedom*, mimeographed in faded blue, but she didn't give them a second glance, instead fixating on a half-cracked black and white photograph with a serrated edge. The photograph was taken in Chicago, by the lake. The two girls were both wearing polka-dot dresses and broad-brimmed hats, One of them held her hand up to her hat to keep it from flying off her head, drawing her arm into a graceful curve. Her dress was pulled against her body by the wind. How could a wind only blow on one of the sisters? "They're relatives," said Tamara with conviction. "Which one's grandma?"

Beth pointed. "That's her. The pretty one. Grandma Vivian. The other is Aunt Beatrice. They were the Neuman sisters. Like Neuman's Department Store in Center City."

"She'd be my great aunt," said Tamara, "and I'd be her great niece." She was pleased with herself for knowing this information. "Does she own Neuman's?"

"No, sweetie. I think the stockholders do."

"Are we stockholders?"

The question startled Beth. If Tamara were a little older, this would have required an explanation, but for now, she just said, "No. We're not."

"Where's Great Aunt Beatrice now?"

"I don't know, honey," said Beth. She tried to get back to those French quizzes, but Tamara wanted to know the last time she'd heard from her, and whether she had any children, then why she didn't have any children. Beth answered all of these questions as best she could, and in the end, she had to say, "Sweetheart, sometimes, you just lose track of people."

Tamara didn't reply. Beth had to admit that her answer had been ill-advised for countless reasons. She turned back to her work and tried not to be aware of Tamara's presence as she attached the photograph of the sisters to the first page of the album. Tamara was so selective that she hadn't managed to fill more of it. The pile of rejected material was enormous, and threatened to spill off the table. Then, out of her silence, Tamara suddenly asked, "How did Grandma Vivian die?"

Beth said, "What?"

"I need to know," said Tamara, "because when I see the doctor to get those shots before I go to Africa, he'll ask me if any diseases run in my family, and I'll have to know what to tell him."

"I'll be right there with you," Beth said. "I'll be able to answer those kinds of questions."

"You won't be with me in Africa," said Tamara.

"Your daddy will be with you."

"He doesn't know anything about your family," Tamara said, "just like you don't know anything about his family."

That wasn't fair or true. Beth kept up good, if formal, relations with Ron's Aunt Theresa, who still sent Tamara a package every month containing tootsie rolls, Archie comic books, and cherry flavored bubble gum, as though those things weren't available in Philadelphia. When Tamara first came to live with Beth, she used to cry at night because she missed Auntie Risa so much. Now, Beth had to reassure the poor old woman that it was perfectly alright for a twelve year old girl to go on a twelve-hour flight all by herself. One particularly painful Sunday, Theresa offered to go with her. Where she'd get the money was anybody's guess. Ron had only offered to pay for Tamara's ticket.

Tamara said, "I'll bet you don't know how Grandma Tammy died."

"Ovarian cancer," Beth said, startling both Tamara and herself. Then she added, "I didn't think you even knew what ovaries were yet."

"Of course I do," said Tamara. "And I know that if she had it, I can get it. That's why you need to tell me this stuff. How did Grandma Vivian die? Did she have what you have?"

"What did I have, sweetheart?" Beth asked, mildly. She knew the conversation was headed in the wrong direction, but she couldn't do anything about it.

"You know. Those pills you took."

It struck Beth, not for the first time, that her daughter would make an excellent detective. As dispassionately as could be managed, Beth answered her. "She might have had what I had. Not everything had the same name back then."

What did they call what her mother had? She'd had been called what? Madcap? Spirited? People had always spoken of the "Two Vivians," the one who'd fly across streets with her shoes in her hand, throw herself into a chair, and chatter until her lipstick smeared with perspiration, and the other one, the sultry Vivian who chose shoes with buckles so she wouldn't have to tie them. When Beth was very young, the first Vivian was ascendant, but really, it was the second one that Beth remembered, the one whose photograph was still probably on Max Fine's desk at Princeton. She hadn't looked sultry by then: more anxious and diminished. Beth could remember her mother saying that Max was the smartest man she ever met and therefore the only man she could have married. Or maybe it was Aunt Beatrice who had told Beth that story, adding that caveat that brains aren't everything and that in fact, sometimes, that sort of fellow shouldn't marry at all.

Maybe there was a sort of girl who shouldn't marry. Perhaps when the sort of fellow who shouldn't marry weds the sort of girl who shouldn't marry, the result would be The Girl Who Does Everything Wrong. These speculations abstracted Beth from her current circumstances, and Tamara had to ask her next question twice before Beth responded.

"Did Grandma Vivian take those pills too?"

"No. Those pills weren't invented yet."

"Maybe if they were invented, she wouldn't have died," said Tamara. Then, blessedly, the questions ended for a while.

Tamara kept going through the box with a fixed intensity that was an essential part of her nature. Her face pulled in on itself like a fist, and she threw aside old syllabi from the first few years of Beth's teaching, programs from plays Beth had seen quite recently, and a lot of Laurel and Larry's letters from Chicago days. Tamara lingered over those letters just long enough to decipher their signatures. She added them to the discard pile.

Without looking up, Tamara said, "You don't have a lot of pictures."

Beth said, "If I'd known you were going to make an album, I would have taken more of them."

She did remember that during the Summer Project, Judy had created a darkroom in the back of the Davis Pharmacy and taught the teenagers to develop photographs. Those photographs might still be in an archive somewhere, over- or underexposed, scenes of children sitting under the tupelo tree behind the church, or drawing with chalk on a patch of concrete; lots of pictures of Laurel playing her guitar with her long hair tossed across a shoulder. Then, Beth remembered that she had a group photograph somewhere in the box.

"Check the bottom," Beth said to Tamara, and she put her quizzes aside to help her look. The rest of the junk fell out in a heap, and together they managed to dislodge a glossy, surprisingly professional print.

It was the morning of the day of the Freedom Democratic Party precinct meeting. Over the door of the church was a banner: ONE MAN ONE VOTE. Beth laid it in the center of the table and took time to point out everyone in the photograph. "There's the lady I stayed with—Claire Burgess. You know, she was a delegate to the convention and went to Atlantic City. And Laurel, of course, and Mr. Davis who always gave us coca-colas. See how the kids all have soda pop in their hands?"

"Where are you?" Tamara asked.

"Way in the back."

"You looked different then," said Tamara. Then she said, "You looked more like me."

"That's because my hair was long," said Beth.

"Why did you cut it?"

The question had an edge, and Beth couldn't quite understand its intensity. "I don't know," she said. "I guess it was too much trouble."

She continued to explain the picture, though she felt Tamara's attention drifting, as though her narrative were a distraction. She told her about the Freedom Vote and how it wasn't recognized by Democrats, but was the only way that black people could participate in an election in Mississippi, how even though they didn't have to face a county clerk, it was still a risk to enter a Movement church, and in particular to be a delegate like Mrs. Burgess. Tamara interrupted, pointing to George Burgess.

"Is that Daddy?"

"No, honey. That's Mrs. Burgess's nephew."

"Is that?"

Tamara had pointed to Larry Walsh. Larry was wearing overalls. His face was slick with perspiration, and his goatee actually had a point like a pencil. He was the only one in the picture who wasn't smiling. "No. That's my project director."

"I thought Daddy was your project director."

"You know he wasn't," said Beth. "I've told you about Larry."

"So where's Daddy?"

"He's not in this picture. It was around the time I met him though," Beth said, and she was prepared to go on talking about all the other people in the photograph, and maybe she would have if Tamara hadn't snapped it up and thrown it in the discard pile. Beth felt a pinch of anger. "Don't you want it for your album?"

"No," said Tamara.

"But your daddy would like to see it," said Beth.

"How would you know?"

Slowly, Beth became conscious of a note in her daughter's voice that went deeper than anger. She looked at her closely. Tamara's eyes were bright, and her lower lip was so stiff that it took real concentration to realize that it was trembling. She sat very still, with the album opened in front of her, the lone photograph of Vivian and Beatrice in the middle of the first page, the rest empty. Beth asked, "Honey, what's the matter?"

Tamara seemed to force the statement out. "Why don't you have any pictures of Daddy?"

Beth reached across the table for her, but Tamara pulled away. "Hey, hey," Beth said. "I told you I didn't take pictures back then."

"But there's nothing." Tamara's voice broke. "You don't have one picture. And how am I going to know him? When he meets me at the airport—how will I know who he is?"

Beth got up and drew her into her arms. Tamara finally surrendered, and Beth crushed her against her chest, feeling, as ever, just how slight the girl was under all her hair, and she buried her face into the curls and whispered, "Oh, sweetheart, listen to me. You'll know who he is. I'll tell you what. There's time. Why don't we call him right now? Why don't we ask him to send us a picture? And you can have it with you when you get there. You can send him a picture too."

Maybe Tamara didn't hear her, or maybe her answer was inadequate, because she went on. "I don't want to go all the way there. I won't know who he is. What if I go with the wrong man?"

For a moment, Beth was tempted. If Tamara didn't want to go, let her stay here. Tell Ron it was her choice. It would be a reasonable enough choice, given her age and circumstances. Beth comforted Tamara and used the time to examine her own conscience. Then she said, "Let's keep looking. Maybe there's something."

But there wasn't. Beth had regrets. She could describe Ron Beauchamp to her daughter, as he was all those years ago. She could close her eyes and see him, just the way he'd looked the night he came to Melody to see what could be salvaged of J.B.'s truck, the long legs in their thick jeans, the white T-shirt glowing, the firefly end of his cigarette, and then the face, its contours almost milky with the reflected floodlight that the Davis boys had rigged up to be sure their father's store would not burn down.

"I'll tell you a story about what happened maybe a week before they took that picture," Beth said to Tamara, as they combed the discard pile. "You know your father knew all about cars. He started fixing cars when he was a boy in Tutwiler, but there was a car in Melody—a truck actually—that was so far gone that it couldn't be fixed at all. The windows—you remember the time you put those jars on the stove? That's what happened to the windows. And that's what happened to the whole truck."

Tamara didn't want a story. She wanted a picture. But habit, or maybe just exhaustion, had turned her passive. She asked, "Did he fix it?"

"I said it couldn't be fixed," said Beth. "There are limits even to your daddy's powers."

"So what happened," Tamara asked. Beth had a feeling that her daughter was humoring her, but she answered anyway.

"They used my car instead."

8

THERE WERE THREE CARS IN all, ferrying people to the church: the Corvair, a '56 Ford Fairlane on loan from Holly Springs, and Harris Johnson's truck which must have dated from the 1930s. The Corvair was the smallest, but it was in the best condition. After being parked on the curb for a month, it had acquired a mystical appeal to the local boys, who fought for the right to drive it.

"Won't you let me take it?" Beth asked Larry, without much hope.

Larry said, "You'll have your hands full making sure people in town get off their porches and over to the precinct meeting."

Beth didn't bother to hide her disappointment. She started off, turning her back on Larry in a way she hoped he'd see as deliberate. He called after her: "Remember to write your aunt. She must know some hotshots in the Democratic Party. When we get to that convention in Atlantic City, we'll need all the support we can get."

It was assumed that the church would be a target of whomever burned the truck, and the Davis boys were somewhere keeping watch. Yet as Beth walked up and down Monroe Street, she found the local people waiting for her on their stoops and porches, or already heading to the meeting. A few of them even said that they were picking up their neighbors on the way to make sure they got there on time. "After what they did to that fine young man and his wife," one elderly woman said, already dressed for that meeting as for church, in a hat and gloves, "after they took away his livelihood, you think I'm staying home? I just hope you all got room in the basement of an A.M.E. church for an old Baptist."

B Y THEN, BETH KNEW, J.B. had approached Larry the night before and said he couldn't be on the slate as a Freedom delegate to the convention. He wanted to lay low for a while.

It had taken Larry by surprise. "What do you mean: lay low?"

"Well," said J.B., "I got an aunt in Mound Bayou." That was colored town in the Delta, and the aunt owned a grocery store where he could help stock the shelves and save a little money. "You know, Mae's pregnant."

"I didn't know," said Larry. "Congratulations."

"It's not the best time, I know," J.B. admitted. "But she's been after me to take a hiatus."

"You take all the time you need," said Larry.

"Aren't you impressed that I used the word *hiatus?*" J.B. said, trying to smile. "I've been reading this book, *Words of Power.* Want all those kids to go back north and tell their friends about the educated businessman they met in Mississippi."

LARRY HADN'T MANAGED TO FIND a replacement. Thus, he seemed even more on edge than ever. He never stopped moving, checking off names of people who'd committed to appear, making sure that the drivers left as soon as they dropped off the passengers, even dipping down to pick up discarded crumpled paper cups of lemonade and crushing them with a short, rough, gesture.

"You got your lemonade?" Mrs. Burgess said to everyone. "You go on to that nice cool basement so we can choose us some delegates for Atlantic City. We're open to all—white and Negro—not like those pagan infidels who call themselves Democrats."

It was true. Judy and Laurel went together to the First United Methodist Church of Melody, deemed the least likely of the white churches to bar them from the door entirely. Somehow, they had both packed decent dresses and even white gloves, wrinkled but clean. They returned early and reported that Judy had stood at the end of the service to announce the precinct meeting, but then, even she had lost her nerve when the minister charged the choir to begin singing right over her, and in the end, they both refused a ride back from the only likely recruit, an old lady pointedly avoided by the other congregants who kept calling after them: "I just love the colored! Why don't you believe me, girls? Ask anyone and they'll tell you how much Miss Gale loves her colored brothers and sisters!"

Freddie later told Beth, "My momma says Miss Gale was a missionary in Africa. She says her brother was eaten by cannibals."

Beth had learned to read Freddie's face when she said that sort of thing. "That's right," she said, "and they were all Algerians, just like Camus. He always found missionaries tasty."

Although Beth wasn't sure if Freddie could follow everything that she was saying, she said it anyhow, and in turn, sometimes, Freddie would say surprising things to Beth like, "I think Judy and Laurel are secret sisters."

When Beth didn't reply at once, she said, "I mean like soul sisters. The way they're always on each other. Like they knew each other before they were born and got to finish their business here on earth."

"Like you and Sweetie and Bobby," said Beth.

Freddie cracked up and said, "Oh, Beth. Come on. They're just who I hang with. I'm like you. I'm still waiting for my soul-mate."

"How do you know what I'm waiting for?" Beth asked. "I might have met my soul-mate already."

"Is he Algerian?" Freddie asked, and they might have gone on all morning, but they were separated by Claire Burgess who turned to face Beth and addressed her fiercely.

"You better write that aunt of yours and tell her that Mrs. Roosevelt would be ashamed of her if she didn't help us. You write just those words. Make sure you say *ashamed*."

So BETH FINE PLANTED HERSELF under a tree behind the church to concentrate on writing her letter. *Dear Aunt Beatrice. I am sorry that I haven't written you since I arrived in Mississippi but I'm bad at doing things when people tell me I have to do them.*

That was a bad beginning. She tried again. *As a lifelong Democrat, I'm sure you must feel ashamed when you consider what your fellow party members are doing in Mississippi.*

The day before, Beth had slipped into Mrs. Burgess's bedroom and dislodged the paper bag with the revolver from underneath the mattress. Somehow, even the simplest thing Claire Burgess had shown them had slipped from her mind, and she damned herself for her distance from what really mattered. Surely even Sweetie or Bobbie could have handled that revolver. Yet there was a chasm between who they were and who Beth Fine could be. Instead, she could only assume the vigilance of men with guns, constant and unasked-for, outside the bedroom window, in the office, in the back lot of the church. Surely, they were in that back lot now. Their silence made her wary. Then she heard a rustle, and her heart lodged in her throat.

Sue Francis emerged from a path through the undergrowth. She walked unsteadily in high-heeled pumps through the grass and across the gravel to the ice-bucket. Her eyes flicked back and forth. Then, she dipped her hand in, took out a couple of ice-cubes, and slipped them down the front of her dress.

Beth made herself visible, and spoke up. "Hey Sue. That looks good."

Sue Francis stiffened, and the ice cubes dropped all the way down the front of the dress and hit the grass before they melted.

Beth asked, "Can I have one?"

"Aren't you supposed to be inside?"

"I'm writing a letter to get support for the Freedom Democrats," said Beth. Somehow, it felt important that Sue Francis knew that she was doing something appropriate, but the news didn't have the effect she'd intended. If possible, Sue Francis looked even more disgusted.

"Can't you do it somewhere else?"

"Larry told me to write the letter," Beth said.

"Not here. And not right now. You find some other place to do it."

"Why not here?"

"Because I," said Sue Francis, "am supposed to keep the area clear."

The hell she was. Yet her hostility had an edge of desperation, almost like pleading. "All right," Beth said at once, and with regret. She left her spot and headed toward the road. What was she interrupting? An assignation. It would have to be. But with whom? Maybe one of the Davis brothers. He'd hand Sue Francis a rifle of her own.

What would Sue Francis do if she got hold of a rifle? Beth thought of that conversation with her father. Yes, the people of Mississippi were nonviolent. All of the people, Bitsy? Had she spoken to them individually? Had they taken off their dark glasses? Beth was so engaged by her speculation that she didn't even see the Packard until it pulled right up next to her. The boy from the dry goods store stuck his head out the window.

"Hey there. You. You Beth."

Beth swallowed her answer. She kept on walking, and she became spectacularly conscious of the sweat that stuck her blouse right to her bra. She tried to cover herself with the letter she'd been writing, all the while feeling the presence of the engine, like a hornet, to her right. The car kept pace with her, going remarkably slowly and taking up the whole of the narrow road, forcing Beth into the weeds in the gutter.

"Look, aren't you gonna answer my question?"

At last, Beth stopped. She couldn't help herself. "Go home."

"I thought this meeting was supposed to be for white and colored both. That's what they told me." He turned off the engine and leaned far out the window. "You tell me—why can't I vote for a delegate?"

"Because," said Beth,. "you aren't registered as a Freedom Democrat."

"Then register me," he said. When Beth didn't respond, he said, "Get in the car."

"You know I can't," said Beth.

He turned pink, and the veins in his neck stuck out. "You think I'm some kind of Klan trash? Look," he said. "I'm sorry about what happened to that junk-dealer. I say, let a man hang on to his business, but nobody asks Cy Cohen."

"You know who burned the truck?"

"Nobody tells Cy Cohen anything either," said Cy Cohen. "But all it takes is common sense. Which you all don't have. Now here you are in a church basement. What if some joker drops a bomb in the window? You got what you call a crematorium going."

"Thanks for the tip," said Beth. Then, more carefully, "Have you heard something? Is there going to be trouble?"

He turned off the ignition. Then, he got out and walked over to the passenger side, and opened the door. He looked right at Beth, defiant, foursquare, with his thick glasses, and his greasy black hair. He had something to tell her, and she would only find out if she had the courage to get into the Packard. That was the bargain. The heat battered down and made it hard to think clearly.

"Come on," he said. "What's stopping you?"

"You know I can't," said Beth, but her eye was on the car's interior, riddled with old newspapers and wrappers from hamburgers or candy. The cushions were torn, and their yellow stuffing showed.

He was about to say something else, and then he stopped. Beth turned around. Larry Walsh stood behind her.

Larry asked Cy, "Can I help you with something?"

"I guess you can't," he said. He glanced at Beth. "Guess I'm not gonna get to vote today."

"Would you like to register as a Freedom Democrat?" Larry asked him, in a voice like steel.

"I think I'll just be on my way," said Cy. He circled to the driver's side and got in. The car stalled. He bent his head over the steering wheel, sweat rolling down his forehead, his glasses slipping down his nose. Eventually, the ignition caught, and he rolled down the gravel road.

Larry said, more to himself than Beth. "That thing's gotta be twenty years old."

"I wouldn't know," said Beth.

Larry gave her a long stare, and it made Beth cross and irrational.

"Listen, I don't even know that guy."

"I do," said Larry. That's Stu Cohen's boy. George said he tried to buy some information from him a couple of weeks ago."

"Buy what information? What secrets do we have?"

"Button your blouse," said Larry. Then, he walked away.

Beth rearranged her damp clothing and wondered what conclusions Larry seemed to draw. She reluctantly trailed him back to the church. He walked with both hands thrust in the pockets of his jeans, looking at the ground rather than Beth. Beth felt compelled to keep up with him, to insist on her own innocence, and all the while she knew it would be futile. The heat battered through her damp hair, and she wondered if he simply wanted her to collapse with exhaustion. After a moment, he paused, and with his back still turned, he spoke.

"You were going to get into that car with him."

"Excuse me?"

"I'm project director here," Larry said. "There are lives at stake. I don't just mean the lives of local people."

Against her better judgment, Beth said, "I thought you told me they never killed white girls."

Larry turned, and he looked angrier than she had ever seen him. "You were about to get into that man's car. And if you did, God knows if we'd ever see you again."

Beth paused. Then she said, "You'd still have the Corvair."

Larry's face wavered, and the anger didn't disappear, but seemed pulled deep below a surface of surprise, confusion, finally resignation. There was no way he could answer what Beth just said, and he was not acknowledging its justice, but its finality. He looked past Beth, at nothing in particular. His eyes narrowed against the sun.

"I didn't mean that," Beth said.

"Yes you did," said Larry. "You think I don't value your life. You think you have my number."

Beth gave a helpless shrug, and he allowed her to fall in beside him as they approached the front entrance of the church. He lingered there.

"Listen," said Larry. "I would put my body on the line for you. You don't believe that?"

"I don't know," Beth said. "I guess," and now she hesitated. Then she found the words. "I guess I don't think I'm worth it."

"When you learn to value your own life, then you'll believe that what I say is true. Until then, this is a useless conversation."

Beth felt intensely visible, standing on the threshold of the church, in her damp, badly buttoned blouse and dusty skirt. From below came the sounds of people singing. "Larry," said Beth. "I think that boy, that Cy Cohen, was trying to warn me about something. I think he knows who burned J.B.'s truck."

"So do we," said Larry. "Come on downstairs."

Beth was startled. "But if you know, why can't you do something about it?"

"We are," Larry said. "We're changing the nature of politics in this country. That's the only way that people like that can be brought to justice. That's what this is all about. Come on downstairs. At least then I'll know you're out of trouble."

"And what if I don't want to be out of trouble?" Beth said. "What if that's what it takes for me to value my life?"

It struck Beth that they had actually begun to hold a conversation. The conversation started at the wrong time. Maybe that was the only way that Beth could really have a conversation. It would have to be when talking wouldn't get her much of anywhere. "Listen," said Larry, "Life isn't—"

A crack. Then silence. The shot came from behind the church. Larry broke into a run, and there was a second shot, and then another. The church erupted, and voters spilled out in time to see Sue Francis propped against the ice-bin. Blood soaked the dust around her skirt. Larry tried to clear some space around her as the crowd converged, and Sue Francis stared at the blood flowing down her leg and dress as though it belonged to someone else.

Larry called, "We need to get her to a hospital. Where are the cars? Where's George?"

"I'm fine," Sue Francis said, a little too firmly. "If you make a fuss, my parents will find out."

Mr. Davis broke through now. "Let me take a look." He gingerly raised the skirt and checked the wound. "The bullet must have grazed it, but she fell right on it. The bone could be broken."

Later, the story pieced itself together. When the Davis boys surveyed the scene, they found a bullet in the gum tree and a few more tracks along the dirt. The shots seemed random. No one was sure how Sue Francis was hit. "Wasn't the lot guarded?" Larry asked Jack Davis.

He gave Larry a hard stare back. "You said you had it covered."

"I was guarding it," said Sue Francis, though her voice was getting weak now. Her eyes grazed Larry's for a moment, and then fixed themselves straight ahead.

Larry's shoulders tightened, and he seemed to have more trouble controlling his breathing than Sue Francis. "I was supposed to meet her here."

"No he wasn't," said Sue Francis. "It's not his fault. It was my idea."

"Don't talk," said Larry. "Where the hell is the Corvair?" Then he felt someone staring at him and he turned around. It was Beth Fine.

Beth had her mouth open, but at the sight of Larry's face, the words lodged in her throat. The sunlight filtered through her wild red hair, the color of rust, the color of blood. Her arms were extended slightly, as though she wanted to keep her balance.

Larry said, "Get the fuck out of here."

"He was trying to warn us," Beth said. "I know he was. If I had gotten into that car—"

"If you had gotten into that car," Larry said, "you think you'd be some hero? Fine, you keep it up, you get in all the cars you want, and all they're going to do is call you a fucking whore."

Beth stepped back. The color drained from her face. Then, she turned and fled. She trembled as she fled, like a chord struck, or a note held for too long. Later that day, the truck and the Ford turned up, parked on Two Street. The Corvair was gone.

SWIMMING
LESSONS

1

ONCE THERE WAS A GIRL who did everything wrong. For example, there was the time she drove to Greenwood, Mississippi and ended up in jail for prostitution. Not that jail, or even a prostitution charge, was a source of shame in those days, not for a Summer Project volunteer.

It happened after Beth Fine hit the cow. It was a Jersey cow, squat and brown, and she hadn't seen it until she was right on top of it, and by the time she slammed on the brakes, the front of the car had caved in, and the cow was down and lowing like a fog-horn.

Beth slammed back and bounced against the steering wheel. Her hands held that wheel in such a grip that she had trouble letting go. When she managed to unlatch the door and stagger outside, she saw, some yards behind her, the car's engine. It had fallen out on impact.

She stood on the road, afraid to pay too much attention to the pain in her ribs. Around her was the Mississippi Delta, light green with cotton. The road was like a line of mercury slipping across a tabletop. It was late afternoon. The cow, the heat, the black skid-marks on the gray road, the way the world seemed to fold itself in thirds, then unfold, shimmer, and fold again, all of this made Beth not quite believe that she was where she was. It was also hard to believe she was alive. She shouldn't have been. There was nowhere to hide, nothing to do but stare up and down that highway. After maybe ten minutes, a truck approached and she flagged it down.

The truck was driven by two elderly Negroes. They pulled over. One of the men very slowly got out and took off his cap. He wore a pair of dark, stained trousers, and the fabric of his shirt was worn to transparency. He had the darkest skin that Beth had ever seen, as black as asphalt. He looked not at Beth, but at the cow. He shook his head.

"Now that's a shame," he said.

Somehow, through gesticulation, luck, or sheer persistence, Beth made it understood that she had to get off the highway and transport herself and her car to Greenwood. The two men took a very long time dislodging a chain from the back of the truck, and then they took even longer to fix it to the Corvair. In the end, Beth sat in her old driver's seat, and her car was towed to the border of Leflore County. The police were waiting.

As for Beth Fine, she was startled to hear that she'd been charged with prostitution. She'd figured they'd arrested her for killing the cow.

THE HOURS THAT BETH SPENT in the county jail were chaotic. The cell was occupied by a girl in a soiled camisole, and an older woman sleeping on a bare mattress whose dress was hiked well above her waist. From the conversation that the girl was having with the prison matron, Beth was made to understand that when the other cellmate got up "there'll be some action." Beth sat on the floor and felt the damp through the bottom of her skirt. There was nothing to look at through the bars but some yellow bricks and stenciled numbers on the facing wall. She had to pay some attention to parts of her body that ached: her ribs, her left shoulder, and the back of her neck where her head had been thrown by the car's impact.

The prison matron kept up her conversation with the girl in the camisole and passed her a cigarette. Beth interrupted.

"Will I get to make a call?" she asked again.

"You don't need to make a call. They're gonna release you in a couple of hours."

Beth shivered. Then she said, "What time is it? Is it after dark? I don't want you to release me after dark."

The matron said, "Can't do nothing about what you want," or at least that's what Beth thought she said.

She was given something on a tray, which she couldn't eat, and she tried to lie down on cement, and thought: let them hold off, let it be daylight, let them forget about me, let me just stay here on the floor. Both cellmates were asleep now, side by side on that mattress, and Beth's thoughts kept turning on themselves as though that conversation with Larry was something that was still unraveling and could only lead back to this cell and to her own damnation. She could have died on the road. Logically, she should have. Why had she been spared? The train of thought was like a circle, and in the center of that circle, tight and urgent, were the papers in the glove compartment of the car that traced it to her father, and that fact that he would soon know everything, and then her mind veered off to Sue Francis, collapsed against the ice-bucket, blood on the ice.

She didn't even realize that she had been called until she was prodded. Then, she sat up.

"Come on. You're free to go," the matron said.

"But what if—"

"Get up. Don't give me trouble."

Beth rose unsteadily, and she wanted to tell the matron that she wasn't capable of getting up and needed medical attention. Instead, she found herself walking along a corridor, past a few stray cells where Negroes slept on mattresses. She wanted to call to them and tell them she was about to be driven off in the dark, but she seemed to have lost her voice.

There were no windows in that corridor, but there were two in the front room, and she was right. It was dark out. Maybe it was after nine. Maybe it was after midnight. Maybe if she didn't move, just stood there, they couldn't make her leave. A man behind a desk handed her some papers, and she asked, "Where are you taking me?"

He was in uniform as well, with the top collar unbuttoned, and he had very pink skin and a transparent buzz cut. "Well that depends," he said. "Are you a good girl?"

"Please," said Beth.

"You can't be such a good girl, doing what you do."

Then, another man said, "Stop it. It's not necessary." Beth turned. The speaker had a New York accent, and he wore a suit that looked as though he'd put it on in the dark. He took the papers from Beth's hand.

"Hey," said Beth.

"Hey yourself," he said to Beth. "You're a pain in the ass, you know that?" He asked her, "Any broken bones? Anything we need to check out tonight?"

Blushing hard, Beth said, "I don't think so."

"You're a lucky fool," the man said. "I wasn't sent here to take care of girls like you. My daughter's your age. She's in Greenville. And if she ever did what you did, I would take her across my knee and give her a spanking."

"You tell her, mister," said the officer.

"Shut up!" said the man, who, as it turned out, was from the National Lawyer's Guild.

THAT WAS HOW BETH FINALLY got to the Greenwood Freedom House. No one met her at the door, which the lawyer unceremoniously opened. Although the front hall was well-lit, the rest of the place was dark, and the lawyer said, "They'll take care of you in the morning. For now, just get some rest."

But where? In the first room, a number of people crashed on couches, and what space wasn't taken up by their bags was littered with loose books and papers. Beth stumbled through, one hand feeling her way, the other pressed against the wall. There was what looked like a pile of blankets, and she rolled into it, but it proved to be a pile of shoes. She was past caring. She lay there for some time and told herself that it was as good a place as any, but then her ribs began to burn, and the pain traveled to her neck, and she knew she wouldn't get to sleep that night.

She heard someone in the kitchen, and that's when she saw Ron Beauchamp, outlined in the dim light of the open refrigerator. It was hard for her to get to her feet, but she did, and she managed to walk across the hall. She said the only thing that came to mind. "I brought the car."

"You kind of startled me, baby," said Ron. He still had the refrigerator door open, and he observed her by its light. "You want a sandwich?"

"No, thanks," said Beth. Then, "You don't remember me."

"Well sure I do," said Ron. "Only your hair's all flat on the side of your head."

Beth said, "I was sleeping on a pile of shoes."

Ron closed the refrigerator door, but the kitchen didn't go black. It was illuminated, softly, by yet another room, where a couple of young Negro men were playing cards.

"I can find you a better place to sleep than a pile of shoes," said Ron.

Beth was afraid to breathe. It took some effort for her to say, "I'm okay."

Ron said, "No, I mean, I could make you up a bed upstairs."

"Don't go to any trouble." Then, she said, "You still don't remember me, do you."

"Sure I do," said Ron, and he seemed to. "You're the one who almost let that cracker kill us on the way to New York City. I wouldn't forget you. Now are you sure you don't want a sandwich? We got bologna and we got peanut butter."

The certainty that Ron did know her, and the courtliness of his offer, maybe also seeing Ron like that, in a T-shirt and boxers, not much taller than she was, with his sharp chin, big ears, and sleepy long-lashed eyes, the sandwich he constructed, all of it got to Beth in a way nothing else had that night. Before she knew it, she was shaking hard, and Ron was putting down the bologna and looking at her. In the effort of holding back tears, Beth's face must have done some pretty outrageous things.

"Hey, hey, it's alright, baby," Ron said. "We got the call; I know about the car. I'm just surprised you didn't break your neck."

"I wish I had," said Beth. Then, "It's not just the car."

"Of course not," said Ron. He wavered. "You want a drink? Maybe a cigarette?"

"I want to be dead."

"No you don't," said Ron. He switched on the kitchen light. He walked to the window, opened it, and scratched the back of his neck, a gesture that brought Beth back to their few hours in the car that day, when she had stared at the back of him and hungered for the front of him. Then he turned and said, "God didn't want you dead. I guess you got to figure out why."

There was a little table and chair in that kitchen. Ron sank into the chair and finished his sandwich. Beth didn't know where to begin, with the French lesson, with Cy Cohen and the mop, with Sue Francis and the ice, and she wasn't sure how much had gotten back to Greenwood, and if any of it could serve as a justification for her current circumstances. At last, she sat down on the other vacant chair and just said, "I didn't think it would be like this."

"Is that so?" said Ron, just as he had back in the car. But he seemed to be listening.

Beth was emboldened. "I thought I'd be in the middle of things, singing and marching and driving people to the courthouse, you know, and the troopers would come, but we'd all be together and there'd be so many of us that we'd just overpower them and fill the jails, but it was just like that time when I was in Chester."

"What time in Chester?" Ron asked.

"When I almost drowned," said Beth.

"Baby," Ron asked, "how fast was that car going when you hit the cow?"

Beth said, "I don't remember."

"If you drove the way you talk," Ron said, "you'd be dead for sure. Now don't you want something to eat?"

"Larry hates me," said Beth.

"Larry?" Ron laughed. "That's just his way. But he's my main man, Larry. Came to us in '61, fresh from the Freedom Rides, and he'd got a lot of Jeremiah in him, and if someone's got a lot of Jeremiah in him, you know he's not gonna put up with nonsense."

Beth persisted. "I wanted to bring you Bluebell as soon as I came, like I said I would. But he wouldn't let me. He won't let me do anything because he thinks I'm useless. He's a racist."

"A what?" Ron didn't laugh this time. "Baby, listen, don't sweat Bluebell. She's just a car. She's not even—you got to forgive me—not even such a good car."

"But she's all I've got," said Beth. Then, amending the statement, with a bowed head and a leaden heart, she added, "She's not even mine."

Ron took this in. "Yeah. It's your daddy's car. And he said you could donate it to the Movement, right, baby?"

"My name is Beth," Beth said, not answering his question.

"Right," Ron said. He rose from the table, and, with hesitation, helped her up. He was shy about touching her, maybe because he knew that she was sore, maybe for other reasons. "Beth, come on. There's a room upstairs. You can make it upstairs?"

"Of course I can," said Beth. "I'm not the one who was shot." Then, with Ron's warm fingers on her arm, she finally broke down and collapsed against him, crying with her whole heart. He let her melt into the stiff cloth of his T-shirt. He still held back, and, sensing it, Beth felt all the more alone and hopeless, and she whispered, "How can I not make things worse? Tell me. I don't know how."

He led her through the corridor and up the stairs to a small room that could have been a closet but was mainly occupied by a table and a bulky printing press. She could make out the shape of the machine by way of swaths of darkness, and Ron managed to arrange some couch cushions in a corner. He laid her in them with a delicacy that broke her heart. She wanted to insist that she was not that fragile, that it had been Sue Francis that needed that kind of treatment, but in fact she did know that she was that fragile, and from her place in the cushions, she looked up at Ron, who stayed beside her. "This okay?" Ron asked her.

"It's fine," she said. Then, "Thanks."

"She's fine too," Ron said. His face hovered above her. "Sue Francis," he added. "Last I heard, she was asleep. Mr. Davis gave her something."

It was like a needle pulled out of Beth's heart. "How did you know?"

Ron said, "It's called a WATS line. Telephone. More like a life-line. Nothing gets past us here in Greenwood."

All Beth could do was to will Ron not to move, to stay right there, crouched over her. It seemed to work. His gaze wandered towards the printing press.

"I fixed that Speed-O-Print around a month ago," he said. "I'm always the one who fixes things here—printing presses, leaky faucets, anything that can be repaired. But mainly, I'm the engine man. My Uncle Walter taught me. He's a driver for a white man up in Tutwiler, but he aims to own his own garage. Uncle Walter always said a man who can take a car apart and put it back together never has to depend on handouts, as long as he's got two hands."

Beth was content just to hear the cadence of Ron's voice, and she wished she could oblige him by falling asleep, but that seemed unlikely. After a while, she said, "What does the press print?"

He smiled. "You're in a historical place right here. This is where we printed up those copies of the Constitution."

"What copies?" Beth asked.

"The ones," said Ron, "that landed me in *Life Magazine*."

Thus, Ron began a story that might have begun, *Once there was a boy who did everything wrong*. It was a bedtime story, though Beth was sure she'd never sleep again. He told her, in that same low, easy voice, about the day he'd been working in Chen's Grocery Store shelving tuna-fish and sliced bread when he heard that Martin Luther King had come to Greenwood, but it was really Bob Moses, about commuting between Tutwiler and Greenwood and spending a month at Broad Street High, but getting expelled when it was clear he was spending too much time at the Freedom House. He was a delinquent, by anybody's standards, the shame of his good aunt and uncle, a crazy nigger who would not behave the way he should because obedience was designed to keep him less than human and he knew it.

"And back then," he said, "we had Freedom Days. You know about the Freedom Days. We brought folks to the courthouse by the river and just like you said—we ended up in jail. And it got so it was hard to find anybody over twenty-one with a job and a family, with something to lose, who was gonna go up to the courthouse. See, in the end, it's all about the children."

"But children can't vote," said Beth.

"But we will. Look at a colored boy and one day he'll be a colored man," Ron said. "That's what we're after in Atlantic City."

"You're going to the convention?"

Ron said, "I'm the one organizing the buses, baby. Can't no one get nowhere without Ron Beauchamp. But we aren't talking about that now. We were talking about this room and the Speed-O-Print we call the Liberator. Frank Court—you remember Frank, the one who met us in Manhattan—he and Jackie Gordon got this notion that somebody ought to go to Broad Street High and hand out copies of the U.S. Constitution. And they managed to get me out from underneath a Valiant and run off maybe two hundred copies and say: Ronny Beauchamp, you got to infiltrate."

Ron had not intended to lead a march, and he hadn't intended to end up at the courthouse. It was not clear what ought to happen next. But then he saw the Yazoo River. It was half a block away, brown and swollen, traveling hard, and his heart seemed to swell too. He told Beth that he thought of the River Jordan, and also of the Mississippi which he'd seen only once, in Greenville, where it flooded a park the way his heart felt flooded now. And his spirit told him to drop to his knees and pray.

That's what he did. It didn't surprise him that all the others dropped to their knees as well. He might have gone right on his belly then, prostrated himself to meet whatever God would give him. The green beside the courthouse was full of those students with their heads bowed and the copies of the Constitution pressed against their hearts, and when the police came to round them up, their prayers carried them through the beating and the dragging into paddy wagons and the hours in jail.

"You hear a lot about singing in the Movement," said Ron. "When we were in jail, we sang so much they said they'd take away our mattresses unless we stopped and there were some who didn't stop singing even when they took their mattresses away. Now me, I like a mattress when I sleep."

"You slept pretty well in that car that time," Beth said.

"I said I like a mattress. But I can sleep anywhere. Guess I'm gifted."

Beth sat up, though her rib gave a twinge. She asked him, "When you went to the high school, did you wear sunglasses?"

Ron seemed bewildered by the question. "You think they'd let me into Broad Street High wearing sunglasses?" But the question was designed to make him remember something else. It did. He looked uncomfortable and said, "You talk too much. What you need to do is sleep."

Beth said, "Stay with me."

He did stay with her, squatting beside the cushions, closing his eyes. Soon, his breathing evened out and carried with it just a little of the scent of peanut butter. Beth had never felt more awake. It must have been close to dawn. Although the room had no windows, the quality of the darkness had changed. It was grainy, diffuse, less night than shadow.

Ron had stretched out his legs now, and they overlapped just a little with the cushion. She cupped her hand around his bare foot, and he stirred. What did she want from him? She wanted him to stay with her. His head was tilted back, and the line of his jaw cast a shadow on his T-shirt. When he had slept in the car, she'd felt irrelevant, but now she felt trusted. What could she give him in return? She too could sleep.

Yet she could not stop looking at him. It was like looking into the future.

2

BUT BETH DREAMED ABOUT the past. Or rather, she dreamed about her mother, sitting behind a white table, her hair brushed smooth, her lipstick dark and precise. She addressed someone, "I was a marvelous domestic in the desert."

The room was full of light, so much light that her mother's face was drowning in it. Only the dark red hair and lips were visible. Then, slowly, lines of chairs, of figures eating, of drapery across the windows of a restaurant formed themselves, and Aunt Beatrice was saying, "Somebody ought to close those drapes."

"It raises too much dust," said Vivian Fine. "It's better to see what you get, and then you clean it."

"I thought you had a maid."

"Oh, she was from the Pueblo, so we had to let her go. They know things we don't know, the Navajo," said Vivian Fine. "Of course we lost her.

Dread followed those words like a blow, and Beth woke up. For a moment, she could not recall where she was or who was in the room, and she wanted to reach out, but hesitated, paralyzed by a fear that had no source but the weird light of that dream. It was all tangled in footage of nuclear blasts she'd seen in high school, memories of her mother towards the end, something about cancer, a word no one said, a death that would have been an explanation. By the time Beth was a little girl, the years in New Mexico were in the deep past, but her mother always talked about the quality of light there, the afternoons in the Pueblo where she'd pass out chocolate to the children, and they'd trade the brightly colored wrappers and follow her around the dirt roads, waving them like copies of the U.S. Constitution.

"They were so warm there," Vivian Fine would say. "They don't mind if you're odd. Not like this place where people get offended if you cross the street against the light."

Who did her mother say this to? Beth could not recall. She did know that Vivian often crossed the street against the light, and when Beth was a little girl, she'd held her mother's hand in wonder and terror as cars came to a honking, screeching halt to let them pass.

Beth's mother said, "In the desert, you know, there's so much space that you can see a car coming for miles in any direction. Not like this place, where everything is hidden."

"Open and hidden are not actual concepts," said Max Fine.

Sometimes, when Beth was supposed to be asleep in bed, she'd listen to her parents, understanding little more than the high cadence of her mother, talking on and on, and then the sudden bass note of her father. They often argued this way, just as Beth would later argue with Max, for the pleasure of his dour approval. Surely, this was her parents' courtship, and the stuff of their early marriage in Los Alamos. Even at first, after they moved to Princeton, she would call him a numbers runner and asked him what he gambled, and he replied that according to his recent research, numbers could not be trusted, and she would laugh and ask if he had read a dollar bill lately: they were supposed to trust in God. When their voices mingled, Beth felt easier.

Then, it was just her mother. "What's life here? Half-life? I can't even fit my paintings on the wall, it's so cramped, and all these people hunched over like turtles with their radioactive brains ticking like bombs."

At some point, Aunt Beatrice spoke to the manager of the Princeton branch of Neuman's Department Store, and Vivian got a job as a window dresser. She would take Beth with her when she was five years old. Beth was told to wait in the storage room. It was full of naked mannequins. Most of them were bald, and a rack of blonde and brown and auburn wigs were shelved by length and color. Beth tried to be brave, but in the end, she came running out, sobbing, "I don't want to be with the artificial people!"

After that, they left her in the window with her mother. "Won't you help me, darling," Vivian Fine asked Beth. She had a bucket of artificial snow, and she had Beth sprinkle the snow along the shoulders of the sweaters, and in a fine layer across the floor. It was August; the sun beat through the plate glass and sparkled.

Afterwards, they would take a taxi home. Vivian gave Beth a change purse shaped like a Scott Terrier. Beth would stand precariously on the edge of a curb and wave that purse to hail the cab, and then her mother would pretend to be a stranger and call out: "Excuse me. I believe you're headed in my direction. Would you mind very much if I shared this ride?"

Beth would reply, "Not at all."

So Beth would sit, with her legs swinging and her frizzy red hair coming out of her ponytail, as her mother told her about Chicago, where people rode the El high in the air, and where you could see everything, not like a taxi where the world was enclosed by the square of a window. There was no El in Princeton. There weren't even buses except the ones that went to Philadelphia and New York, but Vivian said that if Beth ever got to ride the bus, she should sit in the back, because that's where you got to see everything. "That's why colored people sit there. They know things we don't know," Vivian whispered, "just like the Navajo."

Once, Beth and her mother took a trip together to Chicago, for her grandfather's funeral. Beth had never met him, and it was also the first time she met her grandmother, a skinny, trembling matron who swooped down on Beth and terrified her by crushing her to her bosom and braying out to Vivian, "How could you keep her from us? You're a monstrous, monstrous girl!" After the service, Vivian and Beth didn't take the town car to the cemetery. Instead, they walked to the El, took it south, and ended up beside Lake Michigan. It was autumn. Both were underdressed. Beth kept her hand locked in her mother's and tried to figure out why she was being so quiet. Finally, Beth asked, "Mom, are you sad?"

Vivian looked down at Beth and said, "Yes, I guess I am." Her dark auburn hair, so lush that it looked purple, her heart-shaped face, her clear green eyes, even the dark stripes on her sleeveless dress, came into sudden focus. Beth had never seen her mother like this, gentle, present, looking at her. She said, "Maybe I wasn't cut out to have a daughter."

"Am I cut out to be a daughter?" Beth asked her.

"Yes, oh yes," said Vivian. She bent and pressed her lips to Beth's forehead. "You're my good, good girl."

WHEN BETH WOKE UP, SHE was alone. She couldn't gauge the time, but it was probably well into the morning. She could already hear people moving through the hallway, and traffic outside. She propped herself up and managed to get to her feet, and she stood in the doorway of the storage room. A shaggy, grim-looking white boy was passing, and he stopped short at the sight of her.

"You're the girl who totaled the Corvair?" Then, she recognized him. It was Frank Court.

"I guess so," Beth said.

"Crazy! We've got a ride back for you," he said. "You know, you're famous."

"I don't even want to think about what I'm famous for," said Beth.

"You're the first Summer Project volunteer to wreck a car," Frank said. "You know what Larry told us when we called him? He said only you could manage to come out of something like that in one piece."

It struck Beth that Larry didn't mean that as a compliment, and at the same time, that Frank wouldn't hear it any other way.

"Getting out in one piece," said Frank, "is a talent. It's something we have in common, sweetheart. I should have been dead three years ago." He walked her downstairs, where the couches in the front room were deserted now, and in the kitchen, remains of what must have been breakfast were still on the table. There were plates smeared with jam, a few broken crusts, and one cup with an inch of juice on the bottom.

"I could wash up," Beth said.

"I guess you could. No rush," said Frank.

The Freedom House sink was full of plates and coffee cups, and there was a basin of soft soap that fell apart as soon as Beth laid a sponge into it, but she managed to get everything washed and rinsed. It felt like something she could actually do. A few people drifted in and out of the kitchen, opening the refrigerator, pulling out a wizened apple, glancing at her with indifference or, occasionally, approval. Later, she would discover that she had acquired an instant reputation at Greenwood. She was the girl who washed the dishes.

Ron came into the kitchen just as she was searching for a dishtowel. He was carrying a big package wrapped in butcher paper.

"You staying for lunch?" he asked her, in a way too casual to read.

Beth managed to say, "I don't think so."

Ron said, "But I was going to cook for you." A few people had drifted in behind him, and he said to them, "You all can't leave yet. I got six pounds of catfish and a clean kitchen, and someone who'll wash the dishes afterwards."

"Wash your own dishes," said a white girl. She gave Ron a look that Beth could only describe as saucy. Then she turned to Beth, and in a friendly way, she asked, "Are you the one who hit the cow?" It turned out that they were on their way to the Marshall County Freedom Democratic Party convention and they had space in their Crown Vic, which could hold six. "It would be a crime to waste a seat," she said.

"Isn't it out of your way?" Beth asked.

"No, sister. It sure isn't," said a young Negro man. "As long as you don't mind cramming into the back with a bunch of ignorant fools, we're happy to oblige." He had a mustache and a way of talking up into it that made his voice sound gruff. His name was Will or Bill or something, and he handed her a banana and said, "You'd better eat now because all you're getting on the road is peanut butter."

A Negro girl with a short natural, the first Beth ever saw, held up the remains of a five-pound container with a crack in the glass. "It's the official

SNCC peanut butter jar. Had it since we made the fund-raising trip to Chicago last spring."

"Aren't you scared the glass will get into it?" Beth asked.

"Honey, that's the least of our worries," said the girl. Then she laughed and put her arm around Beth. "Where are you from? California?"

"She's from Swarthmore," said Ron, who had been silent all the time and was sitting backwards in a chair, using a penknife on an apple. "She's a French major. Maybe she'll teach you all some French."

"Have you read Fanon?" asked the man with the mustache. "Every brother in Atlanta's crazy over Fanon." She recognized him then. He had been present at the training in Ohio. He'd torn into a group of volunteers who'd laughed during a film depicting a sweaty, obese Mississippi county clerk. He'd told the volunteers that they should just head home and spend their summer by the pool if they thought this was all a joke. He had terrified her there, but he didn't seem angry now, just a little sleepy. He was the one who would do the driving. He smiled at Beth without recognition.

The Negro girl was Jackie Gordon. "Jackie like the president's wife," she said. Beth ended up in the back seat squeezed between Jackie and the white girl, Helen Forest, who had been working with the Movement since 1961 and had, according to her, fought her way out from behind the desk of the Atlanta office to work in Greenwood and was now working at a Freedom School in Ruleville.

"So what are you all up to in Melody?" Helen asked Beth. "I love the names of these towns: Melody, Harmony—"

"Liberty," called Will from the driver's seat. "And there's our office on Lynch Street."

"So is it melodious in Melody?" Helen asked Beth. She was a plump, sweet-faced girl no more than five feet tall. Her brown hair was cut unevenly. She told Beth that she let one of her students cut it. "I know there's not much in the way of rules in Ruleville."

In the front seat, another young black man thumped his leg and started in.

We're on our way to Melody—oh yeah.
We're on our way to Melody—oh yeah
Don' let those cops get hold of me
Befo' we get to Melody—

"Harry Belafonte here," said Jackie, "thinks he can write songs."

"I never said I was Harry Belafonte," the man said. "Just tryin' to wuk up a little enthusiasm about this trip. Jus' tryin' to show a little reshpect for our sista Beth here. After all, she's gotta work with Larry Walsh and that would drive the spirit out of anyone."

"Larry's my man," said Will. "Don't say a word against Larry."

"But you've got to admit, he's hard-line." The man turned in his seat and smiled at Beth. His name was Sylvester. He had a broken nose and most of his front teeth were missing, and there was something ugly and appealing about him. "It's 'cause he's from Boston. Those cats from the North, they got an attitude. Even when they cool cats, like Shtokely. They tink they got shomething to prove. Now me, I don't have a ting to prove because I was born right here in Ruleville."

"What about me?" Helen asked him. "What about my white skin?"

"Oh, fa'get about your white skin, suga'," said Sylvester. "You've rishked that skin so many times it mightus well not be there at all."

The conversation kept on going, as Beth leaned back in the seat with the enormous, mostly empty, jar of peanut butter on her lap, and they talked about the convention in Jackson and the way that so much energy was going into preparing for Atlantic City that it was hard to remember that they once had no use for those sorts of politics. "Remember, I warned you," Jackie said. "Turn away from direct action, and before you know it, you're not dealing with ethics, you're dealing with politics."

"Jacks," said Will, "it's strategy. You ever hear of strategy, or is that against your precious code of ethics?"

"The question is, can we bring morality to politics, or are we going to end up bringing politics to our morality? They're bound to try to make us play their game and offer us some kind of compromise."

"The point is," said Helen, "this *is* direct action. We're taking the struggle north. And if those folks in Atlantic City can't be moved by Fannie Lou Hamer talking about the beating she took for having the audacity to try to register to vote, if it can't make them see the light, then I'm just packing up my bags and moving to Katmandu."

Sylvester asked, "Was' in Katmandu?"

Helen said, "Mountains. And a little peace and quiet."

"Girl," said Jackie, "you'll just end up organizing—who d'ya call it—Katmandoodles?"

"Tibetans," said Will.

"Oh, he's a college boy," said Jackie to Beth. "Trust him to know that. I dropped out my junior year after the sit-ins and never looked back. And if a Katmandoodle starts to crow somewhere, I'll just fly over there and join him. You know how it goes in the Movement. It's all waves. Like, when we started it was with those sit-ins at Greensboro, that was a wave. Then it was Nashville, and then the Freedom Rides, then Albany and McComb, we just ride these waves of freedom."

"But Atlantic City—thas' a tidal wave," said Sylvester. "Headin' to that convention, thas' calling America's bluff, baby. You really think we'll win?"

"I guess you can't stop a tidal wave," said Jackie. "All you can do is just get really wet."

Beth tried to think of whether she should join in the conversation, but then she realized that she didn't have to. It wasn't that they ignored her. Rather, it was assumed that she must be all right because she knew Ron Beauchamp.

"So, Ron recruited you," Jackie said, archly, Beth thought.

"Kind of," said Beth.

Will said, "Jackie was Ronny's neighbor. She was the one who got him arrested."

"No—he got himself arrested," Jackie said. "Let's get that straight."

Helen said, "What I heard was that Ron had told everyone he was going to get arrested with you, Jackie. He had a crush on you."

"Well, everybody has a crush on me," said Jackie. Beth believed her. Her skin was the color of dark honey, and her hair framed her face like a halo.

Jackie told them about the buses Ron had arranged for the convention. The greatest coup of all was the yellow school bus from that same high school where he had caused the trouble back in '62. "That must have been the last time I saw Ronny in a suit and tie," she said. "But he'll have to dig them up again. We've all got to lobby, and no way they're gonna look at us twice in our overalls. Now me, I've always dressed respectably."

"Thas' cause yo' daddy ownsh a funeral parlor," said Sylvester. "Talk 'bout a growth industry."

The four chatted away, driving at a reasonable speed in a Crown Vic, a ten-year-old model that Ron had refurbished, preserving the red upholstery. They seemed so comfortable in that car that they might have easily kept going through to Alabama, maybe all the way across the country. Helen Forest had driven from Texas to the SNCC office in Atlanta the night Medger Evers died.

"I just couldn't sleep," said Helen. "You know how it is? You've got to do something. And all I could do was drive. I was teaching—I'd just gotten my degree and I was at a Negro school talking about Medger. I'd already gotten into trouble for that. And I knew I couldn't face those kids in the morning."

"You should have seen her when she showed up in the office," Jackie said. "She'd taken so much No-doze, she was twitching like a rabbit. We were about to call the funny farm. But Mrs. Ella Baker got her calmed down and put her to bed, and in the morning, we found out she knew how to type."

Sylvester said, "Helen's a little crazy, but we love her anyway."

"I'm not crazy. I'm high spirited," said Helen.

Jackie asked Beth, "Are you high spirited too? Because if you are, maybe you can understand half of what that girl says, because I sure can't."

"Oh, I'm not high spirited," said Beth. "I'm high strung." Then, she felt delighted with herself.

"Great, great," said Sylvester. "Sherves us right ta be in a car with a couple of white girls. Will, can't you go any faster?"

"Can't, man. You know Her Majesty will not be rushed. Ron's got her wired so if she goes over eighty, she'll explode."

"Don't even joke about that—don't even joke," said Jackie, though she was smiling.

So Will talked about the high speed chase down Highway 51 the week before and how he managed to get off the road before Amite County, and Sylvester asked him about the car's new paint job, and how unlikely it would be to keep the highway patrol from spotting what so clearly was a Movement vehicle, and Jackie reached over to take the jar of peanut butter off Beth's lap. She scooped some out with a cracker. Then the crackers were passed around.

Beth leaned into the damp, red vinyl seat. Her thighs pressed against the thighs of the two women. Jackie handed Beth a small, white tube, leaned over, and parted her afro just above the ear.

"Honey, could you put some disinfectant on for me and rub it in real good? I'm supposed to do it every morning, but I forgot."

Gingerly, Beth squeezed a strand of cream into the cut.

"Hey, how'd you get that one?" Helen asked Jackie.

"Oh—that's an old one. You know, from that time in January. Opened again," Jackie said. Then, she said to Beth, "Why are you being so careful, honey? I told you to rub it in."

3

MR. DAVIS WAS SHELVING STOCK when Beth was dropped off at the pharmacy. The moment she opened the door, he stepped up and laid the flats of his hands behind her neck and then down her back and the sides of her rib cage. He watched her face for signs of discomfort. "You know," he said, "it's a miracle they're not taking you back here in a hearse."

"Please," said Beth. "I'm really okay. Just a little sore."

"So those hard-headed kids in Greenwood figure you're good to go?"

"I've got a pretty hard head myself," Beth said. "Where's Larry?"

"He's in Holly Springs at the Marshall County convention," said Davis.

"But I want to see him," said Beth.

Mr. Davis said, "Maybe he doesn't have anything to say to you just now, Beth." He told her about the call from State Farm Insurance they had received this morning, just as Larry was about to drive to Holly Springs. "Seems that Corvair wasn't in your name."

"I never said it was," said Beth. She tried to keep the note of defensiveness out of her voice, but it was hard work.

"You need to understand," said Mr. Davis. "He's got plenty on his mind right now. When J.B.'s truck got burned, it kind of brought us together, but Sue Francis getting shot, well, nothing like that's happened here before. In broad daylight."

"But it's not my fault," Beth began, and then immediately added, "Don't tell Larry I said that."

"Why not? It's true," said Mr. Davis. Then, he said, "Beth, you need to go pack."

Beth said nothing.

"You're being sent home," he said. He pulled a bus schedule off the wall and handed it to her. "There's a Greyhound to Memphis, leaves at ten in the morning, and another one at two. Stops just the other side of the tracks. I can get George to help you with your bags."

"Thanks," said Beth. "I may need help."

Mrs. BURGESS WAS IN HOLLY Springs as well. At supper time, George came over from Mrs. Turner's house with a covered dish of chicken and rice. Laurel, Beth and Po sat together and Laurel spooned portions onto plates and tried to keep up a bright stream of conversation.

"Look," Laurel said to Po. "There's a wish-bone. You want to make a wish?"

But Po just went on tearing chicken off the bone, chewing with an open mouth and spitting its skin onto the floor, and, with Mrs. Burgess gone, what had seemed simply eccentric seemed more sinister, somehow.

Not for the first time, Beth wondered about Po's father. The more she looked at him the less he looked like Mrs. Burgess, or like anyone else in town. If she laid her arm right next to his, he wouldn't be much darker. Meanwhile, Po got up from the chair and made it to his regular place on the couch, the cushion he had worn out through the summer, the soiled pillow by his head. There was still chicken grease on his fingers, and he rubbed them against his shirt.

"You think we ought to wipe him off?" Laurel asked Beth.

"Why are you asking me?" Beth said.

"Why do you sound like that? Like you're mad at me?"

"Oh, hell," said Beth. She started to clear the table and take the dishes to the basin. "I'm not mad at you. To be honest, I'm not thinking about you at all."

"I know," said Laurel. Then she started to cry. Of course, Beth had to turn to her and listen to her start in about how she wished she were leaving too, and how when none of her students came that morning she'd gone to the houses of their parents but none of them even opened the door, how the most recent letter from her fiancée implied that he was going to spend another year in Ghana, and how Judy had been so distant, hadn't even spoken to her since the shooting, not even all the time they'd waited by the church.

All of this came out of Laurel in a strange, high-pitched stream. Beth just stood there listening, and after a while, she said, "You ought to go find her."

"I don't even know where she is," said Laurel.

"She's looking for you," said Beth, and as soon as she said it, she knew it was true. She looked down at her greasy, soapy, dripping hands, and although Laurel could in no way understand her, she added, "When I wash dishes, I'm always right. Go on."

As though in confirmation, Po said, "Uh."

Laurel slipped her long hair over one shoulder, a gesture of recovery.

"Are you sure you'll be alright?"

"Why wouldn't I be alright?" Beth asked, and now she actually did feel angry. "Just get out of here. Take your guitar. Go sing with your soul-sister, okay?"

"I can't take my guitar in the rain," said Laurel, because rain was falling now, in thick, fist-sized drops, and she put on a blue slicker before she rushed off.

Beth looked after her for some time. Meanwhile, she scrubbed the dishes. Mrs. Burgess had the same soft-soap they used in Greenwood, the kind that clung to the rims of the plates, and as Beth drew the dishrag around and around, she wondered if life could take the form of a series of necessary tasks that would present themselves to her and that she would learn to do just well enough: to wash the dinner dishes, to pack a suitcase, to read a bus schedule to Memphis, to occupy herself on the long trip east, to greet her father—and then Beth lost her train of thought. What the hell would she say to her father?

She moved into Mrs. Burgess's room and pulled her suitcase out from under her bed. The room was almost black now, and distant thunder seemed to carry the evening with it. She could hear Po move back and forth in the front room, dragging his feet, making the sad, low, "eh-oh" sound in his throat that sometimes meant he was scared.

"It's okay," Beth called in from the bedroom. "I'm right here."

"Eh-oh," Po said again, faint but persistent. Beth knew she was avoiding packing. Then, lightening struck close by. Or something like it. Silence followed.

Beth called to Po, "Are you okay in there?"

She stuck her head out of the bedroom door. One white man held a high-beam flashlight. The other had Po by the neck. She shrank back, but they'd heard her, and the one who wasn't holding Po eyed Beth with amusement. "Hey, girlfriend's here."

She drew back, heart racing, shrinking against the wall of the bedroom, ears humming, and even so, she could hear the sound of the cushion wrenched from the couch's box-spring and the shriek of Po as he was torn from his place, the laughter.

"Look at the mess you made. Where's your momma?"

"With the other coons? At the coon-convention?"

Beth felt her hand slip under the mattress. There was a white place in her head where, piece by piece, the revolver constructed itself, chambers, the safety catch, the way the fingers of Claire Burgess were positioned on the trigger. The pieces fell together with a maniac precision that engrossed Beth Fine so thoroughly that she hadn't even noticed that she'd stepped into the front room with the pistol cocked and pointed.

The lowered flashlight tossed a beam into the rain. "You don't even know how to hold it, you cunt."

"Easy does it. You don't know what you're doing."

"Yes I do," said Beth. Her left hand kept the right one steady, and she moved forward, as though her feet were in a groove in the floor and some-one had given her a soft push from behind. "I do know. Yes, I do."

One of the men pulled out his own gun and pointed it not at Beth, but at Po. "You're not the blonde. You're Cy's girl, honey. You two-timing Cy with this nigger?"

The other man released his hold on Po to grab hold of his own fly. "I got a gun too, honey. You want to see my gun?"

That's when Beth pulled the trigger. The impact threw the pistol from her hand and she scrambled for it, managing to grip it and step backward and to shoot again. There was another gunshot—from one of the men—and it hit the couch. Beth raised her gun and shot right through the pas-sageway, and she could hear them stumble off, slam a car door, tear off through the rain.

Beth's hand shook. The gun dropped near the couch cushion. Then she reached for it and something in her stomach cracked. She vomited. The effort made her weak, and in the end, she doubled over and pushed the gun out of the way before she closed her eyes.

Po WAS THE ONE TO go for help. He pounded on Mrs. Turner's door, and when she opened it and saw the drenched, mountain-ous figure, she didn't recognize him at first. She threw on a robe and pad-ded over. Beth was still on the floor with her cheek next to the gun.

"Honey, honey," Mrs. Turner said.

"Don't call me that," Beth said. "Don't call me honey."

"Well I've got to know. Are you all right? This boy here's all right," she said.

"I'm fine," said Beth. She propped herself up and in fact, her head felt so clear it hurt. "I just need to take a bath."

Her movements were stiff, not awkward, but more as though her body had stopped belonging to her. Mrs. Turner had a tub in the back. "Why don't you wait until the rain lets up."

"I'd rather do it in the rain," Beth said. She understood this woman was afraid, and she respected fear just now. She understood it. In a way she never really had before, she knew why people acted on fear. She disrobed, climbed into a tin tub of the cool water made cooler by the rain, and swore she would never be afraid in the same way again, would not act on fear. She would let no one persuade her otherwise. She looked at the gap between one house and another. The rain stopped at last, and now there were a few stars scattered through the floss of cloud, and also a hazy moon. To bathe like this, in a tin tub in the moonlight, was a remarkable thing. Through the sheets laid over the tub, she could see the outline of her body, hazy as the moon through those clouds.

George must have been standing near her for a while. It wasn't until she got up with the wet sheet around her that he made himself known. "Miss," he said. "You okay?"

Beth turned and looked at George. "Everyone keeps asking me that. Yes, I am."

George kept his eyes lowered, and Beth knew he felt responsible for what happened, that he resented the responsibility, and that he had come out to see Beth in hopes of absolution. "I guess," he said, "you hit one of those bastards."

"I doubt it," said Beth.

"Maybe you shot his balls off," George said. "Maybe he'll die, even."

When George said all of this, Beth recognized a decision she had already made. She wasn't going to Paris. She wasn't even going back to college. The rest of her life was hazy, but she knew that the way to live that life was going to be like driving through the fog with headlights on; she would see what was in front of her, and direct herself with that resolve in mind. "George," she said, "I need to be by myself for a little while, okay?"

George said, "Yeah. I hear you."

Beth watched him turn to go, and she said, "I didn't even aim, George. I didn't know what I was doing."

George turned around, and he said, "Yes, miss. Yes you did."

4

THE BATH WAS THE LAST moment of solitude Beth would have until she got on the bus, where she would spend twenty hours and have more time than she wished to have to think about that night, and also to resist thinking about what would happen next. At sunrise, she went back to the Burgess house and found Laurel sitting cross-legged on the bed. She looked up at Beth with her dour, long-lashed eyes and said, "I left you here."

"If I could spend," said Beth, "less time telling people that they're not to blame, I could actually finish packing."

"So you're alright?" Laurel asked. "Really?"

"Look," said Beth, as she started towards the door, "We came here knowing something terrible might happen to us. But I guess the black people here face that kind of shit every day."

The language clearly startled Laurel, who straightened and made an awkward gesture of protest with a single raised hand, as though she were tracing a signal in the air. Then she said, "So, should we call someone?"

"I can't think that far ahead," Beth said. She crossed the hallway where Mrs. Turner was sweeping up debris from the couch, and Po sat on an unharmed edge, with his head bowed. His face was pock-marked, ash-jawed, sorrowful, and because Beth didn't want to talk to Laurel again, she sat next to him, and she began to feel a little of what Po might feel, as though the world was overwhelming and, really, there was nowhere to go, nowhere safe, so you might as well not move.

This was a feeling that would return in the future, and Beth had a tiny foretaste of it, like a drop of medication that makes the tip of the tongue numb. But that day, Beth did manage to rouse herself, and in spite of the gravitational pull of Po and those broken springs, she got up from the couch, folded her clothing, and took her suitcase to the door.

There was Larry. He wore a sleeveless T-shirt that he must have slept in. One arm was braced against the wall; the other hung loose beside him. His eyes were red. "Fine," he said, "Where do you think you're going?"

Beth rubbed her eyes. "What? Why?"

"Listen," said Larry, "What do you have that suitcase for? Are you crazy? Why are you standing there?"

"Why are you here? You're supposed to be in Holly Springs."

"Where's Po?" He pushed past her, straight into the house where Mrs. Turner was still stuffing the white ticking back into the sofa-cushions. The damp patches on the floor had been mopped up, and the gun had been cleaned too, and was resting on top of its paper bag on the kitchen counter. Larry stopped, put a hand on the wall—again as though to keep himself from falling—and then he closed his eyes. "Alright," Larry said. "I guess nobody thought about evidence."

Mrs. Turner asked him, "You want some coffee?"

"Where's Po?" Larry asked again, and then he seemed to realize that he was standing right in front of him." He backed up. "Your momma's on her way," he said to him. "She was in a car right behind me."

Mrs. Turner settled Larry at the kitchen table and poured him a cup of coffee, and after a moment, Beth sat across from him and said, "I think he's okay, but it's hard to tell."

Larry didn't seem to hear her. He put his coffee cup against his forehead and to Beth's mind, he seemed years older, shaky, all the animosity burned out of him. Then he set the cup down and said, "And you?"

"I wasn't the one they were after," Beth said. "You were right."

Larry seemed bewildered. "What are you talking about?"

"I wasn't the one they were after. But I was the reason they came for him. Because we were living under the same roof." Beth said, "I should stick to cleaning up the pharmacy."

"Oh Lord, Fine," Larry said. "You want me to say it. All right. I'll say it. You could have stayed at home this summer, sure, all of you. You could have said it wasn't your business. But it is your business, what happens in Mississippi, and you knew it, and you came."

"I guess the spirit moved me," Beth said, in such a way that Larry wasn't sure how to respond. She added, "I'm glad I didn't end up shooting myself."

"Now you wouldn't have said that a couple of days ago," Larry said.

"People change," Beth said.

"Yes, they do," Larry replied. Then he sank backwards into his chair. "You want to know why I told you to clean up the pharmacy? When I first showed up in McComb, maybe three years ago, there were a bunch of us—black and white—mostly from the north, who couldn't stand how slow those folks in Mississippi were, thought we knew just how the Movement ought to go, and James Forman—that's SNCC's Executive Director—he watched us make fools of ourselves for a while, and then he told us to clean up Quin's Cafe."

"So he tried to make you humble?" Beth asked.

"No, that's not Jim's way," said Larry. "I think he figured Mrs. Quin had other things to do and could have used the help."

"Where did you get the mop?"

"Oh, Forman showed us. Seems he'd cleaned the place the week before. And I should have shown you where that mop and bucket were, that day," Larry said. It was dangerously close to an apology. Then he seemed to come back to himself. "Why did Mrs. Turner mop that floor? And who cleaned that gun? If we want a chance in court, we have to get the FBI here while there's still some evidence."

Beth looked at his eyes, which were blood-shot, narrow, intelligent and nervous. It was clear what Larry expected of her. It was also clear that Beth was looking straight though those expectations. He took another awkward sip of coffee and then pushed the cup aside.

"So you're not going to stay and testify?"

All Beth could say was, "I can't think that far ahead." Larry nodded, and he seemed to recognize that logic and accept it. Somehow, if she could just cling to that phrase, if she could say it, again and again, then the choice would be postponed and no one would call her anything but sensible.

IN THE END, BETH DIDN'T need George Burgess to help carry her suitcase to the bus stop. Her bag seemed to have gotten lighter since it sat in the trunk of the Corvair. She laid the bag down and looked at the road that rose over a hill. It swam in the sunlight, but unlike the Delta highway, it played no tricks on her eyes. It was just a road.

Then she saw Freddie. She was on a bicycle, huffing up the hill, and she pulled up beside Beth and dismounted. "Glad I caught you," she said. "I thought—I figured you could use—" and then losing her words completely, she pulled a cloth sack out of the wicker basket between the handlebars. "Just some apples," Freddie said, "and some of that pie that Sweetie says you like."

Beth took the sack. "Thanks."

"And I wanted to tell you," Freddie said. "I really do like the book. The one you showed me, I mean. It's interesting. Only," she said, "I can't figure out why you gave it to me. I don't want to be a doctor."

The mid-morning sun pounded on Beth, and the dust of the road rose around her ankles. Without warning, Beth pressed her face into that sack and began to cry. Freddie looked at her, and then hesitantly put her arms around her.

"Hey, hey," Freddie said, "Don't do that. I could be a doctor if you want me to."

Beth looked up. "You have to be rich," she said. "Management, Math and Money. Promise me. Don't let anyone talk you into doing something else if that's what you really want to do."

A car was coming down the road. Beth recognized it, and was glad that Freddie stood with her. Apparently there would be one more goodbye. Cy Cohen pulled up in his Packard, and rolled down the window. He saw Beth's suitcase, and he said, "So it's true. You've been run out of town."

Freddie said, "You leave her alone, Mr. Cohen."

Cy ignored Freddie. He was in a state of agitation. His glasses were askew and his shirt was plastered to his chest with perspiration. He had obviously been looking for Beth for some time. "I had no idea they'd go after you like that. If I had known—"

"You would have done what?" Beth asked. Her eyes were dry now, and she kept a hand on Freddie's shoulder, holding her back. Then she said, "Cy, when you showed up at the church that day, what were you going to tell me?"

"Get in the car," said Cy.

"No," said Beth. Then she said, "Sorry, I can't."

"When are you gonna realize I'm not Klan trash? I just got things to say to you."

Then Beth said. "Why don't you get *out* of the car?"

The words had come of their own accord, and they took Cy by surprise. He hesitated, looking first at Beth and then at Freddie, and then at Beth again. After a moment he said, "Why? You gonna shoot me too? It sure is a good thing you're going back to Philadelphia."

"I'm not from Philadelphia," Beth said again, fruitlessly.

"Yes you are," said Cy. "My momma's got family in Philadelphia. You tell them I said hey."

The bus had arrived, and Cy Cohen gunned the motor and disappeared. Beth felt in her pocket where she'd put the wad of money her father had given her. She managed to peel off another five to hand the driver, and while he was making change, she stood for some time with the rest of the money in her hand. It wasn't as thick as she'd initially suspected. She moved into the back of the bus, took a seat by a window, and worked off the fives, like layers on an onion. Then she sat with them loose on her lap. There were perhaps a dozen other people on the bus, all of them Negro. She was the only white girl, and she knew she was conspicuous, but she was well past caring. For the first time since Max Fine had handed her the money, she counted it.

5

THE BATHROOMS IN THE GEM Hotel in Atlantic City had strips across their toilet seats. The first time Larry saw one, he walked right out and said to George, "You want to see something to tell your grandchildren about?"

George, who was changing into a suit he'd borrowed from a sympathetic reporter, said, "My grandchildren aren't gonna want to hear about no bathroom, man." Still, he let himself look, and he shook his head. "Sanitized for your protection."

"Just like this convention," Larry said, more to himself. "That is until we showed up."

George said, "Well, I hear white folks never wipe themselves."

"Come on," Larry said. "You played cards with those volunteers all summer. You should know better."

"I might have played cards with those cats but I never followed them into no toilet," said George. Then, he asked Larry, "You know how to tie this tie?"

Larry helped him, though the telephone rang, and he had to clamp the earpiece under his shoulder while he finished George's knot. It was Frank with more news about some deal floated by the Democratic heavy-hitters to prevent an open vote on seating the Freedom Democrats, and Frank said, with satisfaction, "They must be shitting in their pants, they're so scared."

After all, the Freedom Delegates had gotten a powerhouse of a lawyer, a real insider who worked for the United Auto Workers, and suddenly, well-connected Democrats opened their doors to them. And there were all the parents of those summer volunteers, calling their delegates and telling them that little Suzie Q or Howie—or, as Frank reminded them, Mickey or Andy—didn't go down to that hell hole for nothing. Finally— and this was Larry's real theory—here was L.B.J. uncontested, at a convention that had no real issue. Now the Mississippi Freedom Democratic Party was the issue.

Sometimes it would be Jackie on the other end of the telephone line. She was making the rounds of hotel suites in a smart little sweater set, and she had a notebook in her purse where she made a point of writing down even the faintest of endorsements. Jackie was always good at getting people to make promises. Or it was Helen with an update on the impact of testimony on the Credentials Committee. Frank didn't like this sort of work and said so. "I can't deal with people I don't respect. And there's nothing to respect about these party hacks."

"When's Ron up to testify?" Larry asked.

There was a pause at the end of the line, and then Frank said, "Did you hear something?"

Larry said, "With everyone coming in and out of here, I'm lucky I hear you."

"No," said Frank. "An echo." Then he said, "I'll see you later, sport." He waited a beat before hanging up, just long enough for Larry to hear what Frank heard.

Who was tapping their phone? The list of hotel rooms occupied by Freedom Democratic Party delegates and supporters was not exactly top secret: after all, the point was visibility. Even if they'd wanted to be discreet, it would have been impossible. Larry's particular room saw so much traffic that he probably would have gotten more sleep on the floor of a church. The delegates from Marshall County made it a headquarters of sorts, and one skinny old lady from Holly Springs got sunstroke during the vigil on the boardwalk a mile away and ended up convalescing in one of the beds.

There was one room with six phones hooked up, full of Movement people calling delegates. The front veranda of the hotel looked like the porch of a Freedom House, full of discarded signs, kids playing guitar, girls fixing each other's hair. Still, to most of the delegates, the strangest things remained those hotel bathrooms. They took long showers, and the hot water never ran out. They used the tiny soaps in their hair before they even saw the bottles of shampoo. Then there were the full length mirrors. A few of the SNCC field secretaries hadn't looked at their own reflections in months. Most of the men had dropped weight, and their skin had the ground-in ashy look common in men twice their age. They straightened their spines to make their suits sit right. Those suits were borrowed.

Another source of fascination was the television. There were a few of them in Melody, usually rigged up to clothes hangers. The ones in the hotel had spotty reception, but they all worked, and they were always on. Convention coverage started in the morning and ran into the afternoon, and, as Larry said, they were the only big story. Mrs. Fannie Lou Hamer's testimony before the Credentials Committee was cut short by a "special message from the President." Then, Johnson appeared on screen, braying out some nonsense like the ass he was. But that only meant that Mrs. Hamer's testimony was shown, in full, that night, when everyone was watching.

"Aunt Claire ought to be on TV too," George said to Freddie and Bobbie who had been standing in the sun all afternoon next to the shell of Mickey Schwerner's burnt-out station wagon. The girls had been out there since they arrived, holding whatever signs came to hand, both wearing their good Sunday dresses.

Freddie and Bobbie had never seen so many white people before, and all so nice. Strangers came up to them and thanked them for being there. A lady delegate from Washington state had handed Bobbie five dollars.

"Split that with all of us," said George.

"Why?" Bobbie asked.

"It goes here," said Larry, producing an envelope. "Checks, cash, everything anybody hands you."

"No," said Bobbie. "I didn't have to tell you. Why shouldn't I keep it?"

Then, they were blessedly distracted by the television where a reporter spoke, at length, to Jackie Gordon, who was probably the first girl to appear on television with a natural.

"Will Beth be here?" Bobbie asked Larry.

Larry said, "I don't know."

"She's on her way to Paris, France, I bet," said Bobbie. "I wish she was here. She would understand about the five dollars."

"I'm reading that book she gave me about that plague. It's really good," said Freddie. "There's this part where the doctor asks this guy if he has a code of ethics, and you know what he says it is?"

"Comprehension," said Larry.

"You read it already," Freddie said.

"It's my book," Larry said. He was tired. The trouble was, both beds in the room were occupied, one by the lady with the heatstroke, and the other by Po Burgess. Although Mrs. Turner said she'd be happy to look after Po back in Melody, understandably enough, Claire Burgess refused to leave town without him.

Because Po seldom left the room, Larry was forced into a kind of proximity. It struck him that he'd never realized before that Po was a grown man. He had to be shaved in the morning. He had a lot of hair under his arms and on his legs. He smelled. At some point, Mrs. Burgess and George put him in the shower, and he screamed and carried on so much that if the FBI had wired the room, Larry wondered what they'd thought was going on.

Claire Burgess asked, "How can we open their hearts? How can we move them? If Mrs. Hamer can't move them—if those lives of those three young men can't move them—"

"We'll move them," said Freddie. "Mrs. Burgess, you should have been on the boardwalk with us, the way they looked when we held up the pictures of those three boys who died. They understand. We're going to win."

IT DID SEEM THAT WAY. In the convention hall, Larry felt his elbow gently taken by a number of white men wearing delegate badges who told him that they'd heard there was a way to get those badges to Movement people so they could go onto the convention floor. There was a runner who took them, they said, disguised as a Young Citizen for Johnson. Did Larry know where they could find her? And barring that, maybe he could take the badge himself. One of them said, "No one seems to understand how all of this looks internationally." Another said, "I've gotten calls non-stop since that Hamer woman testified on television last night, the one who got the beating." Then, there was a light-skinned Negro from Ohio. He had tears in his eyes, and he said, "I just met her. I met Mrs. Hamer, and she shook my hand. And I had to tell someone that this is where history is beginning, right here at this convention."

Yet for Larry, the greatest moment came when he was crossing the hotel lobby and saw J.B. sitting at the bar. He practically leapt in his direction, threw his arms around him, and said, "What are you doing here, man?"

"Where else would I be?" J.B. asked. He disentangled himself and laughed. "I guess that's what you kids call the SNCC hug."

"What happened to your hiatus?"

"Well, I'm taking a hiatus from the hiatus. Mount Bayou's a foolish place to take one anyhow," J.B. said. "You know how many Movement people come through that town? It's like the only integrated resort in Mississippi. And there was this guy—Sylvester—and he was with this white girl who's based in Ruleville, and they had an extra seat on the bus—"

"No need to explain," Larry said. He pulled up a stool next to J.B. and ordered them both beers.

"Watch out," said J.B. "I don't know how much liquor costs here. I've been sticking to coffee. At least that's not going to run more than a quarter."

"If we sit here for long enough, some guilty white delegate from Oregon will pay for us anyhow," said Larry. Then, he felt a little guilty himself. "Listen," he said, "I haven't told anyone else yet. I'm moving to the Atlanta office in January."

J.B. put down his coffee cup. "No kidding. You gonna be a big shot?"

"No. Just need a little time out of the field. We'll be needing someone to head the Melody project."

"And you figure if you tempt me with that ten dollar a week salary, I'll be sure to come home." J.B. laughed. "Man, you make it so attractive." Then, he said, "Isn't Atlanta where Sue Francis wants to go? You know she lost that scholarship to Tupelo."

"I'm not surprised," said Larry. "She wasn't exactly Honeybee material."

Their beers appeared in the silence that followed. Or it was not precisely silence. There was always noise in that lobby, delegates talking over each other, the press pushing their way towards conference rooms, piped music. Then, J.B. said, "She's on crutches, but she gets around pretty good. I think she wants to see you."

"My door is always open," Larry said.

THAT WAS NOT PRECISELY TRUE. He closed it once. It was after Ron Beauchamp's appearance before the Credentials Committee that took place in the middle of the afternoon. Momentum for the Freedom Democrats was cresting, and it was time to bring on the boy who got his story in *Life Magazine*.

But Ron Beauchamp was exhausted. He had slept, not at the Gem Hotel, but on the back seat of the Crown Vic because he'd seen a few rough looking characters casing the parking lot and wanted to make sure nobody let the air out of the tires of all his buses. It was Jackie who had pulled him out of that car, told him that his country paranoia had no place at this convention, and managed to get him up to a room and into a decent suit before he realized that more was going to be asked of him.

Ron said to Jackie, "What do I got to say to them?"

"You'll find out," said Jackie. "Remember what Pastor Holden says, Ronny. The Lord will put words into your mouth."

"I can't stand the way they all look at me," Ron said.

"How do they look at you? Ronny, those people love you. They want to take your picture, shake your hand."

"They look at me like they don't see me," Ron said.

Jackie lost her patience altogether. "This isn't about the seats anymore, Ronny. It's about the future of the Movement. If they don't see us now, they're never going to see us. Nobody's going to care about black folks in Mississippi after this summer."

IN HIS ILL-FITTING SUIT, RON didn't look much older than George, though he tried to alter the effect somewhat by putting on his dark glasses. The room was packed with reporters. He sweated through his jacket. As soon as he took his place at the head of the table, a dozen flashbulbs exploded.

"You all have been hearing a lot about voting in Mississippi," Ron said. "You all have been hearing a lot about justice in America."

He paused and bowed his head as he poured a glass of water from a pitcher by his elbow. It spilled a little. There was another brutal flash. He looked up.

"I am nineteen. Can't vote. I guess I can't say I was turned away from a courthouse, like Mrs. Hamer. But I've been beaten in front of one. See, I'm a mechanic. I fix the cars that carry people to the courthouse. I believe things can be fixed, if you got the will to do it. So I guess I'm here to testify that the cars I fix carry folks to the Leflore County Courthouse in Greenwood, Mississippi who have got the will to register and vote. It takes will to go up those courthouse steps. You all know the story, when I was struck down, when I was on my knees—"

"Could you take off your glasses?" a photographer asked him. "They reflect the light."

Ron obliged, laying them on the table, and blinking as the flash went off again. He kept both palms of his hands flat on the table to keep himself steady. "When I was struck down, that afternoon, I was praying by the river. I was on my knees before the water."

"Ron!" a reporter called. "Could you bow your head again, like you did before? We didn't get that scar."

Ron looked confused. His eyes darted as he tried to figure out who posed the question.

"Show us that scar again. Move the hair out of the way."

"I'll try, man." He took a step back, and almost at once started to stagger. He braced a hand against the wall, and grazed the other through his hair, and then seemed to be having trouble finding the thread of what he'd intended to say, maybe something about Gideon's army and the kneeling and the water, but the sweat stood on his forehead, and he reached out, feeling for the chair.

The photographers moved closer. "Just bow that head," one called out. "That's the ticket. Just like you did in Mississippi."

Helen Forest stepped between them. "Give the man some space. He's not a fucking performing monkey."

In the wake of the silence that followed, the reporters watched the fierce, tiny white girl lead Ron Beauchamp to an elevator. None of them took photographs.

RON AND HELEN ENDED UP back in Larry's room, and Helen kept up a furious monologue about Jackie's insensitivity, and Po Burgess was sitting up in bed, staring at the television, and the heat-stroke woman was running the shower, and Larry thought: if one more person comes in here, I will get out a gun and shoot them. That's when he shut the door.

Helen said to Ron, "Look, after this is over, one way or another, it's clear you need a break. You've heard about Harry Belafonte's offer?"

"He's gonna write a song for us?" Ron asked, trying to smile.

"No. He's going to send some Movement people to Africa, for a tour."

"The State Department would love that," said Larry. "I've heard they use pictures of integrated sit-ins to show Africans what an advanced society we have here in America."

"I don't give a shit about what the State Department loves," said Helen. "A lot of people are going. I'd go if I could."

But Ron just said, "What would I do in Africa?"

"Just give it some thought, okay?" Helen said. "I'm going to visit some friends in Delaware and Washington. Ron, you should come along. There's a bunch of them at the vigil. It's a big world out there."

Then, Helen invaded the bathroom to get a wet towel for Ron's forehead, and Larry said, "Maybe a break wouldn't be a bad idea, Beauchamp."

"Man, I'm not an African," Ron said. "I don't carry a spear. I don't beat a tom-tom."

"Don't you want to see where you came from?" Larry asked him.

"I come from Mississippi," Ron said. He lay down on the empty bed and stared at the ceiling. "Oh man, I need to get back home. Whenever I leave, I go to pieces. It's like I can't do anything right, like I don't know the game. And then I start to get angry and ashamed and confused like all the grace is running out of me. Like the last time I came east. There was this girl from Swarthmore. Ended up in your project."

"Beth Fine?" Larry said. "What did she do to you?"

Maybe Ron would have clarified if Helen hadn't returned just then and arranged a towel on his forehead. She said to Larry, "What about you, Mr. Marcus Garvey? Are you saying you're not an African?"

"Helen, I don't know, all right? Don't press me. I'm taking things one hour at a time now. We've still got the convention."

"No we don't," said Helen. "There's no way they're going to unseat the Mississippi Democrats, and we both know it. It won't even be brought to a floor vote. This is nothing but a circus."

Larry did not reply for a moment. Then, he said, "You know, this room is probably bugged."

"Those people on the Credentials Committee," Helen said, "last I heard, they were getting these phone calls. Like this one guy has a wife up for a judgeship, and somebody asks him how much he really wants his wife to be a judge. Jackie thinks they're going to offer us two at-large seats—not with voting rights, of course. And the rest of us will all be honored guests of the convention. Our lawyer's behind the deal. So's Dr. King. They're calling a meeting to announce a victory."

"Our people won't accept it," Larry said.

"They're not *our people*," said Helen.

"Maybe not yours," said Larry, and he realized that he was angry. "Why don't you just go back to Texas and do your missionary work with Mexicans! Just get out of my face, all right? Get out of Ron's face. Unless you want him to show you his scars!"

Helen looked as though she wanted to say more, but she held herself in, shaking with badly suppressed emotion. She opened the door and walked off, leaving that door ajar, and into that room came stale air and the smell of whiskey spilled on the hallway carpet.

Ron sat up, and the towel slipped from his forehead. He said, "She didn't deserve that."

"I'm sick of taking care of these white people," Larry said. "I'm sick of having to make allowances for them. I'm even sick of being angry at them."

"So don't be," Ron said. He rubbed the towel across this face. "Man, that feels good. I want to just lose myself in a nice, clean towel, you know? Just plain stop thinking. Could you turn up the TV?"

Larry obliged him, and then he turned and he just stood, for a little while, in front of that open door. He leaned his face against the frame and dug his fingers into his goatee. Behind him, journalists droned, images flickered, and the late afternoon sun fought against the air conditioner. Larry realized he didn't want to move. If he stood there for long enough, someone was bound to come down that hallway. Something would happen.

6

"SO," SAID BEATRICE NEUMAN, "YOU'VE had quite an adventure."

She laid her hand on Beth's. She had taken off her white gloves and put them on top of her purse, and the entire ensemble was on the side of the table, as though she could, at any moment, put herself together and leave in a hurry. Beth was intended to take note of this. Beatrice Neuman had pretended not to notice that her niece hadn't written to her all summer, and that the one phone call she'd gotten had been from the National Lawyer's Guild who had requested money to pay a substantial fine. Beth said, "I wouldn't call it an adventure."

"Well, why not? A fabulous adventure," said Aunt Bea. "I'm sure it's something I would have given my eye-teeth for at your age." She smiled in such a way as to reveal the whole range of her teeth and gums, as insincere a smile as Beth had ever seen. She was clearly furious.

"Well," Beth said, "I just hope our hard work won't go to waste. I guess you know what's going to happen in Atlantic City."

"Funny you should mention Atlantic City," said Aunt Bea. "I'm heading down there tomorrow. It's very important, you know, that the Democratic platform has a strong plank on the U.N. It's such a terrible world out there, and if we don't have the institutions to make peace, well, my dear, then where are we?"

Beth knew what she had come to New York to do, and she was determined to do it, but there was, frankly, no right moment. There was only the sense that she knew so well, that she had nothing to lose. "You've heard about the Freedom Democrats," said Beth. "You must have. It's been in all the papers."

"All real Democrats are Freedom Democrats," said Aunt Beatrice. "Now, I don't have much time, dear. We could talk after we order lunch. I'm sure you must have lots of tales to tell."

"They're not tales," said Beth. "They're things that really happened."

"Don't get so worked up," said Aunt Bea. "You'd think I needed convincing."

The waiter took their orders, and during that interval, Beth used the time to frame her words with care. "Aunt Bea," she said, after he'd gone, "the woman I was living with risked her life trying to register to vote. And her son almost died because I lived there, because there were white people in that town who see two white girls living under the same roof as a black man and think that's grounds for murder."

"You never told me you were living with a young Negro man," said Aunt Bea. "And will this boy be in Atlantic City too?"

"I don't know," said Beth. "But his mother, Claire Burgess, is a Freedom delegate. And Larry Walsh—"

"I believe that was the director of your project," said Aunt Beatrice. "You see? I do know something."

"Then you know about the challenge, that we're trying to unseat the segregationists."

"I know some people are standing on the boardwalk to honor those poor dead boys," said Aunt Beatrice. "It strikes me that they'd make better use of their time at the Republican convention. But of course, Goldwater's people wouldn't be terribly open to that sort of display."

She'd told the waiter to bring the check the same time as he brought their salads. They were lovely salads, with crabmeat, avocado and pimiento, and Beth suddenly found her fork too heavy to lift from her napkin. She said to Aunt Beatrice, "I don't think I can eat this."

"Then you shouldn't have let me order it," said Aunt Beatrice. "Perhaps it's a little rich for you, after Mississippi. What did you eat there? A lot of cornmeal and molasses, I suppose. The price of that salad would buy a lot of cornmeal and molasses. With Max Fine for a father, I'm sure you can do the math, dear. Of course," she said, "Johnson has more sympathy for the poor than any president since Roosevelt. But if we make a lot of people at the convention angry and we lose the south, we get Goldwater, and we all die in an atom blast, and then a salad, here or there, won't make a difference."

SINCE BETH RETURNED FROM MELODY, she had been staying with her father. When she appeared after her two-day bus trip, Beth put down her suitcase and knocked on the door of her father's study. The door remained closed. She had to open it herself, and found him, startled, standing at his blackboard with a line of numbers trailing from a corner. He looked older than she'd remembered, and more gentle.

"Bitsy," he said. "I thought you'd call first."

"You're glad to see me?" Beth asked him.

"I'm your father," he said. He extended his hand, not a paternal gesture. Beth shook it, but that wasn't his intention. He said, "I need the key."

"What key?" Beth asked him.

"The car key," he said. "I'm afraid you aren't listed on the insurance anymore. Not that I think you're reckless, Bitsy, but there are certain technicalities."

"I don't have the key," said Beth.

After a pause, Max said, "I see." Then, he looked at the hand she had just shaken, and both of them realized it was caked with chalk. He wiped it on a soft cloth and said, "Why don't we sit down, and you can tell me about all of those nonviolent people in Mississippi."

That was when Beth realized that no one had told him what had happened the night she left Melody. She also knew that telling him was her responsibility. But what would be gained by it? What would it prove? Furthermore, it was so outside of the parameters of ordinary discourse that it was, simply, impossible. She sat down in the hard chair intended for his graduate students and said, "I met all kinds of people, dad."

"Of course you did. As you could have anywhere at all. So what was the point, precisely?"

Then, she saw what he wanted her to do. He wanted her to argue. She didn't have the strength. She just wanted to go to bed. "No point, I guess," she said.

"You don't look very pleased with yourself, Bitsy," her father said. "You don't look as though you're happy you went to Mississippi."

"Maybe I'm just not happy at all," said Beth. The answer felt dishonest, but it made a certain look pass across her father's face. "I need to rest, Dad. If there's nothing pressing."

"Nothing pressing," said her father. "Your bed's made up."

Because she'd barely slept on the bus, because she hadn't slept the night before she left; because in some ways she hadn't really gotten a full night's sleep in all her time in Melody, Beth hit the bed without looking at it. That was where she spent most of the week that followed.

BETH'S ROOM HAD UNDERGONE A few changes since she'd left for Swarthmore. The Formica nightstand was still there, the flimsy desk she'd owned since fourth grade, and the bookshelves lined with contact paper. But most of her books were gone now, and some of the overflow of journals from her father's study were stuffed into the shelves sideways. On the wall was the Picasso print of Don Quixote that she had purchased at a sale for Princeton students. She'd fallen asleep on top of the

Dale Evans bedspread. Even recently, she'd rubbed her face into the chenille of that spread, which her mother had brought back from Los Alamos when Beth was still a baby. Perhaps her mother had taken it along in the hopes that something of the cowgirl would remain in Beth, some kind of gaiety and recklessness and skill.

Now, Beth could not imagine how she'd managed to spend eighteen years in that house. Her father had hired a Romanian maid who cleaned her room every morning and put fussy little folds around the pillow. She'd leave dinner in the oven before she went home, and as Max Fine was clearly at a critical point in his work, he'd seldom emerge before Beth went to bed. There was a television in the kitchen. The maid always had it on. If Beth came in to get herself a glass of water, she felt as though she was interrupting a conversation.

Not long after Beth came back from the lunch with her aunt, she asked the maid, "Is that the news?"

It was an afternoon broadcast of the convention, and she thought she saw—just for a moment—J.B. Powder wearing a suit, but it was someone else. Then, filling the whole screen—she almost cried out—Jackie Gordon. The announcer was saying something, and the maid started to run the garbage disposal. Beth pulled her from the sink.

"Stop it! I need to hear this!"

The maid gave her a hard look, and left the room. Whatever Beth had hoped to hear had passed, and now they were interviewing a delegate from Minnesota. Beth sat at the table, fearful that she'd miss something, and that was when her father emerged and said, "I need to talk to you, Bitsy."

Beth turned in surprise. "Can it wait?"

"Now," said her father. He pulled up another chair and faced her, and she wondered if she could manage to continue watching the broadcast of the convention without his knowledge. He said, "You know, you frightened Daria just then."

"Sorry," said Beth. There was coverage from the boardwalk now, a vigil. Was that Bobbie? How did she manage to get there? She was holding one of the placards with a picture of Andrew Goodman. "I know that girl," Beth said. "The heavy one. I taught her French."

He turned off the television.

"Hey," said Beth. "I was watching that."

"Bitsy," her father said, "I need to know your plans."

"What do you mean?" Beth said. "I just want to sit and watch the convention coverage, and then I figured I'd get the paper."

"I mean," said Max, "You are frightening Daria. She says you are always in whatever room she's cleaning. She says you look like a raccoon.

Now, I have always trusted you—implicitly, Bitsy. You're my daughter. You're a reasonable person. But when you go crashing cars—"

"I'll pay for the car," Beth said immediately.

"That's not necessary and also impractical. You have a week before you leave for Paris."

"I'm not going to Paris," Beth said.

Her father said nothing for a moment. He made a cradle out of his hands and seemed to spend a long time looking at the hair on the backs of them. "Alright," he said. "I must say, this takes me by surprise, but alright. Then I suppose we'll have to make other arrangements."

"Why?" Beth asked him.

"That, daughter, is a question designed to provoke. And of course, you must answer it yourself. However," he said, "I must insist, again, that you do your best not to frighten Daria. I've become quite dependent on her."

He left Beth sitting there and she immediately turned the television back on. There was Lyndon Johnson, his face filling the screen like a side of pork, and she stared at it for a while, but what she'd lost when her father switched off the television was irretrievable. The maid lurked in the parlor, waiting for Beth to leave the kitchen. After a while, she did. And characteristically, she took her father's question with her.

He could still do that much to Beth—draw her in, make her do a double-take, scrape the fuzz off of her fuzzy logic. For hours, she would lie on the hard couch in the parlor, and try to make her way through her father's copy of Pascal's *Pensées*, a book he'd clearly never read. He'd pass her by on his way to fill his coffee cup, and look as though he disapproved of her position or the couch or her choice of reading material. Sometimes, she couldn't bear another day in that house. Sometimes she was afraid, really afraid, that she would never leave again.

WHEN BETH WAS NO MORE than six, she emerged from the department store with her mother and ran off to hail their taxi cab. It was a bright late-summer day, like this one, where the sunshine seemed to slam off everything like metal sheeting, and she didn't see that cab until it pulled over. She opened the door, and shimmied inside. Her mother didn't join her.

"Mommy," she called out. "Don't you want to share the ride with me?"

She replied, "I prefer the bus."

Then she walked off, leaving Beth to scramble out of the cab and run after her. Her pace was leisurely, and it wasn't long before Beth overtook her at the corner. She was looking at her watch. A curtain of dark red hair fell across her face.

"It's usually here by now," she said.

Beth knew that there were no buses in their neighborhood, but she stood rooted there, hot and anxious, because she knew very well that her mother was sure there was a bus. Beth's lip was trembling ominously. If the bus that didn't exist didn't come soon, her mother would see her cry. Beth could just walk away. Then *she* would be the one everybody worried about. Still, she couldn't bring herself to leave. She had no destination. Instead, she stood, swaying, holding her Scott Terrier purse and running the zipper up and down its spine. It struck her then, and also years later, that people only get lost when they start to look for something.

BETH WAS ON PRINCETON'S CAMPUS when she saw the headline through the window of an honor box: *Mississippi Negroes Offered Historic Compromise*. She bent down to read the first paragraph of text visible through the glass:

According to attorney Joseph Rauh, the quest to unseat the Mississippi delegates has ended with a promise of two at-large seats, to be filled by Aaron Henry, a Negro and Chairman of the Mississippi NAACP, and Ed King, a white minister. Supported by such luminaries as Dr. Martin Luther King, the announcement of the terms caused the all-white regular Mississippi delegates to walk off of the convention floor as a body.

Two seats? They wouldn't have settled for two seats. She knew she ought to buy the paper, but that would mean knowing how it all ended. She settled on crouching low to read what she could through the glass of the honor box.

It is as yet uncertain if the compromise will be accepted by the so-called Freedom Delegates. However, pressures are being brought to bear to move, as one of their leaders put it, "from protest to politics." Among the observers, CORE field secretary Martin Weinglass spoke for the majority of the supporters when he said that the compromise did not enjoy widespread support among the Freedom Democratic Party delegates.

Beth sank onto the sidewalk entirely and gave in to vertigo, and then somehow, she found herself in a phone booth dialing Long Island information, where she managed to get the number for Marty's parents. "I'm his old girlfriend," Beth said. "I just want to know if you've heard from him."

"You're Missy?"

"No," said Beth, appalled to realize that she was blushing. "I must have been before Missy."

"Well, I'm sure that Marty would love to hear from you, but he's in Mississippi just now and away from any sort of telephone."

"He's nowhere near Mississippi," Beth said.

"I don't see how you know that, dear," said Marty's mother, whom Beth had never met, and who had—according to Marty—a special mask she wore to keep from getting smile-lines. "He just sent us a telegram from Mississippi yesterday. He was driving some of the delegates back home."

"No he's not," Beth said, trying to stay calm. "Marty's not in Mississippi."

"He's in McComb, Mississippi. We're scared to death, of course, but very proud of him."

Beth said again, "He can't be in McComb." Then, she realized what a fool she was making of herself, and she hung up.

7

THE NEXT DAY, BETH FINE arrived in Chester. She'd brought no suitcase, as she hadn't planned to spend the night. She had the address of the place where Marty had moved the previous winter, which may or may not have been called a Freedom House.

Just to be heading towards a Freedom House gave Beth courage. When she'd told her Aunt Bea that she didn't want to work for the Eleanor Roosevelt Foundation, when she told her father that she didn't want to transfer to Rutgers, and when she had to field a phone call from Neuman's Department Store and insist that she was in no way interested in their management training program, she listened to herself, as from a distance. Her voice had faltered. It must have cost her father something, to contact these people who despised him, and she could sense in it an appeal to her compassion.

He might have hoped that this was what had drawn her, at last, to open his office door, but that was not the case. She told him where she was going.

He said to her, "What precisely is in Chester?"

"I have unfinished business," Beth said, knowing this would not satisfy him. She added, "I promise, Dad, when I come back, you can do what you want with me. Sign me up as a research assistant. Send me to live with Aunt Bea. Just let me do this thing. I'll be back tonight."

Max shook his head. "Bitsy, you always have the best intentions. But I know you well enough by now to be surprised you came back from Mississippi in one piece. Logically, you should not have. Frankly, I wouldn't let you go to France now even if you wanted to, or not until you showed some sign of good sense."

"This is my sign of good sense," said Beth.

There must have been something about the way Beth said it that gave Max Fine pause. He turned in his seat and opened up his desk drawer. Removing the money clip, he asked, "How much do you need?"

"Dad," Beth said. "I mean it. I have unfinished business. I should be back on the last bus."

He didn't turn. She knew that he was sorting through those bills. The gesture was dismissive and hard to bear. He was waiting for an answer.

"I don't want any more money," Beth said at last. She wanted to cry. "I still have fifteen dollars left from what you gave me two months ago."

"Do you?" Max spoke through a thickness in his throat. After a pause, he went on. "That ought to be more than enough to get you to Chester and back." His voice sounded strange, and he turned his chair back to his desk before he added, "Keep the change."

GETTING OFF THE GREYHOUND BUS at the Chester station and asking for directions, she looked at the expression on the white shopkeeper's face and knew: she was headed for the Negro part of town.

"You're sure that's the address?" he asked her.

"Yes," she said. "That's where I want to go."

The blocks were crammed with row houses, porches piled with half-rotted furniture. Everything was luminous with decay. The address in Beth's hand was just beyond a vacant lot where a white girl lay on a bed sheet on a patch of blighted grass.

The girl sat up and shook out her curly golden hair. "Hello, hello, hello," she said, "and welcome to our revolutionary barbecue."

Beth drew back, and asked, "Excuse me. Is this the Freedom House?"

"Everybody say Freedom!" cried the girl. Her voice slurred, and she cocked her head. "You're from the college, right? You might as well go around the back. Everyone's hanging out there."

"I'm looking for Marty Weinglass," said Beth.

"What do you want with him? He's not good for much," said the girl. That's when Beth realized that she was probably Missy.

Beth said, "I hear he was at the convention. I'm an old friend of his. I was part of the Summer Project."

Missy's eyes focused. "You're the girl with the gun."

"I just want to talk to him, okay?" Beth said. She started towards the house, a detached gray clapboard monstrosity that looked as though, in another age, it might have been a mansion or garage or a barn. The door was open. Missy had told the truth. The house felt empty. Smoke billowed in from the kitchen, and she started towards it and found a back door open and a number of white teenaged boys huddled around a grill.

They all looked at her at once. "Shit," one of them said. "Who sent you?"

Another held out a wiener on a stick. "You hungry?"

Beth asked, "Is Marty home?"

"Martin the Martian? He's in his spaceship." They all giggled, and when Beth didn't join in, they looked bewildered.

As it turned out, he was inside after all, in a room off the kitchen where they kept a pile of cardboard signs from demonstrations, a few enormous velveteen cushions, and a television. Beth tried to physically prevent the blood from rushing to her heart at her first look at Marty Weinglass in months. He was sitting on the floor with his back against one of the cushions, skinner and shaggier but unmistakably himself.

He looked up with an evil smile. "Hey, I thought I'd see you at the circus."

"So you really were in Atlantic City?"

"So you were really in Mississippi?" Marty patted a space next to him on the cushion. "You want to watch the riot with me? It's really something else."

"I don't want to watch the riot," Beth said. She was conscious of how stiff she sounded, but she would not be shamed or intimidated. "I came here to find out what happened."

"The riot's what's happening," Marty said. "It's all one big ball of bubblegum anyhow. Look at Philadelphia going up in flames. Last month, it was Harlem in flames. Next month, it'll be Washington. You want to get high?"

In spite of herself, Beth watched the screen for a while, and said, "How did this start?"

"Some Philly cop pulled a pregnant Negro lady from a car and beat her. Sound familiar?"

The smoke from Marty's joint made Beth's eyes smart, and she couldn't quite make out whether the people running on the screen were black or white. The image was obscured all the more by the television's poor reception.

Then, Marty said, "Of course, they were betrayed."

Beth said, "You mean the lady?"

"I mean the Movement."

Beth positioned herself closer, because he'd dropped his voice to a whisper. "Can't we turn off the television?" she asked him.

"I'm telling you," Marty said. "It's all one big ball of bubblegum."

"Stop saying that! You're trivializing it!"

"It *is* trivial," Marty said. He pulled her beside him and put his arm around her in a way that seemed sheer condescension. "Man, you summer volunteer-types, Joe and Judy College, you're in some fuzzy-wuzzy world where the feds will step in and take care of everything. But that's not our world. You're not a complete idiot. How can you possibly believe that it's in the interest of the President of the United States to unseat white southern delegates? Why should he listen to a bunch of Mississippi Negroes?"

"He has to listen," Beth said. Then she realized the she was sobbing.

Marty said, "No he doesn't. It's that simple. He does not. He can pull his strings and talk about how they should all be so happy to be honored guests at his convention, and he can get big guns like Humphrey on his side and even get Dr. King to lay some pressure on them. That's politics."

"Why can't people—" Beth began. Tears welled up and cut the statement short. She wanted to throw up, and it was only through her tears that she could say, "Why can't people just have some fucking courage?"

"They do," said Marty. "Just watch them on TV."

Marty, even Marty stoned, assumed a snake-like charm, and he lay, prone in the dim room full of scrawled poster board. There was something wrong with what he said, some fault of logic that Beth should have been able to catch, but she didn't have the strength.

"Is it true?" he asked. "The rumor going around, I mean, about that gun?"

"What rumor?" Beth asked.

"That you protected your black lover from the Klan."

"He wasn't my lover." Beth sat up. "It wasn't the Klan."

"But there was a gun. That part's true." He propped himself on one arm, and his hair was all over his face so that he had to peer through it to meet her eyes. "You look different. Your hair is lighter. It's very sexy."

Beth said, "Did you see Larry Walsh in Atlantic City?"

"Larry? Sure," Marty said. He pushed himself forward so his thigh was pressed against Beth's, and she peeled it away. He didn't seem to notice. "You know Larry?"

"I wrote you. He's my project director."

"He hates white people," said Marty. He gave a laugh like a gulp, anxious and unpleasant. "But that doesn't stop him from hanging with this yellow chick on crutches—"

"Sue Francis was there?"

"Talk about a bug up her ass," Marty said. "Hey, how much do you know about guns?"

"Would you stop it about the gun?" Beth said. Whatever hold Marty had on her was gone, and she realized that if she didn't leave soon, she would, in fact, be forced to spend the night, and it would be unpleasant, and maybe even impossible, to avoid sleeping with Marty. She got up too quickly, and stumbled against the poster board signs: *One Man One Vote, U.S. Out of Indochina, Chester Committee For Freedom Now*, and an enormous drawing of Andrew Goodman that fell out of the pile and skittered halfway across the floor. What the hell was she doing here? Then she remembered: this was a Freedom House. And Beth knew that if this was, indeed, a Freedom House, and she walked away, she would not know where else to go.

Marty seemed to know it too. He was in no hurry to convince her to do much of anything, but he didn't seem to know how to stop talking. "You know," he said, "you ought to get into the spirit of things. Join the party. Missy scored some really high quality hotdogs, and Helen says she knows you."

Beth just looked at him. "What are you talking about? You can't mean Helen Forest."

"Why can't I?" Marty asked her. "You think you're the only one with any fucking friends in the Movement?"

Beth ran outside, but the grill was untended and the smoke crawled through the night air like a net. Later, she'd realize that she had probably inhaled too much smoke from Marty's marijuana cigarette, but just then, the net had its own logic. It trapped her, thrashed her back and forth, and when she freed herself and started up the stairs, she almost broke the loose banister, and managed to make it to the second floor in time to see one of the teenagers flushing something down the toilet. He gave her a strange smile, and closed the door. Later, she would realize he thought she was a Narc.

"Helen!" Beth called. "What are you doing here? Where are you?"

She knocked on a door, and then another. She had her hand on the knob of a third, when it opened from the inside. There was Ron Beauchamp.

He was holding a bottle of Coca Cola, and he wore a T-shirt and blue cotton boxers. His sunglasses were pushed up on his forehead. Twilight spilled in from behind him, the first natural light Beth had seen since she'd entered that house, and Beth felt his proximity like a soft blow to her stomach.

He said, "I knew that was you calling, but I thought it couldn't be."

Beth asked, "Why not?" Then she said, "I woke you."

"I can't sleep forever," Ron said.

Again, Beth asked, "Why not? You like to sleep."

"You're crazy, baby, you know?" Ron opened the door all the way, and hugged her. She hadn't expected that. She was so drained that it took effort to wrap her own arms around him, but once she did, she fit her chin against the crook of his neck and just stayed there. His hands stayed on her back. A minute passed, maybe more. Beth let go. Ron said, "Aren't you glad to see me?"

"I'm glad to see you," Beth said. She was afraid she'd start to cry again, but instead, she took his soda, drank too much of it, and then wiped her mouth. "It's hot in here."

"I thought you'd be in Atlantic City," Ron said.

"I'm glad I wasn't," Beth said. "I don't think I could have stood it, seeing you all take those two seats."

Ron said, "Where'd you hear that?"

"You didn't take them?" Beth asked. She laid her hand on Ron's arm, and then blushed at the self-conscious gesture. Yes, he was there. She took it off again. "I thought you didn't have a choice."

Ron looked at her as though she'd lost her mind. "You think we came all the way to Atlantic City to have someone else tell us what to do? We could do that back in Mississippi, baby. Sure, we were pressed—sure we got some people angry—but the delegates all talked it through, like we always do, and in the end we told them: we're nobody's honored guests. We *are* the delegates from Mississippi."

Beth asked, "But what about Dr. King?"

"It was hard to go against the word of a man like Reverend King," said Ron. "But no offence to the Reverend, he's not from Mississippi."

Beth wanted to touch Ron again, just lay a hand on him, and if he left it there, then it would mean that she wasn't dreaming, but she couldn't bring herself to test the circumstances. What if you were strong and clear enough to know what you wanted, and what if it was something that you couldn't get, but you kept on wanting? What if clarity was its own justification? What if people lived like that—what would life look like? While all of this rushed through her head, Ron just stood there, watching the expression on her face, and smiling.

"Well you're sure glad," he said. "So's Helen. But you know, she wants to send me to Africa."

"What are you talking about?" Beth asked. "Helen would never say that."

"She's right downstairs," said Ron. "You can ask her."

They both realized that they were standing, but there was nowhere to sit except a single mattress on the floor, which was covered with what looked like an embroidered tablecloth. The logical thing would have been to go downstairs and find Helen, but there was something in Beth, and maybe in Ron too, that made the logical thing seem impossible. Instead, they stood there, like two lampposts, feeling too hot in their clothing.

Ron said, "Mrs. Burgess was asking for you. She never got to thank you for what you did. That took real courage."

"No it didn't," said Beth. She stood inches away from him, and she said, "That wasn't courage. This is." She kissed him.

She felt his lips part with surprise, and then soften, and he caught her by the waist. There was a pull, almost like a lock clicking in place, and she was pressed against the closed door by the weight of him. Then they came up for air. A sob broke in her. She didn't know where it came from.

Ron's eyes were closed, and he was sweating.

"Are you okay?" she asked him, and she didn't even know what she was saying.

Ron opened his eyes; the sunglasses were pressed crookedly against his forehead. He spoke with difficulty. "Yeah, baby. I'm okay."

"Your eyes are so opaque."

"So what?"

"Opaque," Beth said again. Then, "I know I'm blushing."

"You do that a lot," said Ron, and Beth's face burned all the brighter with the knowledge that he'd paid attention to her body and he was letting her know that was the case. Then, they both realized that they had overturned the bottle at some point, and they were both standing in a pool of Coca Cola. Ron said, "Oops."

"We've really made a mess," said Beth.

"I know," said Ron. Then he asked her, "When you blush, do you turn pink all over?"

Beth sat on the mattress and began working her T-shirt over her head. It was so sweaty that it got caught mid-way, and then she could feel Ron pulling from the top. His fingers were clumsy and hesitant. Beth shimmied out of the wet shirt and when he started on her shorts, she pulled him down and said, "I'll do it. Let me."

"Baby," Ron said, "I want to."

"I want to," Beth began.

The whites of Ron's eyes were showing, and maybe he was too lost to hear. He pulled her down on the mattress, and then Beth lost the definition between wants. She laid her hands somewhere on Ron's body and kissed his eyelashes. Those lashes pulled against her mouth. A fan was beating a meter downstairs, and she wanted to make her own heart beat at just that rhythm.

8

WHEN BETH WAS SEVEN YEARS old, she went to Paris with her mother. The circumstances of that trip were mysterious. It took place during the school year, so she had to miss two weeks of class, but it didn't seem to matter. Her mother was sent by Neuman's Department Store, to look at the new spring fashions. Beth knew that her mother was already not who she had been. She wore too much lipstick and kept applying layers on top of layers, often in public and without a mirror. She mismatched clothing, which Beth noticed, though she sensed that she should keep the information to herself.

Beth knew: there were two Vivians, the slim and energetic heiress who gave up her fortune and threw herself into a new life with the smartest man in the world, and the other one, the Vivian that Beth knew now, the one who never said a word, and sometimes would notice Beth beside her, and treat her like a random fellow passenger on a journey that didn't interest her much. Beth let things pass, and passing, they accumulated and just became her life. Was it so unnatural for Vivian to order a Manhattan on the airplane, and for Beth to take little sips of her mother's drink? Was it so unusual that the hotel on the Seine had little keys on hooks and that Beth and her mother each got one?

"Darling," her mother said, "you're old enough to entertain yourself, aren't you?"

Although Beth wasn't sure what that meant, she agreed that she was. While her mother was gone, she spent the first days in that room standing on the narrow balcony, watching tourists and couples promenade along the river, and vendors sell ice cream or balloons or artificial flowers made of cloth and wire. Her mother returned at four in the afternoon, and she would ask, "So are you enjoying yourself?"

Beth would say that she was. Then, her mother would kick off her shoes, roll up in the big, mauve coverlet, and nap until dinnertime.

On the third day, Beth finally left the room. She closed the door and walked down the thin, striped carpet of the hallway, downstairs, and past the lobby where the day clerk, a short man with a mustache like a smudge, took her key and replaced it on the hook. She stepped outside.

Beyond the door was an avenue quite different from that view on the balcony. Big black cabs, a crush of people, the chaos and the heat and grittiness of Paris made Beth know that she shouldn't have been out there alone. She had taken her little plastic purse shaped like a Scott Terrier, and she held it against her chest with both hands and walked a few steps forwards. Then, she stopped.

Beth had seldom been alone on a street before. Maybe it was because this was a different country, or because she'd spent too long in the hotel, but the outside felt just like death must feel. It was too big, and she was small and lost. And like death, the state was irrevocable. She couldn't face that clerk again no more than a moment after she'd walked out of hotel.

So Beth just stood there on the sidewalk, with her fingers twined around the black patent leather of the purse, and her pale face turning this way and that. It was hot. Somehow, if she could only find the promenade by the river that she had seen from her window, she would be all right.

Then, she saw something glint between two buildings. It was the Seine. She started down the alley and was surprised that no one stopped her and asked, "Little girl, where are you going? Are you lost?" No, they just let her go. The alley was narrow and the consciousness that she was in dangerous circumstances was counterbalanced by what her body did, which was put one foot in front of the other. She was a brave girl. Before long, she would be in the open once again, and she could tell her mother how she'd found a secret passage to the vendor who sold the artificial flowers.

Then, all at once, a newspaper flapped in her face. There was a girl, just Beth's size, dirty and black-haired, who swung that paper back and forth and forced Beth towards the wall, and when Beth raised her arms to guard her face, she felt her purse snatched from her hand.

"Hey!" Beth called. The dark girl turned and loosed a line of spit that landed on Beth's cheek, and Beth reeled back. That's when she knew that there were two girls, because they shot out of that alley and took off in two directions, and by the time Beth reached the open, they had disappeared.

Beth found one of the iron benches she'd seen from the hotel window, and she sat there, shaking. She felt weird and foul, as though the stuff had come off of the newspaper all over her. Her heart was pounding, but it wasn't fear. It was rage. Rage made her blood hum all the way through her heart until she felt too big for her own body. She couldn't master it. She crumpled up and cried. People walked by without turning, perhaps discreet, or perhaps because she wasn't loud enough for them to hear.

Time passed. She realized someone was sitting next to her. It was the man from the front desk of the hotel. He might have been on his break. He was slight, and didn't take up much space on the bench. He must have had gentlemanly instincts, because although he must have been conscious of Beth's tears, he didn't look in her direction. Instead, he lit a cigarette and smoked companionably next to her, as though she were a self-possessed young woman.

Beth was grateful. Years later, in Mississippi, she would hear Claire Burgess tell the story of the prophet Jonah who, after his trials inside the whale, rested under the shade of a gourd and was thankful for that gourd, and Beth's mind went back to that gracious clerk who didn't hand her a handkerchief, who knew that it meant enough that he was there to cast a shadow over her and keep her company. She couldn't tell how long he sat there, but once she'd gained control of herself, he took his leave without a word.

She sat, wiped her nose on her sleeve, and looked at the Seine and the promenade for a while. The sunlight mellowed just enough to imply that some time had passed, and she could be sure her mother would be home.

In fact, her mother didn't seem at all surprised that Beth had not been there when she returned. She was already taking her afternoon nap, characteristically still in her work-clothes. During the first few days, she had taken them off, but as time passed, she would just lie down in her straight skirt and her jacket. A stocking had come out of a garter. When Beth appeared, she sat up and took a moment to adjust the stocking. Her lipstick was smeared, and it made her look drunk, although she wasn't. She didn't freshen up before dinner that night. Beth was very conscious of her own face, but if it had changed, she couldn't see it in the mirror.

THE NEXT DAY, BETH WENT out again, and the next. Each time, she would negotiate a new route to the river. Slowly, the avenue became less startling. Slowly, she dared herself to make a wider circle. She discovered a bakery window where she could watch cakes being decorated. She walked through a toy store where a set of wooden ducks could be pulled on a cord. She took pride in making herself cross a new street, or turn a new corner, and so many streets ran towards the Seine that she stopped thinking hard about a destination, and when she saw the river sparkle, she would turn, and be there before she so much as cared if she'd run into those filthy dark-haired girls again.

One day, along the promenade, she found a market where vendors sat behind card tables or laid-out blankets. On those blankets and tables were wares for sale: tools, shoes and boots, hats, record albums in yellowed sleeves. Beth lingered, passing from one vendor to the next, and then, among debris scattered on a folding table, she saw her Scott Terrier purse.

She stopped short. The words were out of her mouth. "That's mine!"

No one seemed to hear her. Of course, she was speaking English, but they must have understood.

"That's my purse. How did it get here?"

The question, or maybe her expression, did draw some attention. A few people who were idly sorting through the wares looked over, and one of them posed a question to the vendor who gave an articulate shrug.

A lady in a tailored suit asked Beth in English, "Is there something the matter?"

"That's my purse," said Beth again.

She became an object of amusement, as people chattered away in the language she didn't know, and again, she felt despair and fury. The vendor, impassive, went on fiddling with a number of folded playing cards he'd lined up on the table.

One of the Frenchmen spoke to the vendor. He pointed first at Beth and then at the purse.

Again, a shrug. The vendor mumbled something and pushed a card sideways with the flat of his hand. His fingernails were dirty.

The Frenchman reached over and thrust the cards to one side. He put his face close to the vendor's and said something sharp. Everyone got quiet.

The vendor didn't shrug this time. He gestured towards the purse and rolled his eyes so high that they were all yellowish whites. The Frenchman picked up the purse and gave it to Beth.

The sun beat down. From the man who'd given Beth the purse came an unpleasant odor of aftershave. The purse was warm, and the little mobile eye of the terrier rolled up and down as Beth held it unsteadily. She felt the urge to drop it, somehow discard it, but everyone was looking at her now. She was supposed to do something.

Then she said, "It's not mine."

The lady who knew English said, "What are you talking about?"

"I made a mistake. It's not my purse."

At once, she realized that this was true. She had thought it was her purse, but now that she was holding it, she could see that the lining was lighter, and the zipper had a different clasp. She stood her ground.

"I can't take this purse. It isn't mine."

Now the grownups were bewildered, and the man who had given the purse to Beth leaned in, forcing her backwards. The lady asked, "Little girl, is it or is it not your property?"

Beth fought back tears and cried out, "I don't know!"

Then she dropped the purse and ran. She took off down the river for some distance, below a bridge where the air turned dank and clammy, through a park, and ultimately to a part of the embankment where there was a little wharf. She stood there panting, and that's when she spotted the morning clerk from the hotel, the one with the mustache.

He was sitting on a bench with a young woman, and they were chatting companionably, watching someone fish. Beth rushed up to him and said, "Mister, please, I'm lost."

He turned to her and smiled. "You have come far. But the way back is not difficult." He glanced at his companion, a slim, brown-skinned girl who, like the clerk, seemed incapable of condescension. She addressed him in French, just a few words. Then, he said to Beth, "Would you care for company?"

Beth nodded, and tried not to seem too eager.

They walked Beth back to the hotel, and on the way, Beth saw the grubby vendor at a distance, headed in the other direction, with the table strapped to his back. With what she hoped was a casual air, Beth asked the hotel clerk, "Where is that man from?"

"Gypsy," said the clerk, "I would think, from the look of him. Though he could be from Algeria."

The woman made a harsh sound and said, "Come on, man. He's a Frenchman, same as you." She spoke English, clearly intending for Beth to hear.

"The Arabs in Algeria don't consider themselves Frenchmen," the clerk replied. "Of course, we could ignore those distinctions, my dear, and we would live in a very different world indeed."

"Indeed," said the woman. She continued, though now in French, and the two grownups walked along, arguing with great animation and affection that cast a glow on the entire promenade. Beth would have given anything to be able to follow that conversation. It might have been that day that she became determined to learn French. In any event, when her mother came home that night and kicked off her shoes to lie down for her nap, Beth waited to see if she would ask her if she'd had a good time that day. When she didn't, Beth volunteered the information herself.

"I met the desk-clerk's girlfriend."

"Goodness gracious," Beth's mother said. She turned her head on the pillow. Her face, compressed and caked with the day's make-up, looked shapeless, and she kept her eyes closed. She asked Beth, "Was she nice?"

"Mostly she spoke French," Beth said. "She's a Negro. And she gave me this." Beth then produced one of the cloth flowers she had seen so often from the window, a red pansy. Beth said to her mother, "It's for you."

9

"I DON'T KNOW HOW SHE died," Beth said to Ron. "I mean, it should just be a simple answer, right? Like, your mom died of cancer. They never told me."

Ron rolled over and leaned his head on his arm. They were lying together on a blanket in a little picnic area just off the turnpike in Ohio, and they had just made love. Ron said, "You know, I got a father in Chicago, and I could find him if I set my mind to it, but to tell you the truth, I just don't think it matters."

"You're not curious?"

"I got other things to do," said Ron, "like you know, I need to cook for you. I wanted to that day, but you were so all-fired-up to get back to Melody. You had a boyfriend there."

"I didn't," Beth said, and she started to laugh. "My God, Ron, who would my boyfriend be?"

"I know it wasn't Larry," said Ron. "He doesn't dig white chicks."

"And you do?" Beth slid herself against him and they kissed, though part of Beth continued to wonder what she wanted him to answer. That he dug white chicks? That he dug her in particular? Maybe it was fortunate that they both heard a car approach just then and scrambled for their clothes.

They didn't stay in hotels, and once they crossed the Tennessee border, Beth, without prompting, moved to the back of Hercules, a baby blue Rambler station wagon loaded with donated books and three new mimeograph machines. Hercules was big enough for Beth to stretch all the way out in the back and catch up on some sleep. A few hours later, Ron handed Beth the keys and said, "Don't hit any cows." He moved into the back, lay down, and gave an audible and friendly yawn.

Driving Hercules was a new experience for Beth. It was a little like navigating a boat. Well, they were moving onto uncharted waters. From Chester, Beth had written, rather than called her father. "It's better that way," Beth had said. "He's no good over the phone." Ron thought that maybe he could find something for Beth to do in Greenwood. But when Beth called Larry from a phone booth in Delaware to ask if there was a place for her in Melody, she'd gotten Freddie on the phone instead, and it seemed impossible not to at least spend a few weeks there.

"Yeah I know Freddie," Ron said. He spoke so casually that Beth was tempted to take her eyes off the road and give him a direct and dirty look. He seemed to read her anyway, because he said, "Come on, baby, she's just a sweet kid."

"What about Jackie?"

"Oh, Jackie," Ron said. "Now Jackie's another story, but you know, she likes those college boys. Jackie and Will, they make sense. Only, you know, he's a hard-liner and she's a floater."

"What's a floater?"

"Folks on that freedom high. You know like Jackie, Helen, Sylvester. The ones who do when the spirit say do. Like you."

The car bounced just a little on its wheels as Beth turned onto a state highway. She couldn't shake the giddiness, not quite. But she knew that she was going to have to face Larry. For all that Freddie wanted her in Melody, she couldn't know who else would. Least of all Larry, who would surely draw his own conclusions when she appeared again. Would he expect her to press charges? Would she have to face that night and those men?

When she pulled into Melody, Ron was still lying on the back seat, and she felt a wave of dread that could have only been vanquished if he was holding her. But they were in Mississippi. He couldn't hold her. The impossibility of their circumstances closed over her so that she had to struggle to keep believing that she wouldn't spin off the road. She bypassed the white center of town, crossed the tracks, and pulled up to the pharmacy.

Larry was sitting on the stoop, with his hands in the pockets of his overalls. His goatee was pointier and his frown deeper than Beth had remembered. He rose when the car pulled in, and then his face lit up.

"Fine! Goddamn!" he called. Then, he bounded over and she couldn't even make it out of the car before he'd caught her up and nearly knocked the air out of her.

Ron poked his head up, shook the sleep out of it, and said, "Well then, I guess you're home."

THE FIRST THING LARRY SAID after he let her go was, "I got you a room." It was in a boarding house in a section of town where the children in the Freedom School had once told Beth not to go. The room, small and surprisingly clean, had a single bed, a wash-basin, and a hot-plate on which she cooked enormous pots of beans she purchased from her ten dollar a week salary from SNCC.

Beth turned that room into an office. That's where she stored her maps of the county, and where she wrote her letters to office supply stores in the north to get them to donate slightly defective typewriters. She sent off well over a hundred letters, and two months later, fifteen typewriters appeared. She found stands for them by writing to her Aunt Beatrice—she did this regularly now, once a week—drawing her attention to a government surplus warehouse, and filling what room was left in a moving van heading from Washington D.C. to Memphis.

"I met that aunt of yours at the convention," Larry said when the typewriter stands arrived, courtesy of Harris Johnson's truck. "She cornered me and asked if I wanted—personally, mind you—to destroy the Democratic Party."

"What did you say?" Beth asked him.

"I told her I figured the Democrats were already doing the job pretty well themselves." Larry hoisted the stands out of the truck-bed, and he and Beth arranged them in the basement of the church. "Yeah, your aunt's sure a piece of work."

"So am I," Beth said. "Remember?"

Larry didn't disagree. He adjusted a stand and put a piece of paper in the typewriter closest to the door. Crouching, he began to type with two fingers: *What a piece of work is Fine.*

"I thought it was *Every Good Boy Does Fine*," said Beth, and then she blushed.

"*Deserves Favor*," Larry said. "What kind of typing class did you take anyhow?

Beth felt a nervous flutter. "How come you're being so nice to me?"

"I always was nice to you," Larry said. "You just never noticed."

SOMETIMES, BETH WONDERED IF HER presence was a liability. She knew that Claire Burgess's house was guarded every night now, sometimes by one of the Davis brothers, sometimes by George, who was still learning how to keep himself awake, and who would shoot one of the hollyhocks if it rattled. She wasn't sure if the room she occupied was guarded too. It seemed foolish to hope that she could be inconspicuous. She wondered if they would ask her to carry a gun. The possibility wedged itself into her throat. But it never happened. Perhaps, she thought, they just assumed she'd brought her own.

Beth took to having a beer with Larry at the end of the day. They found each other pleasant and undemanding company. Larry listened to Beth's theory about washing dishes, and told her about a visit he had made to a Zen temple just outside of Boston.

"What really struck me was that nobody seemed to see my color. And there was a kind of seriousness to everything they did—I mean sweeping the floor, laying a cloth on a table. And the silence. You couldn't have stood it for a minute."

"Why couldn't I have stood it?" Beth asked, with some impatience. "I know how to shut up."

"Well, there's also the matter of detachment," Larry said, with a smile.

"I can be detached."

"No you can't," said Larry. "You've got to know yourself. Detachment takes discipline. You keep an endless vigil. Think of Harris Johnson. You know, he sits on his porch all night, with his light burning."

"So Harris Johnson is a Buddhist?"

"He's vigilant," said Larry.

"But he's not keeping a vigil against passion. It's against somebody burning down his house. I wouldn't call that detachment."

"You just don't get it!" Larry shouted. "Vigilance *is* detachment!" And for emphasis, he slammed his fist down on the table.

This caused Beth to smile, and counter, "You don't sound very detached to me."

Then she'd order another beer she didn't want, and they would talk about Larry's unfinished dissertation on Algeria, and he would expound on neocolonialism and its relevance to Mississippi. She would ask him if a liberation movement could look, to a sick system, like psychosis, and Larry rejected the metaphor as too abstract to be of use to anyone but a psychotic, and the force of the argument washed over them both and made them laugh. They drew some stares.

Beth said, "I don't want to get you in trouble."

"Hell, Fine," said Larry. "I'm the one keeping you out of trouble. If I don't keep an eye on you, you'll be off to see your boyfriend."

Beth held her breath, and something about her face made Larry clarify.

"You know. That Cohen boy. The one who ought to be subpoenaed."

"Cy Cohen doesn't have anything to do with what happened," Beth said.

"Hey, hey, don't get bent out of shape," Larry said. "We all know how much you love little Cy Cohen. We know you came back for him."

"I don't love Cy Cohen," Beth said. "Larry, you know why I came back."

Larry looked hard at Beth, and lowered his voice to the point of near inaudibility. He said, "Please watch yourself. He's a good kid. But he's a kid."

Beth didn't answer. Ron had been appearing a few times a week, to check on Johnson's truck, supposedly, or to deliver something to the office. Most recently, he'd brought an Oldsmobile and left it with George after instructing him about the automatic transmission. Until then, Larry had let those visits pass without comment.

Beth said, "He's not so young. Only a year younger than me."

"Beth," Larry said, with an earnestness that rattled her, "He's been out of Mississippi twice. The first time, you got him lost in New Jersey. The second time—well, I think you both got lost."

"Not lost," Beth said. She sounded petulant, even to herself.

Larry continued. "He's not used to meeting white people on a basis of equality." The plate of rice and peas they were sharing was getting cold. Larry lit a cigarette. Then he said, "Are you sure you're over it?"

"Over what?" Beth asked.

"You know what. What happened. What you won't talk about. Consider that, okay? Consider why you got into this. Before it goes too deep."

Beth wanted to ask: what is too deep? She thought of a song: *So high you can't get over it, so deep you can't get under it, so wide, you can't get around it.* What was the source of the ease between her and Larry now? Did he think it came from nowhere? What Beth said instead was: "Larry, he's just giving me swimming lessons."

IN THE STRETCH OF INDIAN summer that lasted, in Mississippi, well into October, Ron would take Beth to a pond he knew. The pond was in Mound Bayou, and once, when she ran into a grocery store to get a bag of chips, Beth saw J.B. and a very pregnant Mae. J.B. said, "Hey! I heard you were back, kid! You want to come over for a cup of coffee?" and Beth had to make some very awkward excuse, and with a thrill of secrecy, slink out to Hercules, which was parked behind a stand of pine trees half a block away.

The pond was deep and clear, never quite exposed to sunlight. It was full of minnows. Ron would take Beth's hand and say, "Step in."

"It's cold."

"Not too cold, baby. It's been warming up all summer, warming up just for you. Come on. Just your foot."

The edge was so muddy that her legs sank in to the ankle. The bottom was half-liquid, syrupy, and it shaped itself around her feet like socks, and rose in a smoky cloud. Then, the ground shifted. There were Ron's feet, near her own.

"Another step."

She took that step. The water reached her knees. "You'll trick me," said Beth. "I'll be in over my head."

"If you already know that, what's the trick?" Ron asked her. He looked sly, with his narrow, not-quite-open eyes. Such was the shade and sunlight that he seemed both there and not there, flickering. But his hand was on her arm, warm, whole, closing around her elbow. With a thrust, he let go, and went under.

She watched his body, like a shadow, like an absence. She watched weeds part, and all those silver, darting minnows with their trails of bubbles. It was magnetic, her need to be with him. He must have known. It wouldn't be long before she found the water closing in over her head.

Ron taught Beth how to float, how to let her legs rise, how to relax her shoulders—didn't she know how to relax?—how to turn her arms into wings and push her body forward. Then, she would make her way across the pond and stand, flushed but also very cold, on the other side. He'd come around with a blanket, and they would warm up in the car.

Hercules's expansive and slightly ragged back seat was big enough for one, but not for two. They never noticed the discomfort when they were making love, but afterwards, Beth hated that she could never see his whole body. The bathing suit she'd borrowed from Jackie Gordon hung over the window and dripped in her face, and she felt boxed-in and cross.

"We can't keep doing this in cars," Beth said.

"Can't see why not," said Ron. He groomed her wet hair and pulled it back with both hands.

"We'll get too old," said Beth. He gave her a look of such tender exasperation that she had to laugh and kiss him. She wished they didn't have to be so careful. Maybe they could spend a week or two up north, in Chicago or even New York, stay with some of Ron's friends from the Movement and make love in a bed with sheets.

"Yeah, baby. But you got to know something about me by now. I don't wear well outside of Mississippi." That was a little too close to what Larry had said for Beth's comfort, and she didn't pursue the point. Besides, Ron felt an urgent need to keep the Sojourner Fleet running. Although Greenwood was still a Movement stronghold, discipline had dwindled to the point where Ron found it easier to move from project to project than to run a functioning garage. In most of the places where Ron landed, he found cars abandoned, or turned over to local teenagers, or just plain gone with their field secretaries to points unknown.

Ron would be away for days at a time, trying to track down those vehicles. "I just don't get it," Ron had said to Beth. "You know how long it took us to get all those donations? And the other day, I caught this kid from Greenwood taking Her Majesty for a joyride up 51. I swear, if he gets himself in jail, ain't no one from the National Lawyers Guild gonna fly here to bail him out again."

"You were that age once," Beth had said to Ron.

"I wasn't ever that age," Ron said. "I always knew how to take care of my cars. And I never depended on some white man from New York to save my behind. Those boys don't care if they break up my fleet."

"It isn't *your* fleet," said Beth.

He sulked after that. As far as he was concerned, what those field secretaries did just wasn't right, and that boy who drove up 51 was brought up badly. A whipping from his father would have been in order. Then, he would talk about the type of father he would be, and how he'd teach his son to shift gears as soon as he could understand the alphabet. He said, "One day, you know, I got to introduce you to my people."

"Your people?" Beth asked him.

"Aunt Risa, Uncle Walter. I wonder what they'd make of you. Probably think you're too skinny. But they're the best, understand? The best there is. They took my momma Tammy in with a baby and no prospects. When she took up with my daddy, Aunt Risa said, 'Tamara, how do you know that Ronald Beauchamp doesn't have a wife back in Chicago?' And you know what she said? 'Risa, I'll be woman enough for him. You mark my words.'"

"She sounds kind of wild," said Beth.

"And smart. Took the cancer to slow her down. See, Risa was the younger one, but she always felt like the older sister. And then she and Uncle Walter saw her through a sickness that wasted her down to nothing. They're true Christians."

Ron still went to church in Tutwiler every Sunday morning, and sometimes on Tuesdays as well. He invited her to join him once after a swimming lesson. "Jackie comes sometimes," Ron said. "She was brought up hearing Pastor Holden. Now, some people say she's strayed, but in her heart, she'll always be a Christian."

"I'm not a Christian," Beth said.

Ron nodded, unruffled by what Beth had intended to serve as a confession. "You're one of the chosen people. No need to apologize for that."

Beth shook her head. "That's not what I mean. That's irrelevant. It's just—I don't believe in God."

The words brought on silence. To cover what might have been embarrassment, Ron felt for his jeans and T-shirt and got out of the car to dress. All the while, Beth tried to figure out some way to give the statement context. She'd spoken with the sense that she was coming clean to him, yet at the same time, the words were not what she'd meant at all. Ron had his jeans back on, and he was pulling the T-shirt over his head. Beth called out through the window, "I'm sorry."

"Baby, I don't know how you can live like that," said Ron. "But I'm not here to live your life for you." Then he kissed her through the open window, a brief kiss, before he got into the driver's seat to start the car. He was somewhere else. It was that way sometimes. He might as well have been wearing those dark glasses.

Yet it was like the letter she had written to her father from that Freedom House in Chester, while Ron fried up their breakfast. She had her stocking feet up on the table, and the pad propped on her knees, and after a moment of worrying the pen with her teeth, she could only think to quote a line from Pascal that even he might recognize: *The heart has its reasons, which reason does not know.*

WHY DIDN'T RON WANT TO know about his father? If he had no father, what sort of father would he be? Beth knew better than to raise those questions, and her own father had cursed her with logic enough to turn them on herself. If she had no mother, what sort of mother would she be? In the end, what did Beth know about her mother, if she couldn't even know how she had died?

During her last year, Vivian had been home more often. She no longer seemed to work at Neuman's. For a time, she always seemed to be in the middle of cleaning the house or making dinner or paying bills; she was ceaselessly, endlessly active. Her hair was pulled back tight and there were hard creases in her blouse where she had ironed it in a hurry. When she walked Beth to school, Beth would have to say, "Mommy, slow down."

Once, she went away without saying goodbye. Beth's father said to her, "She had to take a rest, Bitsy."

"She didn't have to work so hard. I could have helped her," Beth said. "If she'd asked me."

In fact, when Vivian returned, there was an air of accusation about her, a line between her eyebrows that hadn't been there before. She wore her hair in a stiff, new style, parted right down the middle. There was a scar on her forehead, just a shade lighter than her very white skin. Beth rushed up to kiss her, and Vivian suffered it briefly before gently pushing Beth aside.

"Mommy," said Beth, "I'm going to help you from now on."

"Mommy's just home for a visit," said Vivian.

"But why do you have to go away again to rest? You can rest here." Beth said.

Vivian shook her head, and the hair moved, just a little, to the left.

That's when Beth asked, "Mommy, are you wearing a wig?"

"How clever of you to notice," said Vivian. She readjusted it and said, "I thought, why should my hair always look one way? I thought your daddy might like to be married to a brunette or a blonde."

"He just wants to be married to you," said Beth, heavily, and she hugged her mother as though to forestall a kind of falling that seemed to go on and on, even as they both sat on the couch in the living room. The couch, pea-green, low-backed, bought in installments when Max had arrived in Princeton with few prospects, now paid for, a permanent part of their living room, would be there when Beth found out her mother wasn't coming home, and it was as though Beth, even then, knew what else would happen in that place. She hung onto the cool, lax body of her mother, and she was not surprised to see her father join them, holding a cocktail in each hand and glancing at the two of them with one of his half-smiles. Later, Beth would characterize those smiles as ironic, but when she was very young, she thought they were like smiles that forgot they were smiles, or smiles that stopped too soon.

"Viv, you still like ice?" he asked her.

Beth's mother looked up and said, "What makes you think I've changed? Yes, of course I still like ice."

"It's okay for you to have this?" Max said, and there was a note in his voice that Beth couldn't classify.

"Perfectly fine," she replied. "It'll do me a world of good, sweetheart. Now darling," she said, addressing Beth, "why don't you go get that jar of olives out of the fridge and bring it out here, and you can have one yourself."

"I don't like olives," said Beth. She did not let go of her mother.

"Well, that's the first I've heard of it," said Vivian. "Then why don't you get something you do like, baby. There must be something you like best."

After her mother said this, Beth left the room without a fuss and went to the kitchen, but as soon as she was alone, she started to cry and didn't stop until she heard someone approach. Then, she hurriedly opened the refrigerator and found the jar of olives. She was holding them by the time her father came in.

"Bitsy," he said. "Forget about the olives. She's asleep."

Beth asked, "Can I look at her?"

If the question seemed strange to Max, he didn't show it. He stifled a yawn and moved past her to return the olives to the refrigerator, and she took that as permission and hurried back to the living room before he changed his mind.

Beth stood some distance away now, watching her mother as she lay on the couch with her shoes on the floor and her stocking feet propped up. Her yellow dress had traveled and bunched around her knees, and her arms cradled her head, as though to keep the wig in place. Beth sat on the floor and tucked her hands into her mother's shoes, which were still warm and slightly damp with perspiration. She fell asleep that way, holding those shoes like puppets. At some point, her father found her there and led her off to bed.

10

AS THEY APPROACHED WAVELAND, BETH saw her first southern live oak trees. Their bark was black, and their limbs were curved, like elbows. They grew along one side of the Gulf highway; on the far side was the sea. Down that narrow strip, she rode with George and J.B. and a few people from the Holly Springs project. Larry was already there. He'd left the night before.

She wished Freddie could be with her. Freddie had taught Beth how to identify magnolias, elms, holly-bushes, bindweed, and an imported English Ivy which had somehow overtaken every fence and Freddie claimed would turn deep crimson when the air turned cold. Freddie was still in high school, and even if she could miss class, it was unlikely that her parents would let her to go to the conference, but she said to Beth, "You got to keep an eye on George for me."

It was November, but as balmy as mid-summer, and the smell of the sea made Beth think of home, and rare trips to Asbury Park when she was a little girl. After a rainstorm, the Jersey boardwalk would be the color of those live oak trees. Smokey the Oldsmobile was just the size of Max Fine's wide, steady car. J.B. drove.

"Does the water in the gulf get cold?" Beth asked J.B.

"I sure don't know," J.B. said. "We never went down here. Seems to be a lot of folks fishing, though. Look at those wharves."

The wharves jutted out every few yards. They were as black and shaggy as the live oak trees, and some were so long that the ends of them were lost in haze.

"How's it for swimming?" Beth asked.

George broke in. "What kind of fool wants to swim in November?" He lit a cigarette. "Can't you drive any faster, man?"

"Not on your life," said J.B. "Maybe you wouldn't mind getting your ass thrown in jail, but I'm gonna be a father."

Mae was due by Christmas. J.B. was always back and forth between Mound Bayou and Melody these days, patching holes in his roof, checking the wiring in the fuse-box, and in general reoccupying his own house gradually. He was also looking for work, with no success. He admitted to Beth privately that he hoped he might run into someone at the Waveland conference who had Washington connections and could set him up with a federal job, maybe with the poverty program.

George said, "Where is this place anyhow? Looks like we're miles from any colored people. Gives me the creeps. Where are we supposed to go to cut loose?"

Beth had gone over the schedule with Larry. "Well, the meetings go on pretty much all day."

"Then you can bet there'll be some serious cutting loose at night," said one of the boys from Holly Springs, a long-time SNCC-person who'd been to a few of these gatherings. "And you can bet nobody's gonna sleep."

Beth hadn't slept much these days anyway. She couldn't bear the four walls of her room when outside, the moon and stars and soft, cool air were waiting. She would walk down Monroe Street to the outskirts of Melody and lose herself, just stare at the sky. Larry knew she did it, and he dressed her down for it, but he admitted that for no good reason he sometimes felt compelled to join Harris Johnson on this porch all night.

"So you feel it too," said Beth.

"Feel what?"

"Like if you even close your eyes you'll miss something important."

"Fine," said Larry, "You haven't so much as opened any of those books I gave you."

"You know I never read anything someone tells me I have to read," said Beth, a little petulantly.

"You still think you're living in a revolutionary moment."

"Yes I do," said Beth. Then she laughed.

Larry broke in and once again explained that the lack of a distinction between revolutionary discipline and seat of the pants practice was what had brought the Movement to this pass. He told her about Atlantic City, what it taught them all about the limitations of liberal politics. At the last staff meeting, SNCC had decided to take on two hundred white kids who'd stayed after the end of the Summer Project. You couldn't fit all of those fool people in a room.

"Who plans to shut the door?" Beth asked, looking at Larry across a desk, or a shelf of books, or a table at the cafe. That was how many times they'd had that conversation. She'd smile a little, trying to turn the question into a joke. It was no joke.

He grumbled. He gave her full-length lectures on the fate of newly independent African nations, and she seemed, initially, to grant that openness could be manipulated, and that people who have capital and power, people born to privilege, should just get the hell out of the way.

But then Beth said, "I don't have power."

Larry nearly screamed out of sheer frustration. "You still don't get it."

"I can only think of one time—one time in my life when I had power."

"Only one time when you were conscious you had power," said Larry. Then, he left off, though Beth suspected that she and Larry were thinking of different moments entirely. Larry was thinking about the gun. Beth was thinking about the Freedom House in Chester when she had kissed Ron Beauchamp.

"Consciousness is power," Beth said, delighted with the phrase. Larry didn't disagree, but he amended.

"Consciousness is the beginning of power."

George, who happened to be on hand at the cafe during this exchange, broke in. "Man, speak English. Unless that's the way they talk in Boston."

"It depends on which part of Boston," Larry replied. "Listen up. You might find yourself there some day."

THE WAVELAND CONFERENCE WAS HELD in November of 1964, at a Methodist retreat just off the highway. It was supposed to address general questions in the wake of what had gone down in Atlantic City. Just as the numbers of SNCC swelled, liberal support was falling away, and most of the staff were not so sorry to see it go, but if they were, as Beth put it, in a revolutionary moment, what should come next? Who should they organize? Where should they organize? How should they organize? What should be their short-term strategies and long-term vision?

In short, what was the future of the Movement? These were, as Beth put it, existential questions. After Larry had received the notice, Beth asked, "They actually expect us to figure out these things in one conference?"

"People are presenting position papers," Larry said. "They're supposed to keep us more on track than usual." Smiling, he added, "Want to write one?"

"About what?" Beth asked him.

"How about power and consciousness."

"Very funny," Beth said. But then she wrote one, which she refused to show to Larry. She did ask him to arrange to get her a room with Ron.

"You've got to be kidding," Larry said. "This is a Methodist retreat."

"Ron's a Baptist," Beth said. Larry let that pass.

"Look," he said. "Corridors can be dark places at night. No one can tell you what to do in the end. But if you two want to get us kicked off the grounds, don't expect me to think it's cute."

When they arrived and piled their things in the front hallway, Beth checked her room assignment, which included the name of her roommate, and she said, "There's been a mistake."

"No mistake," said the white girl who was staffing.

"But I figured I'd get a room to myself. See, I wrote a position paper, and I might need to caucus." Even as she made the argument, it sounded unconvincing. There were thirty-seven other position papers.

But this was something else again. She would be rooming with Sue Francis. She hadn't seen her since the shooting. Sue Francis had gotten a staff position in Atlanta, and although there were plenty of rumors, including an involved story about her parents driving to Georgia to try to force her to go back to Tupelo, she hadn't set foot in Melody since Beth's arrival.

"Larry Walsh left this for you," the girl said. She handed Beth a windbreaker. "He said you'd probably show up without a coat."

"That sounds like him," said Beth, too angry to admit that Larry was correct. With a sinking heart, Beth took the windbreaker, hoisted her rucksack over her shoulder, and walked down the corridor to her room.

Beth found Sue Francis unfolding her clothing on her neat twin bed. She looked up and said, "Oh. Hi."

"You look terrific," Beth said. She meant it. Sue Francis was wearing overalls that illogically seemed to bring out the shape of her hips, and her hair was cut and had grown out into a coffee-colored halo of loose curls.

"I'm not trying to look any way in particular. But thank you, I guess." Then she said, "You look different."

"Thank you too, I guess." Beth said. She nearly said more, but Sue Francis interrupted.

"Don't touch my stuff, alright?"

Beth let her be, and walked out to look for Larry. She would give him hell. She hadn't seen Ron for over a week, and it felt like a year. The few minutes she'd spent with Sue Francis made her desperate for friendly company, and as she explored the grounds, she realized how few of these people she really knew, how in the end, she remained an outsider. She hoped to run into Jackie, Will, Sylvester, Helen, somebody she'd recognize by sight, but the people pulling into the lot were all strangers. Beth walked past the broad live oaks and crossed the highway. There was the ocean. She pulled on the windbreaker, which, admittedly, she needed. Seagulls swooped so low that she could see their legs tucked in.

Then, she stuck her hands in her pockets and felt a slip of paper. There was something written on it.

Room 28. Midnight.

She closed her hand around the note and smelled the sea.

THAT NIGHT, AFTER THE MEETING where James Forman spoke, she managed to untangle herself from Jackie's company, and even to evade Helen who was excited about a position paper about the role of women in the Movement. The mood was frantic, breathless, and from room after room came the sound of arguments or laughter or guitars and singing, clouds of cigarette smoke. The conversations were elusive and circular as smoke-rings, and at any other point, she might be drawn in, but not that night. The corridor, she realized with some despair, would not be a dark place. These people were like her; they never slept. Still, when she peered into her room, she was not surprised to find Sue Francis already in bed and snoring softly, looking gentler than one would expect, like a sprung trap.

She took her chances in the hallway. The room was one flight up: *24, 26.* The door she wanted was ajar.

Ron lay in one twin bed. The other was empty. He had been waiting for her with his head propped on his arm, and when he saw her, he smiled like a sleepy little boy. She closed the door behind her, stripped, and climbed in. All of his limbs closed around her like four corners, and it was so easy and so happy that she didn't even mind that they had to be quiet and that he blasted all of his shouting into her hair. The damp sheets in that little bed got so tangled that they had to climb all over each other afterwards just to lay side by side.

"We got more room in Hercules," Ron said.

Beth said, "I like it in a bed."

They kissed again, and Ron laid his hands between her hips, and touched her just enough to make her fall into sensation of a piece with every detail of the room, the clean single-framed window, the moonlight filtered through the leaves and clouds into a gray that filled the cross-hatch of the windowpanes.

"What about your roommate?" Beth asked him.

"Larry?" Ron smiled. "Baby, don't you worry about Larry. We got it all worked out. He's in your room."

"I don't—" Beth began, but then she started again. "Where?" Then, finally, she said, "Oh." It wasn't exactly a surprise. She nestled back into Ron's arm, amused, a little wistful, and grateful that she could stay a while.

Everyone But Beth Seemed To think that SNCC had gone adrift since Atlantic City. In the words of an anonymous position paper that everyone knew was written by Bob Moses: they were on a boat in the middle of the ocean, and their boat had to be rebuilt to stay afloat and had to stay afloat in order to be rebuilt, and to complicate matters, because they were in the middle of the ocean, they would have to build the boat themselves.

The papers were mimeographed on site and distributed before the scheduled workshops. Beth read a stack of them, sitting on the grass in the round courtyard. She could make out the rim of the Gulf, just off the grounds. The edge of the world.

One afternoon, Beth Fine put on a bathing suit beneath her dress. She passed by people sitting under trees and stretched on blankets. She passed a serious-looking group of black women caucusing under a magnolia. She passed Bob Moses himself, who stood alone, leaning against a wall, his eyes closed behind his thick-rimmed glasses, looking so deeply exhausted that it seemed impossible to disturb him. All over the lawn, young people, black and white, did as they pleased with as little self-consciousness as inmates at an asylum. Beth recognized Frank Court lying prone on the grass with his work shirt unfastened at the neck and his arms above his head in a gesture of surrender.

Away from these people, Beth walked, out the gates of the retreat, to the empty wharf. She started across its length. She could feel the wood splinters gather in the soles of her feet; a rush of spray made her right side wet. She didn't care.

She said, "I'm doing this."

The sound of her own voice startled her. Who was she addressing? Or what? The sun was low, hanging just over the lip of the gulf. She shimmied out of her dress and it fell to her ankles. Then, she stepped out of it and walked to the edge of the wharf. She jumped in.

The cold took her breath away, but what she hadn't expected was the dark: above, a light like rubies, below, dark green, no bottom. She remembered then: her arms were wings and they would pull her body up. It never occurred to her that she would drown. Maybe the tide was low. Maybe the wharf was not that long. She made it to the shore before she had time to be afraid.

People at the Waveland Conference spent some time afterwards recounting the sight of a white girl who had walked directly back to the grounds in her bathing suit with her hair dripping and plastered down her back. A strand of seaweed clung to her thigh.

Frank Court jumped up and called, "You're *crazy* sweetheart! You want to freeze to death?"

"It's perfect!" Beth called back. She was shivering, and she was also laughing.

No one else jumped in. No one else had anything to prove, or at least not the same thing to prove. Later that night, they would all sit out on those wharves that jutted out along the coast. They would share a cigarette or a joint and would keep talking about what they had talked about all day, without pretense, as though they had taken themselves beyond judgment or hostile observation. They were on the world's edge. Like Beth, they took delight in not being afraid.

Soon they would be afraid, not just of sheriffs, unmarked cars, and jail cells, or of the federal government. Fatally, they would be afraid of each other. They would think of the times when they could make open challenges this easily, and they would not believe those times existed. The old bond between them would break, maybe because it had to, maybe because they'd planned, from the start, to make themselves obsolete, maybe because only so many people can fit into a room, and no one wants to shut the door.

But that night, Beth, her hair dried stiffly, put on her windbreaker and sat on the edge of a long wharf with Larry Walsh. A few months ago, he'd been her enemy. Now, he passed her a joint.

"And you were jumping to prove what?" Larry asked her.

"That I could." Beth inhaled, but not too deeply.

"You can do a lot of things," Larry said. "But you choose those that are necessary. I don't think that swim was necessary."

"Nobody was asking you," said Beth.

"You're going to get yourself a reputation," Larry said. "Like that anonymous paper of yours."

"How can you know which one is mine," said Beth.

"Oh, I know alright," said Larry. "Who else would actually give something a title like *The Outsider*? It's stolen from Richard Wright who stole it from Camus, and to make matters worse, it sounds like a bad western. You're already known as the Girl with the Gun."

"Is that like *The Beatnik Bride*?" Beth asked him. She didn't want to talk about her paper, which had been soundly dismissed by a group of seasoned Movement people who seemed to have gathered at the workshop expressly for that purpose. They had gone through her dense and self-important prose line by line, and one of them had said, "This had to have been written by one of those college students," and another said, "What's the proposal here? What does this have to do with our future?" Then a third said, "Oh, it has to do with that student's future." Beth sat in silence. Yet, the drubbing didn't make a dent in her conviction that the position was sound.

There are few forces more powerful than the engaged outsider, the outside agitator who can see what is invisible to those caught in the flow of history. The engaged outsider casts himself into a circumstance and creates the opportunity for consciousness, just as a river can change its course through debris, erosion and intervention.

They all misunderstand the line about intervention. They thought it referred to federal intervention, and that really got their backs up, because after that summer, who had faith in federal intervention anymore? In the end, Beth wished that had she hadn't leaned so heavily on metaphor, though she wasn't the only one. Bob Moses had his boat in the middle of the ocean. James Forman had his river of no return. There was a lot of water at Waveland, or, some might say, a lot of floating around.

"Am I a floater?" Beth asked Larry.

Larry laughed. "Where'd you hear that one?"

"You know—like you're a hard-liner, and Jackie and Helen are floaters. What's Ron?"

"A mechanic," said Larry. "What the hell are you talking about? If we start playing those games, then we really are lost."

"Sue Francis is a hard-liner," Beth said dreamily. "I think she was born that way. What's up with you two anyhow?"

"None of your business," Larry said. The air was cool, but somehow, the wood of the wharf had absorbed so much sunlight below its crust of salt that it was comfortably warm.

Beth said, "I thought maybe you'd understand my paper at least. You're an outsider too."

"You'd got things so ass-backwards, I don't even know how to begin to turn you right-side up again," said Larry. "I'm black, okay? I'm always going to be on the outside in white America."

"I'm talking about here in Mississippi. You don't belong here any more than I do. You've chosen this. It takes an outside force to trouble the water."

"Fine," said Larry, "how much do you really know about waves? Look up!" Now they were both looking at the moon. That moon was half-obscured by clouds, not quite full, butter-colored, the color of Po Burgess, the color the baby Beth made with Ron would be. "You think waves are caused by someone throwing rocks? There are greater forces, historical forces—"

"Marxist!" Beth said.

"Damn right," said Larry, "and that's no metaphor."

The two, Beth knew, were stoned out of their minds. They would make an appealing target, a white woman and a black man outlined on that wharf. Their lovers were somewhere else, Sue Francis at a caucus with Atlanta staff, and Ron with friends from Greenwood. Beth had hoped that Ron would let himself be seen with her in public, at least on the grounds. There were plenty of other interracial couples. However, it mattered less to her than she would have thought. Larry laid a hand on Beth's arm, a gesture friendly enough, but highly charged.

He said, "You know, I worry about you."

"I hope you don't," said Beth.

"No, I do." Somewhat awkwardly, he moved his hand to her shoulder. "I mean, all this talk about debris. Pardon me if I extend the metaphor. I know you will. You know what really happens when something falls into a river?"

"It becomes part of that river," said Beth.

"It gets worn down," said Larry. He released her shoulder and just looked at her. "After a while, it breaks apart. Then, it disappears."

THE
BOAT

1

CY COHEN HAD STARTED LOCKING up the dry goods store early on Friday nights, so he could open up the Temple. It meant a real cut in business, because Friday, after all, was payday, and although he would open early on Saturday to make up for the lost time, in the end it was one of those choices you make in life. Either you close early, or the Temple's not set up for services. Then, there was the rabbi, a young man fresh from the seminary, who came in from Memphis once a month and needed a ride from the train station in Holly Springs. The rabbi refused to drive in Mississippi.

"You never know what kind of peckerwoods you find out on those back roads," he said to Cy the first time he picked him up. "You know, they pulled me over just because I had Illinois plates. They said it was my headlight. Who needs that kind of nonsense?"

"Melody's a progressive kind of town," said Cy. He tried not to sound defensive. "You meet a lot of forward-thinking people in Marshall County."

"Yeah, well thank God you're not in the Delta," said the rabbi. "Some of those towns think they won the Civil War."

"So how'd your car get those Illinois plates?" Cy asked him, "Meaning no disrespect, Rabbi."

"I went to seminary in Chicago," he replied. "And if I had any sense, I would have stayed there, but I've got family down here. You know how it is."

"I know," said Cy. He drove the Packard to the Greenfield house where the rabbi would have supper before services. Cy couldn't help but feel slighted, not only by the rabbi's comments about Melody, but also because the rabbi wouldn't stay in his home. That was because of Sherrie.

Maybe Cy could force the issue. After all, how many Jewish girls were there to choose from in Melody? He could have been like his father and gone somewhere else to bring a lady home, but his father had been in the war, and Cy had no excuse at all to get the hell out of town. On top of everything else, his mother had broken her hip that spring and could only get around with a three-pronged cane.

Sherrie got along well with Cy's mother. She got along with everyone. Somehow, Cy thought, he'd found a girl without an ounce of meanness in her. She was tiny, with light brown curly hair and dimples, just like Shirley Temple. They'd known each other in high school, but he hadn't really thought about her in a romantic way until she let him drive her home from meetings of the Chamber of Commerce, where she was recording secretary. Of course, she knew he was Jewish, but her only question was, "You all believe in God, don't you?"

"Sure," said Cy. "It's only I go to church on Fridays instead of Sundays."

"Well, we're all God's children," Sherrie said, "Red and yellow, black and white, each is precious in His sight." Sherrie was a Methodist. Her grandparents had been missionaries in Africa and were buried there. Her parents had retired to the Gulf Coast and seemed to have little interest in her whereabouts. She was living with her aunt Gale—commonly known as Crazy Miss Gale—when Cy met her. In short, she was a kind of orphan, and she gave herself to her new circumstances with an open heart.

At the store, she kept the books, and Cy spent most of his time behind the counter. Sherrie would have preferred to deal with customers. "I'm just wild about Negroes," she said once. "They're so close to God and to the earth. You know, there are a lot of very hateful people in the world but I can only say that life is too short to hate."

Cy would let her talk on and on. It was nice at first. His life had been too silent since his father died. These days, his mother stopped saying much of anything at all. She just clomped around the house with that heavy cane, sat carefully in the chair she always occupied, and spent most of her time watching television.

Millie Cohen had a habit of gripping the furniture to pull herself across the room, and once, they'd come back from work to find her on the floor, holding an overturned chair. He wanted Sherrie to stay home and keep an eye on her, but Sherrie said, "Honey, your mother has such a fierce sort of independence. I don't know how she'll take it."

"Oh, she'll take it alright," said Cy. In fact, his mother put up quite a fight, and in a harsh whisper, while Sherrie was outside trimming the hedges, she told them that she didn't bring him up to have him leave her in the care of a *shiksa* who didn't even know how to tie her shoes, let alone run a household. Cy said, "You don't have a choice, momma. You never stay in one place long enough for that hip of yours to heal."

"If you leave me with that girl," his mother said, "I swear, we'll both end up in traction. I'll break every bone in her body and break both my arms and legs doing it. If you really think I need somebody here, what about a nice colored girl?"

"Momma," said Cy, "she's my wife."

"Well that's your funeral," his mother said. "I'm telling you, get me a colored girl. That boy who works at the Temple, doesn't he have a wife or something?"

"He's seventeen," said Cy.

"Then a sister. We might as well stick to the same family, so we know what we're getting."

Cy was reluctant to press the case with George, who had become pretty strange these days. In fact, there'd been some pressure to let the boy go. Though no one could say precisely how he was involved, it was assumed that he'd played some sort of part in the trouble during that summer. His hair was wild as any cotton-picker's from the Delta, and he always wore the same pair of grubby overalls, even when Cy told him he could stop by the store any time, and he'd let him buy a button-down shirt and chinos at a discount.

"Listen," said George to Cy, "If you give me a discount, give everyone a discount. I know you jack up those prices twice what you ought to."

"So you know what I ought to charge?"

"When we're making fifteen, twenty dollars a week, how can we afford what you ask unless you give us credit?"

"Credit for good manners and good intentions I give," said Cy, "but not for merchandise."

George rolled his eyes. "That's just what I thought you'd say."

"Then why did you bother asking?"

As was his habit, George closed the conversation by turning back to his reading. These days, he'd switched from comic books to paperbacks, and Cy lingered, trying to read the title.

"*The Plague.* What are you on now, son? One of those books where it's the end of the world and there's only one boy and girl who survive?"

George put the book down, irritated. "You got something you want me to do?"

Cy had intended to ask him about finding a girl who could stay with his mother, but now he found himself putting his hand in his pocket for his wallet and peeling off four one-dollar bills.

"What's that for?" George asked him.

"To get a haircut and a shave."

George took the money without comment, and stuck it unceremoniously in the front pocket of his overalls.

"Where'd you get that book?" Cy asked him.

Then, George looked right at him and seemed to make up his mind about something. "You want to borrow it, Mr. Cohen? You can get it down Monroe Street. We got two more of them right there on the shelf, all donated from Boston University. You can just walk right in."

Cy said, "You damned well know I can not just walk right in. You colored boys all have guns. You'd shoot me on sight."

"Oh no. We're integrated," George said. "We even got ourselves another Jew."

"Another what?"

"Another Jew," George said. He looked pleased with himself. "That Jewish girl's been here over a year now. Shame you already got yourself a wife."

CY COHEN WAS THE LAST one to find out that his summer volunteer hadn't gone home. Between his marriage and his mother's health, he'd kept pretty much to himself. Still, it seemed impossible to him that Beth could have been in town all of this time without his knowing. He got a few details from folks in the store: white girl, red hair chopped to pieces on her head, running around in a Mammy sort of housedress and men's work boots, followed by a pack of colored teenagers like she was a movie star.

Sherrie said, "That's such a sad story. I heard she fell in with that J.B. nigger, and he ran off to the Delta after he got into all that trouble, and now her family won't take her back."

"So she's not a volunteer?"

"I'd say she didn't volunteer for anything," said Sherrie. "I'd say she was drafted."

Reluctantly, Cy turned to other sources of information, particularly Barney at the service station who confirmed his suspicions. "That's your slut," he said with a grin that ran across his face like an oil slick. "Bet you didn't know she packed a gun. But the man she shot at wasn't a nigger, so she'll never go to trial. That's just how ass-backwards we are now."

Cy wondered how long he'd be able to stay away. A day passed, then two days, and he told himself that if he could hold out for a full week, then he would be able to just let it pass. However, on the fifth day after he'd spoken to George, he found himself asking Sherrie to take over the register—always a risky proposition—and he walked across the tracks, knowing full well where he was going.

He ran into her almost immediately. She was heading down Monroe Street, dressed just the way he'd been told she was dressed, in those mannish boots and a bulky overcoat, but her hair didn't look the way he'd thought it would. In fact—and it made him ache to know this—it fell in soft, deep, red curls, and her face was round and calm. "My God," said Cy, before he could stop himself, "What happened to you?"

Beth said, "Oh, hey. I guess I should have let you know I was back."

"What are you doing here?" Cy asked.

"Just what needs doing," Beth replied. "Want to help me with the kids?"

"No, I do not want to help you with the kids," Cy said unhappily. "I want to know what you've done to yourself."

Beth looked confused. Then, she said, "Oh. You mean my hair? I let Sweetie cut it. Anyhow, are you going to just stand there, or are you going to help me?"

Flustered, and anxious to continue the conversation, Cy followed Beth down Monroe to the old A.M.E. Church. She led him inside and down the basement, and showed him the typewriters and stands, a couch and easy chair arranged on the far side of a partition, and five shelves of books arranged in rows. The back wall was covered with glossy posters: *Visit Paris, Salutations de Lyon*, and a montage of photographs of children: *Visages de la France*. "Oh, that's Bobbie's corner," said Beth. "She's at Jackson State now, but she gets pretty mad if we move anything."

A number of young girls loitered by the bookshelves, and when they saw Beth and Cy, they started calling out, "Is he your boyfriend? Is he your boyfriend?"

Beth shook her head and said, "Nope. This guy's married. Can't you tell? He's wearing a wedding ring."

Cy felt a little dizzy. "Look, are you gonna come with me and have a conversation about this?"

"About what?" Beth asked him. Then, she said to the girls, "Cy's got a special treat for us today. He's going to show us how he runs his store."

Cy would have protested, but the girls all started talking at once, and so did Beth, right over them, until the cacophony drove all the fight out of him, and he searched for a graceful way out, and couldn't find one. He said, "I guess you all can just follow me. You probably know the way. Your mommas are all my good customers."

One girl said, "I been there plenty of times. But you don't got nothing but clothes for boys."

"Girls can wear jeans," said another, an older girl he would soon know well—Freddie—who was wearing a pair of jeans that looked as though they had been painted on her. "If you knew how to sell jeans to girls, Cy, you'd make a lot more money."

"Didn't your momma teach you manners?" Cy asked her. "My name is Mr. Cohen."

"Beth here called you Cy," said Freddie.

Cy felt his blood burn, and he came close to saying that Beth wasn't anyone's idea of a lady, but he kept his mouth shut. Freddie and the girls started towards the store, and Cy hung back. He managed to whisper to Beth, "You want to get me strung up, don't you. You want me hanging from a tree."

"That wasn't the idea," said Beth. "I figured I was doing you a favor. You know, these girls are going to run Melody one day."

"Yeah, I can't wait," said Cy. "I'll just kill myself right now."

It wasn't until they'd reached the store that Cy remembered that he'd left Sherrie at the cash register. She looked up when the door opened, and it was instructive to see the way her flexible little mouth went up and down as she took in what she saw.

"Why Cy. What a nice surprise. Here I thought you were gone for the day, and now you're back with all these little colored girls." She didn't mention Beth.

But Beth went straight to her and said, "Mrs. Cohen, these young ladies have been taking a course in bookkeeping and business management."

"What on heaven and earth," Sherrie began. Her gaze drifted, uncertainly, towards Cy.

"Honey," said Cy, "mind if I show these girls around?"

"I'm sure I don't," said Sherrie. She seemed to gather herself together, shrugging back the collar of her blouse and patting her hair into place, and she said, "Just do excuse the mess in the office, honey. I just had to stop in the middle and leave the rest for you to figure out because I sure can't." She smiled, as ever, with a thick, weird graciousness that confused the girls. They whispered to each other, but they followed Beth's lead and addressed Sherrie as Mrs. Cohen, thank God.

"Mrs. Cohen," said Freddie, "What's the trouble with the books, if you don't mind me asking?"

"You're cute as a button," said Sherrie. "I don't mind a thing you do."

Beth said, "Freddie here has what you might call a head for figures. You should consider letting her loose on those ledgers of yours."

Cy said, "No, thanks." He turned to find two of the girls had discovered, on their own, his signature pair of blue jeans, the ones three feet across. They were staring at it, and one of them asked, "Can I try it on?"

"We should both try them on," said the other girl. "We could both fit."

"Now that's a novelty item," said Cy. "You might not think that someone could really be that big, girls, but life can surprise you."

Even as he was speaking, the two girls had detached the jeans from the clothespins and were stepping into them with strange little smiles on their faces, and another girl had on one of the jeans-jackets and was looking at herself in a mirror against the wall. Sherrie just stood there with her mouth open, until at last she managed to get out: "Um."

"Now look—" Cy said. "You all know you're not supposed to try clothes on."

"But Cy, it got to fit if we want to buy it."

"But we have our customs, and—oh hell," said Cy. "What do you call this? A Wear-In?"

"That's pretty cool. I like that. A Wear-In. Hey," Freddie said. "You got any pedal pushers?"

"Honey," said Sherrie, caught behind the counter with one hand tangled in her hair, the other drawing towards her mouth. "Oh, honey, what's going on?"

That's when Cy followed the look on his wife's face, and saw Beth Fine crouching over. "Oh God, said Beth. "I'm sorry. I just—"

"What's the matter?" Freddie asked. "You got a cramp?"

"I think," Beth said, but then she stopped saying anything. Her face looked white, and her hair very orange. She formed her words slowly. "I have to get back."

"You're not going anywhere," said Sherrie. She stepped out from behind the counter and laid a hand on Beth's shoulder. She looked at Beth closely. "You need to lie yourself down and take that coat off."

"No. I'm fine," said Beth. Sherrie put her arm in a grip and led her to the office, where there was a couch. "I don't need this," Beth said.

"You need to get off your feet in your condition."

"I have no condition," said Beth. "I'm perfectly fine." Sherrie was not convinced. She had Beth on her back with her coat off and rolled under her head and by then what Sherrie meant became so obvious that Cy couldn't believe he hadn't seen it in the first place.

Sherrie addressed the girls. "You all be brave and tell me, how far along is she?"

"Ma'am," said Freddie, "I don't know what you mean."

"I mean," said Sherrie, "how many months?"

It was the smallest of the girls who said, "I don't know."

Through gritted teeth, Beth said, "Cy, I'm sorry."

"For what?" Cy asked. "What the hell do you have to be sorry about?"

"For what I'm about to ask you to do," said Beth. "I need you to call this number and ask for Ron Beauchamp."

She wrote the number on a slip of paper and handed it to Cy. Her handwriting was hard to read.

Cy leaned over and could smell her sweat and also a thick odor of used clothing. He pointed to one of the numbers and asked, "Is that a four or a nine?"

"It's a nine," she said. Then, she started to cry.

2

WHEN BETH FINE WAS A little girl, she discovered that her body had more courage than she did. It was true in Paris, where the parameters of the world grew wider with each footstep until barriers fell away. It was true in Melody, where she had to get to know a Negro neighborhood that had seemed to her the strangest place on earth. She discovered it again during childbirth, when the pain seemed so enormous that it was like a storm that overtook her. She gave birth in a colored hospital where she was an object of intense scrutiny. With her was Sue Francis, who was unambiguously not a servant, and also not a friend. What white woman would choose to have her baby in a ward where there was little in the way of pain relief, and where all of the doctors and nurses were black?

Still, in some ways, Beth's color meant that she got special care, something Sue Francis was apt to point out in a way that hardly fazed Beth at the time.

"Wait till you have a kid," Beth said to her.

Sue Francis snorted. "If you think I plan to put myself through what I just saw, you've got another thing coming."

Sue Francis, by '66, still hadn't managed to train her hair into a proper afro, so she wore heavy braids bound up in a manner designed to make her look even more imperial. She'd come up from Atlanta to find out what had become of Beth and Ron, who were dangerously close to getting fired from SNCC. Firing staff was a new development, and Sue Francis thought it was about time that someone called people to account. In the case of Ron, she was ambivalent. After all, he was a long-time SNCC-person with a crucial skill, and if he'd come under the influence of floaters, he could be disciplined. Beth, of course, was another story.

But when Sue Francis found Beth alone on her bed and in active labor, even she didn't have the heart to tell her she was fired.

"Where the hell's Ron Beauchamp?"

"On his way," said Beth, though she seemed to be guessing, and her voice arrived from a great distance. "We left a message in Greenwood. They'll track him down."

"Oh, fuck," said Sue Francis. Then, she touched the side Beth's florid face and asked, "So what do you expect me to do?"

"I don't expect you to do a thing," said Beth. "We've got it all worked out. Freddie's going to take me if Ron doesn't get here in time."

"Freddie? That little fool?" Sue Francis rolled her eyes. She wore a distinctly unfeminine army coat, and in spite of all that piled hair, she reminded Beth of one of the boys from the cafe, particularly when she pulled out a pocketknife, though she just used it to open a Coke for Beth to sip while she packed her things to take her to the hospital.

As for Beth, she took sips of the warm Coke and waited for Freddie, who was supposed to come soon, maybe after school, to check in on her, and it didn't seem too hard to just stay where she was. Part of her was hoping Freddie wouldn't show up at all. Then, the pain would shoot right up her, and she couldn't think enough to hope or not to hope. She just gasped.

Sue Francis said, "Okay, girl. Get up. Let's go."

"Go where?" Beth asked, honestly confused.

"Come on," Sue Francis said. Though she was slender, she was strong, and Beth leaned hard on her shoulder to a car that was identifiable as Cleo, the '63 Chevrolet, one of Ron's babies. It had a big back seat, and enough room for Beth to clench and unclench herself all the way to the hospital.

The doctor was surprised, not only by the white girl but by what he called "her nerve." He told Sue Francis that Beth had the constitution of a horse, and for such a little-hipped thing, she hardly gave them a moment's trouble. Given the circumstances, the doctor and nurse weren't surprised when they saw the baby. By then, Freddie had arrived and made a big scene about Beth not trusting her. Beth was beyond listening. She lay, spent and disbelieving, with the moist little baby on her hospital gown. She opened the snaps in front and asked the two girls, "Will she know how to nurse?"

"How are we supposed to know?" Sue Francis said. She turned to Freddie. "See what I mean? And you expect her to run a project?"

"You don't understand," said Freddie.

By then, the baby had latched on, and seemed to fix her clear, jet eyes on Beth, who cradled her and smiled. The smile was strained; Beth's breasts were tender and the little jaws kept working, oblivious to pain. "She knows what she wants," Beth said.

Ron APPEARED A WEEK LATER, and found Sue Francis moved in, Freddie cooking, and Claire Burgess cleaning. He suppressed his first reaction, which was rage—as though his home had been ransacked—and then he knew what it actually meant.

"Well?" said Mrs. Burgess.

"Well what?" Ron asked.

"Aren't you going to ask what's going on?"

"I know what's going on or you all wouldn't be here," Ron said. He managed to keep his voice steady.

Freddie looked up from a pot of stew. "We got J.B. looking for you."

"I was on the road. How was I supposed to know? Man, is this beat-on-me day?"

"No," said Mrs. Burgess. "Praise the Lord, it's Father's Day. Come on, Ronny. Meet your daughter."

Ron found Beth and their baby behind a curtain Mrs. Burgess had slung up to give Beth some privacy. Beth was asleep, and so was the baby. It was hard for Ron to approach two such impenetrable-looking people. This sense of his own irrelevance was compounded when he found out that Beth had already filled out the birth certificate.

"I figured I'd name her after your mother," Beth said that night.

"I told you how many times? Gideon if it's a boy and Corrine if it's a girl. Besides, my mother's name was Tammy."

"What was I supposed to do?" Beth asked him. "I couldn't wait. You weren't here."

"Why couldn't you wait? You had to get her registered with the beloved U.S. Government and Sovereign state of Mississippi?" Ron wanted to see the birth certificate, and Beth, against all logic, couldn't find it. "I just want to know," Ron said, "if you put her down as white or colored."

"I don't decide," Beth said. "You know that."

"Don't you?"

"No," said Beth. "I don't." She was surprised at how steady she kept her voice, and although there was something childish about withholding the news that the certificate, of course, said 'colored,' she wouldn't give him the satisfaction.

Sᴜᴇ FRANCIS CALLED LARRY WALSH, expressing frustration at the turn things had taken, guarded sympathy for Beth, and an uncharacteristic admission that she needed his help. The Atlanta office couldn't spare a car, so Larry took a bus to Melody. He entered Beth and Ron's room without warning, while Beth was nursing Tamara, and Beth gave a gasp, turned pink, and covered herself in haste. Tamara bawled. It was hard to judge Larry's response, as he was wearing sunglasses, but he stroked his goatee, and seemed incapable of moving past the door. "I'll come back later," he said.

"No. Stay. It's just so good to see you," Beth said. "I'm sorry. I've just been kind of emotional lately."

"I hear those things happen," said Larry. "So this is Tamara?"

"Tammy," said Beth. The baby was back on the breast, under a blanket, sucking away, but Beth asked, "Want to hold her?"

"I'd better not," said Larry. "I think I caught something on that goddamned bus. Where's Sue Francis?"

"Oh, fussing about something, probably. What's up with you two anyway?"

"We're married," Larry said. "Where's Ron?"

"We're not married. And he's taking a nap," said Beth. "He's usually out cold, this time of day. He's like a baby himself—always has to eat every couple of hours and sleep every couple of hours."

"So you've got yourself a couple of babies," said Larry. "Should you wake him up or should I?"

"I'll wake him up if you hold Tamara."

"So it *is* Tamara," Larry said. He hooked his sunglasses onto the collar of his army coat and reached out for her. "I'm glad. It's got some dignity."

"So does she," said Beth, and now she pulled the baby away gradually and passed her to Larry. "Give her your finger. Yes, like that. See, girl? Uncle Larry's made of milk."

The expression on Larry Walsh's face was best described as stunned, as one arm cradled Tamara, and two fingers of his free hand were engulfed by Tamara's jaws. She looked right through him. "Fine," Larry said, "Tell her I'm not made of milk."

"Okay. Chocolate milk," said Beth. "Or is that offensive? You know what? I don't care anymore. Did Ron sleep this much in Greenwood?" It didn't take long for her to push the curtain back and let Ron know that they had company.

LATER, LARRY MANAGED TO DISLODGE Sue Francis from the files at the church, and the two of them got down to the serious business of dressing down Ron and Beth. "Listen," Larry said, "it's pretty clear that things have gotten out of hand here. I mean, like, Ron, where were you last week?"

"I got a call from a cat in Lowndes County," Ron said. "You know they got an election coming up there, just formed that new Black Panther Party. They needed an extra pair of hands."

"And who precisely was that cat?" Sue Francis asked him. She was sitting backwards on the folding chair, arms crossed, and her face was so prim that Ron couldn't help but laugh.

"Nobody you'd know, Princess."

"Then you had no business going to Alabama," Larry said. "If you don't get a call from us, you can't trust that call. There's been a lot of provocation these days, brothers who aren't brothers if you know what I mean. You can't know if you're being set up."

"I can tell who to trust," said Ron. "I'm not a child."

Sue Francis broke in then. "Look, we can't afford this sort of bullshit. Either you're SNCC staff or you're not."

"Yeah. Dock my pay," Ron said, with some bitterness. "I haven't seen a check from you people for three months anyhow. What's that about?"

"We've had some financial trouble," said Sue Francis, a little too crisply.

Larry said, "What we need to know, Beauchamp, is what you think you're being paid for? Face it. There's no functioning fleet of cars—hasn't been one for over a year."

Beth broke in. "What about Cleo?"

"Who?"

Ron put his arm around Beth, and pulled her to him. "You can see her from the window. And before you showed up, I changed her oil. That is, until I found out there wasn't no functioning fleet."

Larry frowned. He looked, to Beth's mind, much the way he had back in the old office above the Davis pharmacy, beleaguered and too old. Sue Francis slipped her hand across the distance between their chairs, and tucked it in his pocket. If Larry felt that hand, it didn't show. Beth wondered if they ever fought, and felt a sharp desire to listen to their arguments. They would go at it full-throttle, she suspected. Maybe Sue Francis would throw things. And now here they were finishing each other's sentences.

"Ron," Larry said, "Sue Francis looked at the books today. You know that grant money you all received three months ago? You got a way to keep track of the money?"

"Yeah," Ron said. "Freddie keeps track. Gonna major in accounting up at Rust College in the fall."

Sue Francis broke in. "The books have been doctored. I can tell."

"Bullshit," said Ron. Then, his face froze. Beth had never heard him curse before.

"I can tell," Sue Francis said. "You've got—what—maybe seven kids signed up for childcare at the church. Where did the rest of the money go? Beth, you need to tell me. How did you pay for your hospital room?"

"My aunt—" Beth began, but she stopped herself.

"You mean the one who works for Eleanor Roosevelt?" Larry asked her. "The one I met in Atlantic City? I heard her agency got you that grant."

But the grant was given to the childcare program, not to you."

"Bullshit!" Ron said again, and the curse had a force behind it now. "You people sit in your office and you live off donations, and you tell us we can't do the same? Take a look at this room. We don't even got a proper place to change my daughter's diapers. And your office doesn't even send us checks and then you say we're stealing? Because that's what you're saying, Larry. And Freddie too!"

Sue Francis removed her hand from Larry's pocket and raised it. "I never said that Freddie took so much as a dime, Ron. Keep your cool."

"Freddie did it for me if she did it at all," said Beth. Then she would have given anything to have taken the words back again.

Larry nodded, and he quickly put a hand on Sue Francis's arm to stop her from speaking. Ron sat for a beat, then pushed his chair back and said, "I'm gonna take my daughter for a walk." Tamara had been sleeping in a little wicker carrier they'd gotten as a baby gift, and when Ron pulled her out of it, she started bawling again, and he practically stumbled over himself getting her into the hallway, where, Beth knew, he'd do his best to walk off his confusion. Tamara liked to be walked down the stairs and out the door almost as much as she liked riding in a car. Sometimes, it was the only thing that calmed her down.

LEFT ALONE WITH LARRY AND Sue Francis, Beth lapsed into silence, and she considered questions that she hadn't raised before. Who paid for the room she shared with Ron? How did she get store credit for her groceries? And the visit to the nurse, and the doctor at the delivery. Larry told Sue Francis to see what had become of Ron, and she said, "Why don't you go?" and when he whispered something to her, she made a face and said, "But I got things to say," and in the end, she slowly unhooked each of her legs from the legs of the chair and rested a hand on Larry's shoulder on her way out the door.

Only then, did Beth speak. "I never thought about where the money came from."

"You want a definition of privilege? There it is," said Larry. "Not asking that question. Figuring money is like air."

"But shouldn't it be?" Beth said, though weakly now. She knew that this was not an abstract conversation. She said, "Larry, is Freddie in trouble? I can't do that to her. She was just trying to take care of me."

"Well, that's an old story," said Larry. "Who hasn't been trying to take care of you? Except for me, of course. That's why I'm the one you ought to trust, because frankly, I appear to be the only one who respects you."

Beth's eyes started to tear up, and Larry said, "Don't start, alright? I don't even have a handkerchief."

"What am I supposed to do?" Beth asked him.

"Well Sue Francis, God bless her, she's not a fool. She's got better things to do than make Freddie's life a misery. This kind of thing goes on all the time, and this is small-scale, but I've got to tell you, it's going to be hard on Ron. You see, he's not like you. He's worked his ass off on top of what the Movement paid him ever since he could lift up the hood of a car. Fine, we're asking him to start a project in Chicago."

"He won't leave Mississippi," said Beth.

"Chicago is where we're putting our resources now. We're starting a project on the South Side, tenants' rights, and we want someone seasoned, who's seen action, and someone whose face people can recognize. Everyone knows Ron. He's a good fit, Beth. He'll know it."

"He won't leave his church," said Beth, grasping, and Larry said that there were churches in Chicago, just as she knew he would, and then she came out and said it. "Where am I supposed to go?"

"That's up to you," Larry said. "But this has clearly developed into an unhealthy situation."

Beth wanted to ask, again, what was unhealthy about people taking care of each other, and she knew Larry well enough to hear his answer, that black folks had been taking care of white folks since the first boat of slaves had arrived before the Mayflower, and had those relationships been based on love or on coercion? Then Beth might challenge him, and ask where love ended and coercion began, really, and it would be as though they were again on that rough, wet, dark pier in Waveland, where those abstract conversations were so urgent and so easy, and the questions could be theoretical.

"Fine," said Larry, "have you written to your father about the baby?"

That question seemed to come from nowhere. "Why would I?"

"He has a granddaughter," said Larry. "He might want to see her. Maybe you should head back east, let them meet each other."

"You want to get rid of me?"

Larry sighed and leaned back in the chair. In a few months, he would be in Cincinnati, where he and Sue Francis would move into a ghetto neighborhood to organize the unemployed. The Movement people would leaflet public housing, plaster the walls with fliers that were sometimes torn down and sometimes covered with graffiti, and Sue Francis would give a glue-pot to a volunteer with an elaborate tattoo who turned out to be a member of a street gang called The Young Lords, and would set the glue on fire in front of the Freedom House. Larry would tell this to Beth when she would call him from Chicago, from a pay phone just outside their new apartment. Sometimes, if Tamara was asleep, she would risk leaving her in the apartment, and sometimes she would take Tamara into the phone booth, and struggle to keep the earpiece pressed between her chin and shoulder. She often called in the middle of the night, and he always picked up on the second ring, and addressed her as though they were continuing a long-standing, interrupted, cryptic, conversation.

It was that way now. They spoke in shorthand. "Larry," said Beth, "I can't go back."

"Of course you can't go back. But can't you move on?" Larry asked. He sounded less frustrated than wistful. Beth didn't know how to answer him, but she did her best.

"I could organize white folks in Chicago," she said. "I hear there are a few of them there. And as far as I can tell, white folks never did try to take care of me. Or of each other. Would you call that moving on?"

RON SPENT THE WEEKS BEFORE they moved, primarily, in Tutwiler, and one day, George came running and said, "You're never gonna believe this. I just saw Ron Beauchamp get off a Greyhound bus."

In fact, he had, and appeared a few minutes after George. He asked for Freddie, who was in the back with her adding machine, calculating the receipts, and he said to her, "I got something for you." Then, he took an envelope out of his pocket and said, "Me and Beth, I don't think we ever paid you for taking care of Tammy. I think this should about cover it."

Freddie looked confused. "You know this place is subsidized, Ronny. Besides, Beth here's an employee."

"Oh, I think I know what's subsidized," said Ron. "You gonna take the money or do I have to send the check direct to Washington?"

Although Freddie continued to resist, in the end, the heat of their conversation reached the playroom, and Mrs. Burgess was the one who took the envelope, looked inside, and said, "That's more than it ought to be, son. You ought to take a little of that money back. You got a new life to start in Chicago."

"No. It's just what it ought to be, Mrs. Burgess," Ron said to her. Then, with a spirit Beth hadn't seen in some time, he lifted his daughter from the cradle where she lay and said, "Who's my little girl? Who's my little Tammy? Who's the one who's gonna meet her Aunt Risa and Uncle Walter?"

Once Beth got Ron alone, she had to ask, "What happened to Hercules?"

"Sold him of course," Ron said. Apparently, after a careful inventory of the cars still in the fleet, Ron had discovered that three—including Hercules —weren't on the books, and in fact, for all practical purposes, were his own cars. He took them to a sympathetic dealer in Mound Bayou who probably gave him more than they were worth.

"But how are we going to get to Chicago? With all our things?"

"How many things do we need?" Ron asked her.

"The cradle, the bassinet, the high-chair. You figure we'll fit it all on the Greyhound bus?"

"Baby," said Ron. "I got to talk to you about Tammy."

Ron had already discussed it with his aunt and uncle. They had agreed that given what he had heard about Chicago, it would be best for Tamara to stay with them in Tutwiler.

"No," said Beth.

"You don't trust my people?"

"She's barely three weeks old," said Beth. "Maybe you were sent off to relatives, but Tammy stays with us."

RON'S UNCLE WALTER DID OFFER to drive them to Chicago, and Ron thanked him but insisted that Freedom Riders traveled by bus. "Well, now, you got a point," said Uncle Walter, "but were there little babies on those buses?" In the end, Ron agreed that he could take them as far as Memphis where they would catch an express that left at midnight on Sunday and reach Chicago by noon. Aunt Risa packed a basket with so many provisions that Ron finally stopped her and said, "Aunt Risa, there's food in Chicago."

"Twelve hours is a long time," Aunt Risa said to Ron. "I don't want you to get off that bus at some rest-stop with little Tamara. Ronny, you and your baby girl just make yourself a little home in your seat and eat what's in the basket and you won't have any trouble."

Beth was sitting right there, though Ron's aunt and uncle didn't seem to know it. She said, "We appreciate it, Ma'am."

"Call me Grandma Risa," Ron's aunt said. "Tamara'll call me Grandma Risa and there's no need to cause any more confusion." She said to Ron, "Well, I got to say, I sure am glad you didn't go and name her Corrine. Sounds like a chorus girl."

Ron said, "She was a freedom fighter. Anyone would be proud to have that name."

"Well your momma was the bravest soul I ever knew," said Aunt Theresa, "and Lord knows Tamara's going to need a great deal of courage." She seemed to love to say the name *Tamara*, and when she said it, she gave

Beth a look that was half-sly and half-confused, as though she knew she was responsible for the name and wasn't yet sure what to do with that information.

THE NEXT MORNING, AUNT RISA dressed the baby in a white gown she had made for her and said, "Well you can tell who Tamara's daddy is. That's for sure. It's like you spit her out, Ronny."

Ron was buttoning a white shirt his aunt had just ironed. "I guess she does look a little like me."

"A little?" Aunt Risa laughed. "I'll get out one of your baby pictures and put it next to Tamara and it'll be like she's looking in a mirror."

Uncle Walter found a photograph, and the three of them crowded around it, leaving Beth on the couch on the far end of the parlor. They were all going to church. Beth was supposed to stay behind and "rest up," as Aunt Risa put it. "I've seen you with little Tamara at your breast all night. You sure she won't take a bottle?"

"She doesn't have to take a bottle," Beth said. It seemed to Beth that she had gotten too much rest altogether, and that her daughter had spent all too much time being fussed over by Ron's family. That morning, when she heard Tamara crying in the kitchen and she caught Theresa sticking a sugar tit in her mouth, Beth told her, as politely as she could, that Tamara shouldn't be sucking on a dirty old piece of cloth.

"I guess you know best," Theresa had said. "Mind you, I wouldn't give this baby a dirty old piece of cloth, just a clean linen handkerchief with some sugar water on it. She seems to like it though, don't you, Tamara. It'll keep her quiet during the sermon."

Now, Beth said, "Maybe I should come along."

Aunt Risa looked up. "You want to go to church?"

"I want to go to church," said Beth. Then she added, "If you think I'd be welcome."

Tamara looked up from Aunt Risa's arms. It was true. In the little white button-down gown, Tamara looked as though Ron could have spit her out. Same triangle of a face, same clear jet eyes, same forehead, above which soft hair grew in abundance. Beth took the baby back and felt her go for her breast again. Aunt Risa said to Beth, "We welcome everyone. Only, understand, no offense meant, but will you be modest?"

Beth did take offense. She was wearing a button-down sweater Mrs. Burgess had knitted for her, and a skirt that went most of the way down to the floor. "Grandma Risa," she said, "I don't know what you're asking me."

"I mean, you can't bare your breast in church," Theresa said. "Not the way you've been doing in our home. But you'd be most welcome. Just ask Ron. He's been going every Sunday since he was the age of this little one here. Only missed when he went up north that time." She paused and smiled. "Wasn't that when you two met? I don't recall."

RON WAS NOT HAPPY TO hear that Beth would be joining them at church, and said, in hearing distance of his aunt and uncle, "You told me you don't believe in God."

Beth didn't say that she had changed her mind. She hadn't. But her face turned red, and she whispered to him, "Do they have to know that?"

"You were honest with me. You might as well be honest with them."

"It's not like I've never been inside a church, Ron," Beth said. In fact, she had spent plenty of time at the Methodist and Baptist and Pentecostal churches around Melody, particularly during the heady few months when she'd started the typing and bookkeeping programs. Yet they both knew this was different.

The building itself was unassuming, a clapboard A-frame with an annex where, as Aunt Theresa told Beth, there would be some punch and cookies afterwards. Uncle Walter was a deacon, and thus arrived early. Apparently, they all knew Ron was coming and that this would be his last Sunday at the church, because he was immediately led to a place in the first row, and surrounded by people shaking his hand and wishing him all the best. They seemed to think he would be working for the Poverty Program.

"I'll get you and Tamara settled," said Aunt Risa. She steered them towards the back. "You need anything, honey?"

"I need to be with Ron," Beth said, perversely. She pushed forward and barely saw the people who made way for her, ladies dressed like Aunt Risa, old men, the boys who served as ushers, as Ron must have served long ago. Ron gave her a look, half stern and half-inquisitive, but made room for her on the corduroy cushion of the pew.

Beth arranged Tamara on her lap and felt the crest of her daughter's hair tickle the bare spot just below her neck. She could feel sleep overtake Tamara, feel it even through the ends of the girl's hair. The jolt of the organ woke her up, and she began to cry. Beth tried to rock her to the music and that seemed to do the trick, but eventually, she'd have to nurse. Beth hated to admit it, but Aunt Risa had been right about the sugar teat. She'd also been right to seat her in the back, where she could slip away if the need arose. Aunt Risa had been right, in fact, about practically everything, and now the girl who did everything wrong was taking Tamara away from her and heading to Chicago. Why shouldn't she just leave her daughter with these thoughtful open-hearted people who believed in God? Or, conversely, why shouldn't she take her to Princeton, to suck on a corner of Beth's old Dale Evans bedspread? Beth's thoughts were simultaneously generous and contemptuous, and she struggled to remember why she'd come to this church at all.

She wasn't even aware that the music stopped, and the day's readings had begun: a passage from Paul's letters and a passage from the Prophets, but at the reading from the Hebrew Bible, she felt Ron's presence, like a hand on her arm. Pastor Holden had said something. Beth came back to herself, because he realized that he was looking right at her.

He said, "We have a guest today. Please rise and introduce her."

Beth wanted to get up, but her legs didn't seem to be working. Ron touched her arm for real this time, and he whispered, "Are you okay? Do you want me to answer for you?"

"Hold Tammy," Beth said, and she slipped their daughter onto Ron's lap and managed to get to her feet and say, "I'm Beth Fine. I'm here because I was told I'd be welcome."

"You are most certainly welcome," said Pastor Holden. His hair was dense, on its way to growing into a modified Afro, and there was white in his heavy mustache. He rubbed that mustache and cleared his throat before he said, "But I wasn't calling you. I was calling on the little one beside you, in Brother Beauchamp's arms."

Then Ron rose and held Tamara from behind, so that her white button-down grown fell straight down like a dress shirt, and her hair stood up in its flossy crest and filled with light from the window above the podium. "Pastor," Ron said, "This is my daughter, Tammy. She's going to be a soldier in Gideon's Army."

Ron held Tamara up to face the congregation. She flirted with a little stripe of sunshine that came through the entranceway. Her fist snatched at it. She was laughing.

3

THE FIRST TIME TAMARA HAD returned from Tanzania, Beth had seen the bible in her suitcase. After that, Tamara kept it on her desk, and tucked all of airline ticket stubs inside, pressed like flowers. The next year, she made a point of taking it with her, not in her suitcase, but in a carry-on bag that also held five comic books, a baggie full of Oreo cookies, and a little pink and yellow Flower Power overnight kit Grandma Risa sent her for her birthday.

When Beth and Tamara moved from their battered apartment to a house in a marginal neighborhood and finally to a decent condominium, the bible moved with them. Eventually, it migrated from the middle of her desk to a spot on the bookshelf next to her dictionary, and most recently, to a seemingly random place between two collections of Peanuts cartoons, which Beth perceived, maybe inaccurately, as a demotion.

She didn't give it much more thought until one day when Tamara was fourteen, which also happened to be the day that Tamara told her that Ron had taught her to drive. Tamara was small for her age, with soft, black hair and a little fox-face, and Beth's first thought was that she couldn't be able to see over the wheel.

"You don't believe me," Tamara said.

"It's not a matter of not believing you," said Beth. "Frankly, I have no idea what you do with your father."

She had spoken in anger, and she should have known better, but she still felt thrown off-balance. The months that Tamara spent in Tanzania were always difficult for Beth. She suspected that without a reason to hold herself together, she was sure to relapse, and she taught summer classes, or took on additional committee work, just to give her life a recognizable shape and keep her mind off the once-a-week phone call. Ron had kept his promise; Tamara always picked up at seven a.m. her time. But the connection was so riddled with static that it made her daughter seem even farther away. Always, just before Labor Day, when Beth planted herself by the gate at the airport to greet Tamara, she felt a kind of vertigo. What if, in the course of the summer, something happened to render her daughter unrecognizable?

In fact, the Tamara who returned that August was self-possessed and straight-backed, with her hair out of its ponytail and piled up in a wooden comb. She'd gotten her ears pierced, something Beth had forbidden and which she quietly decided not to make an issue. Tamara had also exchanged her suitcase for a duffel bag, which had been signed by some of the boys in Ron's neighborhood. "I don't know what's up with that," she said to Beth. "They thought I was cute, I guess."

The bag weighed more than Tamara, and when they managed to get it back to the apartment, Tamara began to carefully remove things wrapped in brown paper which she told Beth were the products of a village cooperative. She planned to sell them and send the proceeds back to a woman named Josephine.

"She's really cool," said Tamara, and all the while, she kept unwrapping the mysterious objects and setting them in a row on the living room couch. "She's American, but she's not hung up, you know?"

Beth didn't let herself speculate on how much time Tamara had spent with this Josephine, and who she was to Ron, and if she was responsible for the piercing of her daughter's ears. She had planned to take Tamara out to her favorite restaurant, a cafeteria that served something she always called Slippery Chicken, but somehow, the dinner hour passed, and by nine, Tamara had unpacked the last of the batik cloth, the ebony back-scratchers, and the stacking bowls. There were also a lot of little soapstone men with exaggerated phalluses that didn't seem precisely appropriate for a little girl to cart around.

Tamara got Beth to drive her to shops all over the city. Some upscale galleries specialized in "ethnic art," and some run-down South Street places catered to aging hippies, and then there were the storefronts in North and West Philadelphia with the African flags in the windows and bins full of incense by the doors. It took tremendous restraint on Beth's part not to go in with Tamara, but she knew she shouldn't cross that line, not now. Tamara usually came back with at least a few pieces gone, and once somebody took all of the back-scratchers. Beth wasn't surprised. She was a charmer, her daughter.

Then, the day before Thanksgiving, a shipment arrived that took up the whole front hallway of the building. Boxes, plastered with exotic stamps, were piled like a ziggurat against the wall. Beth said to Tamara, "That's it. Tell Josephine that you've done your part for self-determination."

"But this is for the Christmas rush, mom. I've got booths at two crafts fairs."

Beth fought back weariness. Just the thought of lugging those boxes up the three flights to their apartment made her weak. "Sweetheart," she said, "we don't have anywhere to put all this junk."

Tamara said, "I guess you think I'm junk too."

Beth hesitated. If Tamara had been a year younger, Beth would answered by taking her in her arms. She'd raised a tough kid, she knew, but also a transparent one. Yet now, when Beth looked at Tamara, she saw not an appeal, but a challenge. Her daughter, thick hair stuck high on her head, gold hoops in her ears, her face more like Ron's than her own, her daughter seemed to believe what she had just said, that if Beth didn't want that stuff in the hallway, she didn't want her either.

Tamara said, "I'm moving to Tanzania."

"Come on," said Beth. "Let's get these away from the door."

"I mean it, mom," Tamara said. "I'm an African. Maybe you'd rather I wasn't, but I am."

"Listen," said Beth, "give me a hand here." She lifted the first of the boxes, which may have held some of those stone sculptures. It was breaking apart at the bottom. Tamara didn't move, and continued to give Beth the grimmest of stares.

"Give me your car keys," Tamara said.

"Come on, honey."

"I'm not coming on. I'm getting out of here," said Tamara. "Give me the keys."

"What do you plan to do with them?" Beth asked. That was when she discovered that Tamara had learned how to drive.

Later, Beth would find out that Tamara had been driving between Josephine's village and her father's apartment in the capital all summer, in a jeep that Tamara owned part of already, and that she was selling the things that Josephine sent her so she could own the jeep in earnest. But just then, there was no time for details. There was only time for Tamara to storm upstairs to look for the spare set of car keys her mother kept in a drawer and leave most of the contents of that drawer scattered on the carpet, as Beth trailed her, wondering if being a mother was the sort of thing you needed to keep on doing without pause, if the months away from her daughter had been like a break in the rhythm of a heartbeat, and it would take a shock to make things right again.

It might have taken Tamara in the front seat of the Volkswagen Rabbit, ignition on, lights blazing, arm moving the car into reverse, looking, for all the world, like someone who knew just how to pull out of a parking space, and Beth standing behind the car. The only thing Beth knew that she could do was make it clear that Tamara was leaving the parking space over her dead body.

Tamara let the motor run and waited. Eventually, she'd run out of gas, or her mother would move out of the way. Maybe thirty seconds passed. Then, with a lurch, she put the car into drive and rammed it against the concrete barrier.

Beth ran up to the front of the car just as Tamara turned the motor off. "You don't have your seat belt on," Beth said.

"They don't have seat belts in Tanzania," said Tamara. She didn't meet Beth's eyes. "Now you'll never believe me about driving."

"I always believe you," Beth said. "Sweetheart, always. Always, always." She asked Tamara if she was okay, and when Tamara said yes, Beth had to believe that too.

THAT NIGHT, THEY SPENT SOME time calling people with attics and basements, and by the next morning, they had found space for all of the boxes. Beth drove the car with the crushed fender. Tamara said, "Will it cost a lot to fix?"

"I have no idea," said Beth.

"I'll pay for it," said Tamara.

"No you won't," Beth said. She had remembered that she could say things without hesitation. That morning, for the first time since August, Tamara had asked her mother to braid her hair, a goodwill gesture. She even helped her cook corn casserole. They would have their usual Thanksgiving dinner at Laurel's place in Lower Merion, a big stone house full of lesbians and their children.

The casserole was a one-person job, and once Tamara had opened the cans of cream of mushroom soup and grated the American cheese, it was hard to find a way to keep her busy. She leaned against the counter and kept opening the oven to see if the cheese had browned. Then, out of the blue, she asked, "Mom, why did we move out of our old house?"

Beth said, "You remember. It was much too big. Cleaning it was like painting the Brooklyn Bridge. You finish one end and have to start right over on the other."

"I could have helped," Tamara said.

"I never knew you missed that house," Beth said. In fact, when they had moved to the condominium in Mount Airy, Tamara had seemed delighted, particularly by the balcony, where they both stored bicycles they could ride right up a dirt path called Forbidden Drive all the way to Center City. Beth had told herself that she was in a part of Philadelphia that was deliberately and defiantly integrated, but the fact was that most of the neighbors were white therapists, social workers, and academic types. Still, when she started to classify her own behavior, she was stopped in her tracks by that time a man exposed himself to Tamara back in West Philadelphia. Who wouldn't want their child safe? It was a faultless motivation. And Tamara had seemed happier since the move. Of course, this was before she had to store the boxes.

"You know what Daddy calls you," Tamara asked her. She seemed hesitant, but also powerless to keep the information to herself. "He calls you the Wandering Jew."

"Does he?" Beth said. "Sweetie, you can't keep opening the oven, or the casserole won't cook."

"He didn't say it in a mean way," Tamara said. "He was kind of joking."

"I'm sure he was," said Beth. She looked out the window, past the parking lot, to the green expanse of Fairmount Park. Maybe they could take a walk in the woods while the casserole cooled, and Tamara could finish what she seemed intent on saying. It struck Beth that as Tamara grew older, she'd begun to lose her old directness, and instead approached a conversation sideways. In other words, she had grown less like Beth, and more like Ron.

That was the same day Beth had glanced in Tamara's room and found the bible open on her bed. It was turned to The Gospel According to Luke, Chapter Four: The Temptation of Jesus. "Filled with the Holy Spirit, Jesus returned from the Jordan and was led by the Holy Spirit into the desert for forty days to be tempted by the devil." A faded orange ribbon that must have been tucked in for much of the bible's life marked the place and overlapped onto Tamara's pillow.

So Beth made herself ask, "You know, if you'd ever like to go to church, I'd take you."

Tamara had been staring at the closed oven, and she looked up at her mother with confusion. "What church?"

"I don't know," said Beth, running the possibilities through her mind and fighting back irrational resistance. "Baptist, maybe? You know, in your daddy's church, in Grandpa Risa and Grandpa Walter's church, you get to decide for yourself if you want to get baptized and become a member of the congregation. It's not something somebody else can choose for you."

"Daddy's church?" Tamara looked as though the two words didn't match. Then, she said, "Mom, have you been sneaking around my room?"

"Not sneaking," said Beth. "I just walked right in."

Tamara said, "It's not what you think. I mean, I like to look at it sometimes."

"There's no reason why you shouldn't," Beth said.

"You shouldn't just come into my room like that. It's just not right."

"Sweetheart," said Beth, "since when is this an issue?"

"I just want something that's mine, okay?" Tamara said. "Daddy gave that bible to me, and he said it was all he had left of Mississippi. He didn't say anything about church or Baptists. And I can read it any time I want."

There was a heartbeat of silence before the timer rang. The casserole was done. Beth took it out of the oven.

Then, Tamara said, "I want to make stuffing from black walnuts."

She took a pan along on their walk, intending to fill it with the green hulls, and carry them back to the balcony to peel. As soon as they were outside, the mood lightened. They started across a bridge covered in scarlet ivy. There were few leaves left on the trees, and many on the path, walnut and maple. Horse-chestnut hulls cracked underfoot, and when Tamara spotted the thick green lumps that covered black walnuts, she scooped them up. There weren't many, and she didn't seem to be looking very hard. Beth chose not to remind her that last Thanksgiving, not long after they had moved to the condominium, Tamara had collected a pan full and tried to peel them on the balcony. She managed to work the shells off of a dozen before her nails gave out, and she couldn't get the brown stains off of her fingers before they had to go. She spent most of the dinner with her hands under the table and removed them only when absolutely necessary.

That was the first time that Beth had really seen Tamara self-conscious. Now, of course, the way ahead was hazardous. There would be mahogany back-scratchers, bibles on the bed, crushed car fenders, who knows what. Beth may have to reconsider her belief that if she spoke to her daughter directly and with conviction, it would be enough, and that the world would seem, to Tamara, rational and pleasant. That might not be the case. In a little while, Tamara would look up that same recipe for black walnut stuffing and again discover that it took two hours, and then the two of them would be off to Merion where Laurel, the psychiatrist, would take one look at them and have their number. It was some comfort to Beth that she knew Laurel in Mississippi, where there was no one with less of a clue.

Tamara asked, "Mom, who taught you how to make corn casserole?"

"I got the recipe from the back of a can of cream of mushroom soup," said Beth.

"Oh," said Tamara. She kicked a few leaves out of the way. "I thought it was a family recipe."

"It is," Beth said. "Our family." But that was not what Tamara wanted. She wanted a story about Thanksgivings in Princeton, when Vivian was still alive and making chicken stuffed with chestnuts and prunes, and warming up a store-bought apple pie. Yet what came back to Beth instead

were the later Thanksgivings when her father would send her to Aunt Beatrice who always had a table full of foreign ambassadors, and where, year
after year, Beth found herself gravitating towards the kitchen, where black
chefs and waiters piled plates with food that always smelled and tasted as
though it had been cooked in a military canteen.

"Do you have anything from Princeton?" Tamara asked. "I mean,
anything from when you were a kid?"

Beth kept on walking. Of course, she didn't. Before she could reply,
Tamara tried again.

"Is there something you wish you had?"

"A bedspread," Beth answered at once. "Dale Evans was on it. She's
a cowgirl. It came all the way from the desert, from New Mexico. But it's
gone now."

"How do you know?" Tamara asked her.

"Trust me, it's gone," said Beth. She walked a little faster so that Tamara couldn't read her face and know that some time ago she'd received
notice that everything from that Princeton house had been auctioned off.
The notice was from a lawyer's office. It was still sitting on her desk. She
could have followed up. She might yet. At the same time, as month followed month, the prospect grew increasingly abstract. "I really loved that
bedspread," Beth said. "It was made of something called chenille, almost
like carpet. And Dale Evans had a lasso in the air. I used to hide under it,
sometimes."

"So now you can't hide," Tamara said.

"That's right," Beth said. "Not from you."

She wondered if Ron had told Tamara that she did not believe in God.
She wanted to take that statement back, or alter it a little. Time had caused
her, had compelled her, to believe in something, maybe just in that French
desk clerk with his little mustache who listened to her cry on that Paris
park bench, who didn't make her justify herself, who just believed her. She
swore she'd be that kind of mother, and she tried to be. And as for Max
Fine, maybe she ought to forgive him for not being that kind of father.
He'd never claimed otherwise. But meanwhile, she had walked deeper and
deeper into the woods.

4

RON BEAUCHAMP WAS A SOLDIER in Gideon's army. When Gideon called all of Israel, he told everyone who was afraid to return home, and ten thousand left, and then Gideon called on them to drink, and many knelt before the water, save for three hundred who lapped the water up like dogs. And the Lord said: with these three hundred, I shall defeat Midian.

And a week or so after Ron received in the apartment mailbox a letter from Selective Service informing him that he would be expected to appear at the induction center on a certain day at a certain time, he took a seat on his front stoop and read the letter over, while on the sidewalk, a couple of stringy-looking black girls were playing jump-rope. Ron lit a cigarette.

"Hey, Ronny, can I have one too?" one of the girls asked, kind of flirting.

"Baby, you aren't even old enough to know what a cigarette is. Is your momma coming to the meeting tonight?"

"Only if you take her your own self," the girl, Josie, said. "She said last time she was robbed coming back, because not one boy there was gentleman enough to walk her to her door."

"Well you know I'm a gentleman," Ron said to Josie.

Josie's friend made a face. He returned the expression, but at the last minute, folded it into a smile he'd hoped was winning. It didn't win her though. "You ain't no kind of gentleman, what I hear," she said.

Ron didn't feel like continuing the conversation. He stubbed out the smoke and started towards the high-rise where he was scheduled to meet up with a new kid that a staff member had discovered hanging out in front of a liquor store with his hat pulled over his eyebrows. He was supposed to be a talented organizer, which, as far as Ron could tell, meant that he managed to scare the shit out of the college boy who found him. Ron thought the kid was stupid, but pretty funny once you got him going.

"Oh, yeah," the kid said to Ron, because Ron showed him the letter. "Indoor China. I got a brother and a cousin over there. See, there's Outdoor China, that's the Red one that's got the bomb. Then there's Indoor

China, that's gonna be Red. When they get the bomb, I'm heading there and I'm gonna tell them where to drop it."

Ron had to admit that the kid did know just about everyone at the high rise, a decrepit subsidized unit in Bronzeville. He got his rap going no matter who opened the door, whether it was a grandma with cotton-ball hair or toddler the age of Tamara. He'd stick his foot in the door like he was selling vacuum cleaners, though in fact he was talking people into going to a meeting with their City Council representative, a cracker named Archie Gaydon who managed to get his seat because no one seemed to tell these black Americans that people had died so they could fucking vote.

It felt good to say it sometimes: fuck, fuck, fuck. He couldn't say it in front of Josie or her momma. He couldn't say it, God forbid, in front of little Tammy. But in front of the kid, in the office, over the phone to Larry, it just came pouring out sometimes. Like later that day, he called Cincinnati and said to Larry, "What the fuck am I supposed to do about this draft notice?"

There was a pause on the end of the line. Then Larry replied, "They're targeting us. It can't be a coincidence how many Movement people are getting drafted this year. But at least you have a way out. You're a father."

Ron said. "But you know that isn't right. I shouldn't use that when they're just gonna call up someone else to take my place."

"So you want to go to Vietnam? Or do you want to go to jail?"

"I'm not scared of jail," said Ron.

"I think you've proven that to anybody's satisfaction," said Larry, in his way that always drove Ron a little crazy. But he also added, "You're effective in Chicago, which is more than I can say for me and S.F. here. Ever since the SNCC headquarters moved out of Atlanta, you can't tell who's an FBI plant, and the brothers with the loudest voices are the one who wear the wires. Shit, Ron, I'll tell you, sometimes I miss those all-night meetings. At least I knew everyone."

Ron knew what Larry meant. Aside from a few local people like Mrs. Hamer who started cooperative farms or day-care centers with government funding, what Movement people were left from his part of Mississippi? Frank Court was in D.C., agitating against the war. Last Ron heard, Jackie had disappeared to Seattle—God knows what was in Seattle. As for Sylvester, after he'd come back from Ghana with a new set of teeth, he'd given Beth a SNCC hug that lasted for so long that Ron began to wonder if something else was going on and then said, "Trust you to go against the grain, Beauchamp. Everyone else dropping his white girlfriend, and you go and get yourself one." Helen was supposedly somewhere in Chicago, but when he asked at the Movement office if anyone knew how to contact her, they gave him a look like he'd just asked to fuck her.

There was the word again. Ron opened his bible. He'd tucked a calendar inside so he could figure out just where his church back home would be on a particular day. Off on his own, now, he tended to get impatient with the stories about warring brothers, women after the same man, dimwits who became kings or prophets, all under the supervision of the Lord from whom nothing could be hidden, the Just Judge, who heard Ron curse and watched him father a child out of wedlock and take that child and her white mother to Chicago.

When he told Beth about the letter from the draft board, Beth said, "Well then marry me and claim Tamara. There's your deferment."

"But that's just not right," said Ron, repeating what he'd said to Larry.

Beth gave a laugh like a choke. "Granted, if we get married, I can't stay on welfare. And I'll admit, we won't get too far on your income. What is it, exactly? I don't think I've actually seen it."

"Baby, I got expenses," Ron said.

"You've also gotten a beer-gut," Beth replied, which was true. Well, he had to eat somewhere, and the nearest place to eat happened to be a little bar called Clement's where a man could get himself a burger and trimmings for fifty cents, and a beer for fifty more. He'd had more than his share of meetings over those burgers and those beers, especially since the project office was being staked out by a couple of official-looking white guys in a Crown Vic.

Mr. Clement, the owner and bartender, looked an awful lot like Pastor Holden, and he had the pastor's manner, magnetic, seemed to know everything about you the minute he laid eyes on you, just rough enough around the edges to get you trusting him. Ron had heard rumors that the bartender was an informer, but he said to anyone who listened that the one who started those damned rumors was probably the one who was the informer.

It was at that bar that Ron had planned the meeting that would take place in the lobby of the high rise that night. Mr. Clement told Ron that the neighborhood used to be pretty nice, with some of the only apartments open to colored professionals at a reasonable price, but once those apartments had become subsidized, the schoolteachers and nurses and small business owners had moved somewhere else. Mr. Clement himself lived in a brownstone with his wife and teenaged son, and more than once Ron had wanted to ask him if he was a Baptist and where he went to church, but it seemed to be a crazy thing to be asking a bartender.

Mr. Clement wouldn't serve the kid a beer. The kid said, "Mister, as far as the cops are concerned, I ain't no minor."

"Well, I'm not a cop," said Mr. Clement, mildly. The kid looked dubious. But in the end, he sat across the table from Ron, dipping into a plate of complementary fries, and went over the names of the neighbors who'd committed to appear at the meeting that night. The Movement office hoped to get their own council candidate on the ballot before the week was out, a Bronzeville social studies teacher who had been fired for encouraging students to throw out their twenty-year-old textbooks, and for bringing a member of the Lowndes County Black Panther Party into the school to speak.

The teacher's name was Patrice Parks. Ron met him his first day in Chicago, and the two had been immediately impressed with each other. Patrice told Ron that he'd read about the Broad Street High School walk-out when he was an education major at Jackson State, and he had kept the clipping taped to his desk until it fell apart. As for Ron, he liked Patrice as a sheer presence, tall and dark, with broad clean lines to his face and a habit of wearing white woven shirts that showed just how black he was. Ron was floored and delighted at the thought of someone from Lowndes County appearing in a high school classroom. Ron even knew the speaker, a landowner who carried a rifle and was part of a select group who called themselves the Deacons of Defense. "Black men with guns," Patrice said. "Of course, he didn't bring the rifle with him. Too bad. Pretty soon, Beauchamp, that school is going to frisk the kids, like a prison would. You mark my words."

"But guns don't make you free," said Ron.

"That's true," said Patrice. "But that fellow from Alabama was carrying something else that does make him free. Self respect. I swore when I started teaching, I would arm my students with self-respect. You read about those other Black Panthers, the ones in Oakland who took those rifles into the California Statehouse?"

"Guns are for people who are afraid," Ron said.

"That's true too," said Patrice. In his rather formal way, he shook Ron's hand. "It's an honor to be working with you. Still, I have to ask, do you believe in nonviolence? Even after everything you've been through?"

"Everything I've been through," Ron said, "makes me know where violence takes me. As for the brothers in California, I can't judge anyone. I just got to know myself."

Did he really mean that these days? The source of that statement, Jackie Gordon, had faded into a Pacific mist, leaving Ron to reassess her particular form of Christianity. The kid who ate the free fries at his table had no trouble passing judgment on the sorry-ass tenants who wouldn't sign to put Patrice Parks on the ballot. Patrice himself seemed ready to judge the efficacy of the dough-faced, perspiring member of City Council who would occupy the hot seat at the meeting that same evening.

Surely, that letter from Selective Service had been put into Ron's hand as a test. Yet the terms of the test were unclear. He had been called. A call demands an answer. All of his life, Ron had faced what God had given him.

But sometimes, especially lately, he didn't know what the hell to do. It was that way right now. When he was really low, he wondered if God had gone the way of Jackie Gordon and decided to move to Seattle, if the Just Judge was telling people He'd called it a day and they would damn well have to judge each other. Then Ron thought about what had happened about two months after he arrived in Chicago. He thought about his father.

H<small>E HADN'T TOLD ANYONE HE'D</small> contacted his father, not even Beth. In fact, he wasn't even sure he was going to do it until he found himself in the back of Clement's bar with an open phone book in front of him. There were three listings under Ronald Beauchamp. It was after midnight, and maybe he was a little drunk, and certainly not too anxious to get home. The first man who answered cursed and hung up. But the second one was awake and was Ron's father. He said that he wasn't surprised to hear from Ron, that he knew he was in town.

Ron sobered up completely. "You heard from Uncle Walter?"

"Son," his father said, "I haven't heard from Walter and Theresa in maybe fifteen years."

It was a strange thing to hear the word *son* thrown out so casually, in the lucid, bass voice on the other end, the voice of a broad-chested man.

Ron's father did in fact, have a broad chest. He didn't look a thing like Ron, more like a boxer or a teamster, hulking in an off-white apron when Ron found him at his restaurant not so far from high-rise, a place called Ronnie B's. When Ron appeared at two in the afternoon, just when his father had told him he would be able to take a break, the man scraped grease off the grill with the side of a cleaver, said something to the dishwasher, and gestured Ron towards the back door.

"Can't take but fifteen minutes," he said. He lit a cigarette. "There's always some joker coming in just when I have a smoke, orders everything on the menu."

Ron, who'd been casing the restaurant since eight that morning, had already seen his father sitting on that stoop and joking with the dishwasher and short order cook, and playing with the reception on a transistor radio until he found soul music. He'd turn that radio up until it hurt. The three of them worked their way through at least two packs of cigarettes. Marlboros. Ron knew because he checked the pack after his father threw it in the alley.

Ron asked, "You own this place?"

"Should," his father replied. "It's owned by this little Jew named Meltzer. Had it as good as mine five years ago, but I ran into some debt."

"I cook too," Ron said. "Not for a living, I mean, but I've always liked to cook. Aunt Risa taught me."

"I always said there's a difference between a cook and a chef," said Ron's father. "It's like the difference between a woman and a man. Now when you've got a chef in the kitchen, it's kind of like construction. He does it piece by piece. But a cook's gotta be everywhere at once."

"Yeah," Ron said. "I hear you. Aunt Risa's always got twelve things going, and I don't think she even knows what half of them are."

"The headless chicken syndrome," Ron's father said. He offered Ron a cigarette, which he took. "We had chickens back home, and you know they really do run around after you cut off their heads. It's something you really need to see to believe."

And it could have gone on just like that, for the fifteen minutes his father had set aside. Ron could feel the time passing and understood that so long as they kept talking about cooking and chickens there was a chance that his father would be willing to keep the conversation going, even to see him again. Yet his father's eyes kept wandering to the door to the kitchen, which was still open. Was he checking the clock? At last, Ron had to break in.

"Dad," he said, "How'd you know I was in Chicago?"

His father paused before he answered, and he lit another cigarette. The radio was playing "Get Ready." What Ron had hoped for was an answer that implied that his father knew about the work he had been called to do. It wasn't impossible. After all, the restaurant's patrons probably lived in his district. His father said, "Mind if I turn the volume up? It's a righteous song."

"You didn't answer my question," said Ron.

Again, his father looked right past him, inside, and then beyond the stoop, and without turning, he adjusted the volume on the radio until it was too loud to hear. At the same time, he said, as distinctly as he could, "Son, a little while ago, I got a visit from a G-man. He came by the restaurant, asked me a lot of questions, asked if you'd contacted me. Now I don't know your game."

"My game?" Ron had trouble controlling his voice. "I'm not playing a game."

"I take one look at you, I know you're a straight arrow. But when the FBI comes calling, what's a man supposed to think? I could lose my lease."

"Dad," said Ron again, and it was hard to fight that stream of cheerful soul music. "I'm not doing anything wrong. You can't let them scare you."

"I've already got enough trouble in my life," his father said. "I don't need more of it. Maybe it's better to just go on the way we were."

Ron choked back what he felt. The cigarette his father had given him had burned to nothing in his hand. What the fuck did he expect? This was the man who had sent Ron and Tammy to her sister in Tutwiler the minute she got sick, and as far as Ron knew never once sent a note asking about them, never watched his wife waste down to nothing with the cancer, never came down for the funeral, and now Ron expected what, precisely?

"I'd better get back to work," his father said. "You don't need to go out through the restaurant. There's an alley down the stoop, leads you right back to Michigan Avenue."

Ron turned and said, "Just thought you'd like to know, you got a granddaughter named Tammy." Then, he jumped off the stoop and started down the alley before he could be tempted to see if what he'd said would even touch the man.

RON BARELY SAW TAMARA THESE days. There was something poisonous about the atmosphere in that apartment. Sometimes, the refrigerator would contain nothing but white bread and mayonnaise. Beth lived on that stuff, and you could see the veins right through her skin. Her hair had darkened and thinned. She spent most of the money from public assistance on formula, because her breast-milk had stopped somewhere around the time they'd moved. Ron would feed Tamara her bottle when he came back, which was sometimes three in the morning or sometimes two in the afternoon. Tamara was a scrawny baby, but she was lively, and he liked the little flickers of recognition that passed across her face when he came into the room.

He once asked Beth, "What do you do with her all day?"

"We read *No Exit*," said Beth. "There are four parts, so we switch off."

"We don't have that book," said Ron, unnecessarily, and he was rewarded with Beth's weird, new, cackling laugh. Or maybe she always laughed like that, only he hadn't noticed.

The more he was gone, the less she seemed to mind it. When Tamara started standing up and groping her way across the room, Beth didn't even mention it to him until he saw it for himself. He thought, sometimes, of taking Tamara with him to the office, or even to Clement's. He knew that the bartender would be gentle with children. Yet part of him suspected that if Beth did not have Tamara, she would unravel. That wasn't how he ought to be thinking; the baby was the one who ought to be protected. Yet when he held Tamara on his lap for a minute and let her try to pull off his nose, he knew that somewhere in another room, Beth was drowning.

Maybe that was why he didn't just take Tamara and run off with her, the way any loving and sensible father ought to have done. He would have plenty of time to blame himself, and also to think about what might have come to pass if he'd taken her to a couple of meetings, started some speculation probably, but also made it clear that he had nothing to hide. It might have prevented what happened next.

WHICH WAS: THE EVENING OF the meeting with the City Council representative, just as Ron was making sure the microphone they'd managed to hook up was functioning, the kid appeared. Ron hadn't seen him since he'd finished the plate of fries a few hours before. He had his cap off.

"Hey man," he said. His voice sounded too high. Without the cap, he looked startled, as though someone had yanked it from his head.

"Hey, what's the word from upstairs?" Ron asked him, because last he'd seen him, he'd told him to knock lightly on each door at five or so in the way of a reminder, and instructed him to offer Josie's mamma his arm when he came back for her at eight that night.

"The word from upstairs," said the kid, and now he hesitated, and fiddled, stupidly, with the cord of the microphone. "Did this cost us anything?"

"Yes," said Ron, a little harshly. "Look, just tell me what's going on, man."

"What's going on," he said, "is that we don't have a candidate. Patrice Park is bailing, man. He's gone."

Ron sat in one of the folding chairs. "Listen, kid."

"You don't even know my name," he said. His hands were shaking.

"Sure I do," said Ron.

"No you don't. You don't give a shit. You look—look at what's going around."

Then for the first time, Ron noticed that the kid—that Lucien—was holding something. It was a flier, and Ron took it and felt Lucien sit beside him and watch his face as he read. There was a headline, in block print: *Brothers and Oreos.*

An illustration followed: a crudely drawn black male, prone below a long-haired white female, whose high-heeled boot was on his head. She held a gun.

In the fight against White AmeriKKKa, there are Brothers and there are Oreos. There are some Brothers who look African on the Outside, but when you Twist them a little you see their Creamy Center. Ask Ronald Beauchamp how he likes his Cream and he'll tell you he likes it on top. Some people think Men shouldn't carry Guns but think that Creamy White Girls should.

Is this the Future of Our Movement?

Ron looked up, and there was Lucien, staring at him with wet eyes. "This thing," Lucien said, "is fucking everywhere. All over the office, all over Clement's, must have been fifty slipped under the doors right here in the building. I don't think most of those church ladies understood it, man, but now they so scared they don't even want to come out into the hall."

"Lucien," said Ron, "listen to me. This is all a load of shit."

"Oh I know that. I know. But now Patrice Parks is bailing and I don't know what's gonna go down tonight. It might just be you, me and that cracker from city council."

Ron didn't want to wait and find out. He also wasn't sure where to go to clear his head. All of the usual places had been compromised. In the end, he told Lucien to see if he could get hold of Patrice Parks and tell him he should call Ron at the phone booth across the street. At least that would give the kid something to do. Ron felt weird tingles all across his skin as he walked outside and waited for the light to change, as though he was in crosshairs of a machine gun. Of course, the phone was out of order. Ron leaned his head against the glass of the phone booth and let vapor gather there.

That's where Patrice found him. He opened the door and asked, "Hey. You conscious, Beauchamp?"

Without looking up, Ron said, "Yeah."

"You understand," said Patrice, leaning over a little, "I can't do this. It's not about that shit they're spreading. It's about who's spreading it. Do you have any idea who's managing the office these days? I have some integrity. There are some elements I can't work with."

Ron turned, still on the small wooden seat in the phone booth. "You say you can't do this. I say you won't do this."

"All right," said Patrice. "I won't do this."

Ron thought about the time he'd asked Patrice about his name, if he'd taken it from Patrice Lumumba, the Congolese leader who'd been murdered not long before Medger Evers. Patrice had seemed a little shy about telling Ron how he had taken that name. He called it the gesture of a younger man, but he said that it would have been worse to change it back again, like dismissing the young man he had been. Ron said, "I do have a white girlfriend." It felt strange to be calling Beth his girlfriend, but what other word was there? When Patrice's expression didn't change, he added, "We have a daughter."

"Congratulations," said Patrice. "And you've kept this to yourself, I take it."

"It didn't seem like anybody's business."

"What does the poor woman do? Take bread through a grate in the wall?" Patrice shook his head, in that formal way that always seemed, to Ron, deliberately African, perhaps another tribute to the young man he had been. "When I say that there are some elements that I can't work with," said Patrice, "I was not referring to you. I was referring to people with simple minds. Simple minds can be manipulated. Ask around, Ron. See if you can figure out who produced this thing. You won't find out. But, mark my words, a year from now, every brother in Bronzeville will want the credit. And I don't have the will or the capacity to deal with these people if I run for City Council."

In fact, Ron never did discover who produced the flier. Nobody seemed to know. Apparently, it had appeared tacked on the door of the Movement office, and then, as Lucien had reported, all over Bronzeville. Later, of course, they'd know all about those sorts of fliers. There would be successful lawsuits against the FBI, which would uncover similar tactics used by the agency against what they classified as Black Hate Groups. The name of the operation was COINTELPRO, and it did its work so well that what Patrice had predicted would come to pass. A year after the flier's distribution, every brother in Bronzeville would be so inclined towards suspicion and anger and so anxious for authenticity that he might have written its text, but a year after its distribution, Ron Beauchamp would not be there to bear witness.

That same evening, at a quarter of eight, when a dozen anxious-looking tenants—including Josie's mother—kept their promise, and sat in the folding chairs, someone appeared in the back. It was Helen Forest.

Helen looked pretty much the same as she had last time Ron had seen her, plump and in good spirits, with her brown hair still chopped off as though she'd taken periodic trips to Ruleville and handed her old students the scissors. She stood there, waiting for Ron to come to her. He knew that whoever wrote that flier wanted him to do just that, but he was past caring. He hurried over, put his arms around her, and said, "Oh man, where the hell have you been?"

"Hey, Ronny, what are you talking about? I'm an El ride away, if you care that much. We just heard you were putting on this little dog and pony show, and I figured I would see if you'd make Archie Gaydon sweat. Do rats sweat?" Helen asked, sweetly. Then, because he was still holding her, she said, "Are you going to let go, Ron, or will I have to do it first?" When he still didn't let go, Helen said, "I heard about the letter."

At first Ron thought she meant the flier, and he stepped back, coming to himself and sensing all those church-lady eyes on them.

But Helen said, "What I suggest is Africa."

"What?" Ron said, as though she'd spoken Dutch.

"Africa," Helen said again. "Specifically, Tanzania. We've got a lot of SNCC people over there already. You'll have to raise your own plane fare this time. No more Harry Belafonte."

Ron finally realized what letter she'd referred to. "I can't run away," said Ron. "You know I can't."

"It's not running away," Helen said. "Take what life gives you, Ron. Don't take what death hands you. I think this whole war is just a way for the same people who fucked us over in Atlantic City in '64 to kill us off, Humphrey, Johnson. You know what? It's working. How many times have we told ourselves to stand our ground? And how many times have we told ourselves we won't be moved? We think it's called integrity, but Ronny, it makes us such easy targets."

During Helen's little speech, Archibald Gaydon, the City Council-man, appeared, looking as soft and bald and moist as every other time Ron had seen him. He came flanked by a well-dressed Negro of the Uncle Tom variety, and a plainclothes security guard, obvious as a Pinkerton. Gaydon knew Ron had organized the meeting, and with hesitation, he interrupted Helen, who stepped back with her small, pink smile.

"Young lady," Archie Gaydon said to Helen, "I hope you can convince Ron here to give someone who wants the best for our district the benefit of the doubt."

"Ron's a Christian," Helen replied. "He gives everyone the benefit of the doubt. I however, am a pagan. I eat doubt."

It was very hard for Ron to turn from Helen and step towards the microphone, facing a sudden row of young black men in dark glasses who flanked the back, the scattered tenants who blinked hopefully forward, and Lucien, who wore his cap again. Lucien sat in the front row, and gave Ron a weak thumb's up, as Ron tapped the microphone and began.

5

BETH SAID TO HER AUNT Beatrice, "I need money."

Aunt Beatrice was in Chicago for the Democratic Convention, and she didn't really seem to notice any change in Beth's appearance. Nor was Beth's request different than the requests she'd made since she'd left for Mississippi four years earlier. She just made it more directly. In fact, there was something in Beth's manner that approached a threat, and Beatrice did not respond well to threats. "Well now," she said, "you don't exactly look as though you're at the end of your rope."

Beth was wearing a tailored dress with a short jacket, something she'd picked up at a thrift shop. She had it dry-cleaned after Ron told her that it smelled like a wet dog. The dry-cleaning cost a dollar, and Beth had two dollars left until the end of the week. Now she realized that she should have shown up in a baggy housedress, and she also should have brought Tamara, who was staying with Helen Forest.

Beth needed that money. If Ron wasn't somewhere else in two weeks, he'd have to show up for induction. They could manage to live off public assistance, stray odd jobs, the occasional poverty program windfall, but none of that added up to a plane ticket to Tanzania. Aunt Beatrice added up to a plane ticket. Beth had tracked her down to the Intercontinental Hotel, and it had been surprisingly easy to phone her room and arrange this meeting.

Aunt Beatrice had been so happy to hear from her that she'd come down to the lobby without putting on her hat, and she'd sat them both down and ordered a high tea. The sandwiches were mostly cucumber and cheese on crust-less bread, and Beth grimly stuffed them in her mouth and wondered if she could manage to extend the afternoon to the point where she could order a steak.

"I need money," Beth said again.

The bloom was clearly off Aunt Bea's mood when this was repeated. "I suppose," she said, "that ever since that business last year when white people were banned from your organization, you must have been somewhat at loose ends."

"I'm not at loose ends," said Beth. "And I wasn't banned. We know why we had to leave. We left on our own."

"That's not what I was told," said Aunt Beatrice. "But then again, I suppose you have other sources of information." She looked at the empty plate where the sandwiches used to be, and she asked, "Still eating like a sharecropper, honey?"

"I'm eating like a Welfare Mother," said Beth, "because that's what I am."

At that point, Aunt Beatrice could have said several things. She could have asked about Tamara, whom she knew existed; she had been broad-minded enough to send a rattle and a substantial check to Melody when she heard the news. She also could have discussed how the very concept of public assistance was a part of Johnson's Great Society, and that would lead to a long-winded defense of the Democratic Party, which seemed to need defending these days against young people who looked very much like Beth. Instead, Aunt Beatrice said, "You know who you remind me of?"

"I can't imagine," said Beth.

"Your mother," said Aunt Beatrice, "when she was just back from Los Alamos."

The observation brought on silence. Beth had intended to ask Aunt Beatrice about Vivian's shares in Neuman's Department Store. After all, Beth was twenty-three and should have come into her inheritance. Now, however, she was thrown to the point where she could feel tears coming on, and tears were dangerous. She twisted the cloth napkin around and around her right hand as though she hoped to squeeze something out of it. It was no use. She couldn't continue the conversation. Ron would be stuck in Chicago, he would be drafted, he would die in Vietnam fighting other colored people, and it would be her fault.

MARRIAGE SEEMED OUT OF THE question now. According to Ron, a license would just leave another paper trail, and somebody was following that trail. Beth knew it too. Her father had just sent her a letter saying he had a meeting with the dean of the college, and *strangely* he wrote, *your name came up. He wanted to know if we had much contact and suggested that perhaps I know a little about what you're doing in Chicago and might like to share that information. Contrary to what you may believe, I am not a scoundrel. But what are you doing in Chicago?* The letter did not contain the check that Beth had asked for.

Ron told her that if someone rang the buzzer, she should keep the shade drawn, and not so much as look down to see who was there, unless she was expecting someone.

"But I'm never expecting anyone," Beth said. Thus far, since they'd moved to Chicago, she'd had a single visitor, Laurel, who was in town for a medical convention. She took one look at Beth and said, with the same hesitation Beth remembered, "Would you like to maybe go out somewhere?"

"Out? What's outside?" Beth asked with a grin that she intended to be snaggly. "I've got everything here you could want—hot and cold running water, electricity sometimes. Where's your soul-sister?"

"My what?"

"That girl you hung with, the dyke from Brooklyn?"

"Oh—Judy," said Laurel. "Somewhere, I guess." She looked almost suspiciously at the couch she was supposed to sit on. "Where's Tamara?"

"Asleep at last," Beth said. "I gave her some vodka around an hour ago. It seems to have done the trick."

Essentially, and with amazing speed, Laurel had become a square. She was never so far off, really. Now, she was actually dressed in a periwinkle blue sweater and pressed trousers, and her hair was in what was called a Pixie cut.

"Bethy," Laurel said, "I need to ask you this. Have you seen a doctor?"

"About what?" Beth asked.

"About, well, your skin for one thing."

"This is the kind of skin you have when you're on welfare," Beth said. "You should know. Aren't you a doctor now? Come to think of it, sure I'm seeing a doctor. I'm seeing you."

It was a strange thing to be able to look at herself from a distance and know that the courage she'd so valued was really not a way to gain consciousness, but to lose it, to let something else take over. But there was no one with whom to share this information. Ron just didn't get it, never had. There was a time when she could free-associate to Ron as he listened patiently, without feeling tolerated. That time was over.

She was a mother now. Sitting in the dumpy Chicago apartment—two rooms with greasy windows and linoleum peeling on all four corners—she would hold Tamara, and sometimes Ron would take her, and she'd see the way her little girl looked as though Ron had spit her out. That's how alike they were. If that could be enough, if she could hang on to that baby, then maybe Ron would find a way to take them all to Africa because leaving them behind would be impossible.

Ron ducked into the apartment these days only to open the refrigerator, which contained a jar of mustard and a single hotdog roll. Then, he washed a knife in the sink and made himself a mustard sandwich.

There weren't even any dishes for Beth to wash, nor could she take a sponge-mop to the encrusted floor. There was nothing to do but watch

Ron make his way through the tiny mustard sandwich with his back turned to her. Beth couldn't tell what he was thinking.

Tamara shared their bed, which, Ron said, was a common practice in Africa. Beth would wake up sometimes, in the middle of the night, and find Ron's side of the bed still empty, and her daughter almost on the edge. She rolled up some sheets and built a makeshift barrier around her, and then, close to dawn, woke to find Ron enraged.

"What's this? A wall?"

"For God's sake, she's going to fall off the bed."

"You just don't get it. They don't fall off! If you leave a baby be—don't interfere—they naturally know—naturally!"

"This isn't Africa! This is a bed, not a straw mat!" Beth was shouting now, and Tamara, who was already awake, began to cry.

If only she could raise the money, they would all go—Beth knew. When there was a dark space at the bottom of their broken mailbox, she would jimmy it open with a fork and hope that a check would fall out, instead of an advertisement for a sofa bed, or a bill they couldn't pay. Once, there was a light blue aerogramme from Paris. Beth dropped it, picked it up again, felt a dull pain radiate from the fiber of the paper, and told herself it didn't have a check inside so it couldn't be important, but she opened it anyway, and started reading. *Mon Professeur*, it began. *Je regrette mais je n'aime pas l'histoire. Je l'ai déjà vu.* She read a few more lines. Her hands began to tremble. The letter was in French, and she couldn't understand a word of it.

ONE DAY, THE BUZZER RANG downstairs. Beth had been warned by Ron's friends that a buzzer in mid-afternoon probably meant the cops, but she felt so lonely these days that she couldn't help herself. She opened the shade and looked four flights down to see who was at the door. Marty Weinglass looked back up at her.

The moment her hand hit buzzer to release the lock, she knew she'd made a mistake. She could hear him try the broken elevator, bang on the closed elevator door, curse, and clomp up the four flights. After that, she didn't feel as though she could keep the door closed.

"Shit, you make a brother work," Marty said. He leaned against the door frame, skinnier and shaggier than ever. He had grown a beard, which made him look like a demented rabbi. "Aren't you going to give me a beer or something?"

"We can't afford beer," said Beth.

"Your boyfriend can," said Marty. "I think your boyfriend drinks more than his weight in beer." He threw himself into the apartment and onto the couch as though it were a heroic gesture. "You know, he's gonna get himself a pot belly and then you won't love him anymore."

"Marty," Beth said, "what are you doing here?"

"Everybody's here for the convention," said Marty. "We're camping in Lincoln Park. Missy's here, all the old gang from Swarthmore and Chester, people coming out of the woodwork like termites. Why aren't you sitting next to me? I don't bite."

"I've got to feed Tamara," said Beth.

"So feed her."

"I've got to heat up her bottle."

"You've got a couple of nice bottles on you already," said Marty. "I could heat them up for you."

Beth was too tired to bear this now. She said, "What do you want?"

"I know I haven't been in touch, but that's not entirely my fault," Marty said. "Your man is very protective of you. You don't know what it cost me to even find out where he keeps you. I kept telling him that I want to talk to the girl who sleeps with the nigger, and all he says to me is that I have the wrong number."

That might have been when Beth realized that a switch had been thrown. Marty might or might not have been on that couch. The formula might or might not have been heating on the stove that was two weeks away from being shut off entirely. Tamara—she should have been real—Tamara who had said her first word a week before—was she in the bedroom? Was there a bedroom? Maybe she'd turned on the stove without striking a match, but Marty didn't seem affected. Marty was trying to show her something, the cover of a magazine, a picture of well-built white girls in hot pants. They were holding rifles. He was laughing, but Beth just said, "I need to lie down."

Marty's face seemed to waver. He said, quite clearly, "You look sick."

"I am," said Beth. "Is Larry in town too?"

He rose and steered her towards the bedroom, and he smelled as bad as he looked; he had been camping outdoors for days, he said, and if he could just lie down with her, in a real bed, it would do him a world of good.

"I'm sick," Beth said again, and then she added, "I can't understand a word you're saying. What language are you speaking? Are you speaking French?"

The next thing she knew, it was dark, and the buzzer was ringing downstairs, persistently, in bursts. Ron must have come and gone because Tamara had her pajamas on, but she was awake and wet. There were three diapers left. Tamara bawled, and Beth cushioned her warm, damp head against her breasts, and when the buzzer sounded again, she shouted "Shut up! Shut up!" Then, she felt a wave of panic. It could have been anyone. It could have been Larry. But no power on earth could wrench her from that bed.

6

WHEN CY COHEN HEARD THE rumor that Freddie was in trouble, he didn't want to believe it. After all, she'd been a model employee. He'd taken her on because she offered to balance the books for a store discount, but then she started reading through wholesale catalogs the way Cy had seen that George reading through comic books at the Temple. Freddie had said, "What's the use of a discount if there's nothing here to buy? See these blue jeans with the flared bottoms? All the girls are wearing them now." What she said should have seemed out of line, but Cy had to admit that she made some sense.

These days, Freddie worked for a commission which was higher than what he could have justified by way of salary, and going to Rust College three nights a week, and he had to admit, he couldn't do without her. Maybe he even used just those words—couldn't do without her—to a customer. He shouldn't have. Someone might have taken it the wrong way.

One day, Freddie was selling a jar of some kind of hair cream to a skinny colored boy with one of those wild hair-dos they were all starting to sport across the tracks. Freddie never wore her hair that way. She always looked respectable and must have bought her skirts and blouses at one of the nicer stores that catered to colored clientele. Still, she praised that jar of hair-cream as though she'd made the stuff herself, and threw in a pick with a raised fist on top, and she said, "If it breaks, just bring it back. I tell you, it's impossible to break these things, even in your hair, Clyde." Then, she saw him and said, "Cy, tell this man about our guarantee."

Cy winced. "What guarantee?"

"It's the product guarantee," Freddie said, patiently. "It came with the box. Unbreakable."

"Guess it's guaranteed then. Say, can I talk to you for a minute?" He motioned Freddie towards the office, and Clyde, whoever he was, occupied himself with trying to break the hair-pick, leaving Cy to close the door a little and softly say, "Look, could you not call me Cy in front of customers?"

"But I always call you Cy," said Freddie.

"Maybe you ought to stop," Cy said. "It gives the wrong impression."

"Now what kind of impression is that, Cy?" Freddie asked, just like a fool, which Freddie wasn't. "You mean like you're not my boss? But you know you're my boss, so what does it matter what other people think?"

She certainly didn't look like a girl in trouble. At one point, when a shipment came in, she was bobbing up and down, sorting through white and blue denim jackets, squatting to lift a load of them up to a shelf that she could only reach with a stepladder, and when Cy said, "You shouldn't be doing that, Freddie. You've got to be careful!" Freddie looked at him as though he'd lost his mind.

"What's going on with you, Cy?" Freddie said at last. "Or do you really want me to start calling you Mr. Cohen."

"I don't care," Cy said. It was a quiet afternoon, although in half an hour, a new boy Freddie had talked him into hiring would come in to wash the windows and sweep up. If Cy was going to talk to the girl, he'd have to do it now. "Look," he said, "we've gotten to know each other pretty well, these past two years. I've been pretty straight with you."

Freddie laughed. "Are you about to fire me, Mr. Cohen?"

"No I am not about to fire you," Cy said, and his face began to burn.

"But you look like you've got something you want to say. And I don't know why you don't say it."

So Cy asked Freddie if she was in trouble, and Freddie didn't seem to understand, so Cy said, "Just tell me the truth. Who's the father? You're like a daughter to me, Freddie, and I promise, I'll do everything in my power to make the fellow do the right thing."

Freddie didn't laugh this time. She didn't speak at all. Instead, she walked to the office, seeming to contain an anger that Cy found terrifying. She was there for a while, and Cy could hear the clatter of the adding machine, continuing almost without pause for half an hour. Meanwhile, the colored boy came, and Cy had to deal with him and show him where he'd put the mop and sponge, and by the time he came back to the front of the store, there was Freddie, with a long strip from the machine.

"Look," said Cy, "I'm sorry if you think I insulted you."

"You did insult me," said Freddie. "I figured out my commission for the month. You can write me a check today if you want to and I won't bother you again."

Cy rolled his eyes. "So I insulted you. So I'm sorry."

"What gets me," said Freddie, "is that all it takes in this town is for a girl to be getting married, and everyone figures she's got to be pregnant."

The colored boy washing the windows turned from his work. "Ain't that the truth," he said.

Cy was speechless for a moment. Then, he felt his eyes tear up, and he said, "Darling, that's terrific news. But why didn't you tell me?"

"And I was going to invite you and your wife and mother to the ceremony, but now I'm not so sure."

Cy didn't care who'd see it. He hugged Freddie, and she squirmed in his embrace in a way that made him know that she was herself again. Then he said, "You damn well better have me there. I want to be the one to give you away."

"Cy," Freddie said, "you ought to know better. I've got a perfectly fine father already. I don't think he'd like that one bit."

"So who's the groom?" Cy asked.

Freddie said, "You'll have to come to see."

THE WEDDING WOULD TAKE PLACE in three weeks, and during that time, Freddie refused to divulge the name of the man she would marry. Cy figured he was someone up at Rust College, maybe a doctor or a lawyer, but she dropped a few hints that made him suspect he was from Melody. Yet the only colored fellow in Melody who seemed worthy of Freddie was J.B. Powders, and he was already married. J.B. once came to Cohen's Dry Goods and asked if he could get a discount on some special order khaki coveralls with *Powder's Salvage* printed on the back in blue. He'd brought little Pearlie with him, which softened Cy up just enough to bring the price down a few dollars above wholesale. Word was, J.B. was thinking of expanding. Cy hoped he'd take it slow.

Freddie said to Cy, "You mark this Saturday? It's at the A.M.E. church. You've been there before. It's where you used to hound that Beth."

That's when Cy started to wonder if Beth would be at the wedding. He never did find out what had become of that girl, the one who really got in trouble. Last he heard, she'd disappeared with her colored boyfriend, and if they weren't dead by now they were probably in Philadelphia. He couldn't help but ask Freddie, "Did you send her an invitation?"

Freddie looked confused. "You mean Beth?" Then, she frowned. "You think it's too late now?"

IN FACT, CY FOUND HIMSELF speculating even as he and Sherrie drove to the wedding. At the Greyhound bus stop, he somehow thought he'd see Beth standing there in the dust and sunshine. She'd be there on her own, sun-struck and in need of directions to the church. Then, a bus really did pass, but it didn't stop to let out passengers. Besides, the bus was going in the wrong direction.

Sherrie herself had brightened ever since she'd gotten word that the wedding was at the A.M.E. church. "Why didn't you tell me that girl's a Methodist?"

For Cy, a church was a church, and that long wooden building with the cross on top could have been full of colored Catholic nuns as far as he could tell. They pulled into the lot out back, and he took their gift out of the trunk, a blender that Sherrie had chosen at Greenfield's. He'd wanted to just give the couple cash and let them figure out if they needed a blender, but Sherrie said it was in bad taste to give a check at a church wedding, Cy figured that she knew the territory. He sure didn't. They walked to the front and at the entrance, Sherrie cried out.

"Oh gracious! Look! An African!"

And she was right. In the last row, a lady in a bright orange robe and turban sat with such erect posture that she made the wooden pew look slatternly. She must have heard Sherrie, but she didn't turn. Below the turban, her amber-colored ears were weighted down with heavy golden hoops. Sherrie seemed paralyzed, transfixed. Cy said, "Honey, we'd better take a seat."

Then he felt someone move in beside him. "Hello, Cy."

He turned, and spontaneously took a step back. The colored man who addressed him must have been six and a half feet tall, and his black leather jacket made him seem as heavy as a wrestler. He had a thick beard and mustache and wore sunglasses, and if he knew Cy, Cy sure didn't know him, and didn't want to know him. Sherrie pressed herself against Cy and whispered, "Oh my goodness." As for Cy, just for a moment, he thought: there's the groom.

But it was Larry Walsh, come in from Cincinnati for Freddie's wedding. He also wanted to check about in about a rumor J.B. planned to run for a seat in the state legislature. Granted, J.B. wasn't running as a Black Panther, but as a Democrat, and, as Larry explained to the increasingly spooked Cy, the presence of himself and of Sue Francis was completely unofficial. "What's left of SNCC these days doesn't go in for electoral politics," Larry said. Once Cy heard his voice, he had to admit he recognized him from that business five years ago, though they hadn't exactly made formal acquaintance.

But then, he realized that the African in that last row was Sue Francis. "Mister," he said to Larry, because somehow, the honorific just came out, "What's happened to that girl?"

Larry called into the church, "S.F., come on over here. Look who showed up for the wedding!"

Drawing herself to a height that seemed to match Larry's, Sue Francis floated towards the door with a familiar sour expression on her face, and she flitted her eyes towards Cy and Sherrie and then back again. "You're talking to those people?"

"Cy Cohen's an old friend," Larry. "Can't you relax? Nobody here cares. See," he said to Cy, "my wife is vigilant about political consistency. Is your wife vigilant about your political consistency?"

Before Cy could respond, J.B. came bounding over from the road, wearing a dusty brown suit, and sweating from the armpits. "Man, I'm not too late, am I? I've been speaking at four churches today. Hey Mr. Cohen," he said to Cy. "Glad to see you." He held out his hand, and Cy shook it. Then he turned to Larry. "You can't wear your shades in there, brother. Show some respect."

Larry glanced at Sue Francis, who motioned for him to remove them, which he did, showing a pair of ravaged and soft-looking eyes. "For you," said Larry, "I'll show respect. Even if you're running as a Democrat."

"Always a Freedom Democrat!" J.B. said, and he patted Larry on the back and made to sit next to him and Sue Francis, but Larry gestured him away, towards the front of the church, where a stout, colored woman who could have been Freddie's double sat next to a nervous, colored skinny fellow in half-glasses—They were Freddie's aunt and uncle. The aunt rose and came forward, and took Cy Cohen's hand in both of hers and said, "You dear man. What haven't you done for our Freddie?"

"We got her a blender," Sherrie said. "General Electric model."

Then, the organ music started, and down the aisle came a couple of the girls Cy recognized, Freddie's best friends: Sweetie, a nurse's aide, and Bobbie, who'd just come back from a year in Paris, fat as ever, and according to Freddie, chattering away in French but still barely putting two words together in English. They had gotten the pink organdy for their dresses wholesale.

"Well, I must say, this is in very good taste," Sherri said.

Then came the groom. Cy stood spontaneously. It was George Burgess.

George wore a blue suit that fit him badly, and he was sweating hard. He walked down the aisle alone and stood there, smelling strongly of cologne.

Sherrie tugged Cy's sleeve. "Sit down," she whispered. "Everyone's looking at you."

"They'd look anyway," Cy said, but he sat down.

THERE WAS A RECEPTION AFTERWARDS on the front lawn. It was there that Freddie, still in her bridal gown, cornered Cy and said, "So if Mr. J.B. runs, are you gonna put a campaign sign in your window?"

"If I want to get my store burned down, I'll let you know," Cy said.

"You don't have an ounce of nerve," said Freddie, and she put her hands on her hips and looked capable of making a scene. George stood beside her, amused, handsome, proud to be married to her, like it was a joke he'd planned to play on Cy for years.

"Mr. Cohen," said George, "you just got to make up your mind. I see the way folks look at you. Don't think I don't. And I mean white and colored. And all those dollar bills you give me won't make a bit of difference. It's time you figured out why you give me all those dollar bills."

Sherrie, who'd been standing beside Cy, eating a hunk of wedding cake, asked, "What dollar bills? What sign?"

Cy took off his glasses and cleaned them. "Kids," he said, "you've got to have a little patience."

"Why?" George asked.

Cy put his glasses on again, and said, "Listen, I don't want to be the first one to put the sign in my window. I'd gladly be the second, but not the first."

C<small>Y</small> GRAVITATED TOWARDS A CONVERSATION that went on at a battered picnic table, where Larry Walsh sat in his sunglasses, drinking cold tea with Harris Johnson, the farmer who'd grown all the more taciturn and now seemed like a weathered cedar statue. "Good crowd," Johnson said to Larry. Good spirit here."

Larry said, "I heard about Mrs. Burgess."

"Oh, that was last winter. Sugar in her blood. Her heart." Harris's mouth closed then, and he seemed to have something else to say, but thought better of it. "Her boy's in a home now, down in the Gulf. He's well taken care of."

"I'm sorry," said Larry.

"I am too," said Johnson. Then, he took a sip of the cold tea and it took a long time getting down his throat. "She was a good woman."

"Don't I know it," said Larry.

"She voted—first time—just last year."

"For Humphrey, I suppose," said Larry.

Harris Johnson didn't respond, the implication being that her vote was her business. He turned his head the way an owl might, scouting the territory.

Finally, Larry said, "I'm glad she got to vote. It meant a lot to her."

"It did," said Johnson. Then, he said, "Didn't keep her from dying though."

Cy had wanted to ask Larry about Beth, if he'd spoken to her, where she was now. Yet something about the conversation between the two men felt impossible to penetrate. Larry was talking to Johnson about his work in Cincinnati, where the Freedom House was storing packages for brothers in Cleveland, and where the cops had raided the place and knocked a hole in the wall to look for firearms but hadn't bothered checking the front closet.

"They're strangers now," said Larry. "Not one who was around in '64. The old guard's all in exile—Tanzania, Cuba, Ghana. Maybe that's the way it ought to be. Maybe that's where we should do spade work, where it matters. Maybe there's something about this country that makes you hit a rock—and then you break the spade. You just lose patience. You know, that rent strike fell apart because we couldn't build the trust we needed. And now, we hear about janitors in the school district who have to pay for their own cleaning supplies, and I start talking about starting a campaign, and somebody starts to scream that we should just burn down the damned schools. How am I supposed to work with these kids?"

Harris nodded, and took another sip of tea.

Sue Francis said, "My husband's turning into an old man."

"Well I am an old man," said Larry. "I'm twenty-seven."

She put her arms around him from behind and leaned her chin on his shoulder. "Did Larry tell you I planted a garden? I got the soil prepared. If you've got any seeds for me, Mr. Johnson, let me know. Of course, the cops may just decide to dig the thing up in case I've buried explosives."

Larry shook his head. "Cops? Might be one of those boys who call themselves Black Panthers. Jump the fence and bury explosives there themselves."

Harris Johnson put down his tea, and said, "You all be careful."

"I'm careful," Larry said. Then, he put his hand somewhere on that heavy jacket. He turned to Cy as though he had just noticed he was there, and said, "What are you staring at?"

Cy said nothing. He wished he was anywhere else but there, but he was also scared to turn his back on Larry.

"Leave the kid alone," said Sue Francis. "He can't help it."

"You like to give out dollar bills, I hear." said Larry. "That's one way for a little Jew to increase the size of his manhood. Be a philanthropist. Come down here and save the little colored children. Well, the colored children are throwing the money back in your face, now. Maybe you don't like it—but at least be decent enough to recognize the impulse. You of all people—you should see the point!"

"You want to fight me?" Cy asked him. He found himself tearing his coat off his shoulders, and he stood there in his white shirt and tie, and then, his fingers went automatically to loose the knot and slip that tie into his pocket. "You want to? Or are you going to pull out that gun you've got?"

Larry started to unzip the jacket, and between the beard and sunglasses, his face was like a mask. Sue Francis was saying something, but Cy's ears were buzzing now and who knows what would have happened next if Freddie hadn't called out:

"What the hell are you doing! Cy, Larry, are you crazy?"

They both came back to themselves. Freddie held the train of her wedding gown crumpled in her hands, and tears were running down her face.

"You're spoiling it. You're ruining my day—both of you! Now you stop this right now. You both shake hands."

Larry rooted in his pocket and drew out a handkerchief. He mopped his whole face, and then he wiped his hand before presenting it to Cy. Cy shook it. Then, Cy finally managed to ask: "You ever hear from that Beth, the one from Philadelphia?"

Larry looked startled. "Beth? Not for a while."

"Bobbie told me she sent her a long letter from Paris," Freddie said, "all about that business with the students there last spring. But she never heard a word. And then I sent her an invitation to the wedding. I sent it to that address you gave me, Larry, but she never even answered."

"Maybe it didn't get to her in time," said Larry.

"You think? She and Ron would have come if she had gotten it."

"She might not have the money," Larry said. Then, he was quiet for a minute. "But I haven't heard from her either."

Sue Francis broke in. "That girl's gotten completely useless. She was supposed to make contacts with the Northern Student Movement, but they never heard from her. I always knew she was unreliable."

"We should go there," Larry said suddenly. "Chicago's practically next door."

Sue Francis made a face. "It's ten hours away, baby."

"Well," Larry said, "It just feels wrong, not knowing where she is. I know she'd call me if she was in real trouble."

"That girl wouldn't know real trouble if it knocked her upside the head," Sue Francis said. "You just want to have one of you damned all-night conversations. And where am I supposed to go when you talk about your existential whosit?"

"Stay put," Larry said.

"Why? Because I might learn something?" Sue Francis shook her head so hard, her earrings rattled. "Baby, my education is complete."

In the end, the two of them went back to Cincinnati. Sue Francis promised to send Freddie a gown like hers, and Cy made Freddie promise that she wouldn't try to find a duplicate in one of her catalogs and sell it at the store. "But all the girls thought it was pretty," Freddie said. "And on a big girl like, say, Bobbie, it would be very, very flattering."

THE NIGHT BEFORE THE ELECTION, the light in J.B.'s house was on until dawn, and according to Cy's customers, he seemed so certain that he would be shot that he already looked a little like a corpse. When the results came in, the numbers were closer than they'd expected. If he had just gotten a few more votes in a little set of blocks between the tracks, then J.B. would be on his way to Jackson. As things stood, he was alive, hundreds of blacks in Melody had voted, and nobody—nobody—could say it was a waste of time.

"So here's what's going to happen," Cy said to Freddie. "Powder won't win, because he's an honest man. But they'll find another colored man and he'll be as low-down as the rest of the folks in Jackson, and it won't make a lick of difference what color the man's skin is. He won't care about folks on Two Street, mark my words."

Freddie didn't answer. She'd been distant all day. Maybe she was still recovering from her honeymoon on the Gulf. Then, Cy repeated what he'd said, and she looked up from the catalogue she'd been reading. She was crying.

"Freddie, come on, honey. I didn't mean it about the election."

"It's not—" Freddie began. Then she stopped and took a breath. "I got a call. I don't understand. I just don't."

"What don't you understand?" Cy asked her.

"Sue Francis called me. Said they'd just got back, and their car was out of gas and they needed to get some dinner, and Larry took the car parked out front—it's a Movement car—he took it and it exploded. He's dead."

Cy reached for her and said, "Honey, I'm sorry."

"He was so good and gentle. And now he's gone."

"Well, sounds like he got himself mixed up with a pretty rough crew," Cy began but then Freddie pulled back, shaking with anger.

"A rough crew? You people got the rough crew! You know how much blood you got on your hands?"

But in the end, she sobbed out her heart in Cy's arms. He didn't care how it looked. He loved that girl, and he hoped George Burgess would be worthy of her, somehow.

Then, Freddie said, "Oh, Cy, we'll never know who did it and if it was meant for him or some other black man. Is there some black man, walking around Cincinnati, supposed to be dead instead of Larry? Did he just get in the wrong car? "

7

ONCE THERE WERE TWO VIVIANS. The first could barely bring herself to tie her shoes, and she wore buckles, so she could slip in and out of those shoes without lifting a finger. The second was a dynamo, a harpy who would peck out the eyes of anyone who came too close. That has already happened. They are already ghosts. What can happen has already happened, and what will happen later is of no consequence. Larry knows that. The others can't get the part about later. That is the part that Laurel doesn't get, even though she is the only one who will listen when Beth talks like this.

"You have a future," she says patiently, like a physician. "You have a daughter, Bethy. She needs you back."

"You don't get it," Beth says. "You just don't see what I see." When Beth says things like this to her psychoanalyst, he asks her what she sees. When she says it to the psychiatrist, he prescribes Thorazine. When she says it to her father during his weekly visits to the Princeton Institute, he says, "I hope they're treating you well."

"Fuck you," Beth says to him. "Fuck you for dumping me in this place. Fuck you for saving my life."

"When that turns into a 'thank you,'" the director says to Max Fine, "You'll know she's ready to go home."

She was in the Psychiatric Institute of Princeton, a rambling, eighteenth-century estate with a nineteenth-century lecture hall and twentieth-century state-of-the-art therapies. There was a time when certain surgeries were commonplace at the Institute. Now, a new generation of drugs were administered to patients who, like Beth, had entered with a diagnosis of Schizophrenia.

The psychiatrist who was put in charge of Beth said to Max, "You said there was a family history."

"My wife," said Max. "But she wasn't schizophrenic. Back then, they called it something else, but I'm sure it wasn't schizophrenia. She never had these kinds of hallucinations. But she had mood swings. I don't know if there's a connection here."

"Well, Beth is a very confused girl. Paranoid. Hostile. Resistant to therapy. Has she always had trouble expressing her feelings in words, Dr. Fine?"

"Pardon me?" Max said.

"In words. Some people can't use words. She may be more responsive to other forms of treatment."

For the first time since Beth arrived, Max Fine was weak with emotion. "I don't know," he said. "Don't ask me those sorts of things, doctor. You're the expert, not me. You know what to do."

BETH FINE HAD BEEN DISCOVERED, emaciated and incoherent, in the apartment in Chicago by a neighbor who had seen three and a half year old Tamara wandering alone around the hallway. The neighbor had intended to dress Beth down for her incompetence as a mother, but she took one look at her and her circumstances and called the police, who directed her to the Child Welfare Agency.

They sent a young black social worker who wore African earrings and carried a bag decorated with giraffes. Beth wasn't surprised to hear her say, "That's Ronny Beauchamp's daughter."

The neighbor asked, "Well, where the hell is Ronny Beauchamp?"

The social worker said, "That's not your business."

"If I minded my business, you'd have a dead little girl on your hands," said the neighbor.

The social worker didn't argue the point. She addressed Beth. "Ma'am, do you realize your daughter's walking around the hallway unattended?"

Beth did not shift her position. Her head was on her arm and her spiky hair was so sweaty and had been laying against her skin for so long that it made a rash there.

"Ma'am, do you consider yourself to be a competent parent?"

Stirring a little, Beth asked, "Could you repeat the question?"

"Are you capable of taking care of this little girl?"

"Oh," Beth said. "No. I'm not."

Patiently, it was explained to Beth that the whole thing could go to court, or she could save the city of Chicago a lot of trouble if she could make arrangements herself.

"I'm sorry," Beth said. She was sitting up now, still in the same kitchen chair. There were a greasy spot on the table where her head had weighted down that arm for what must have been a day. "I can't make the arrangements myself."

"Well fuck," said the social worker. "What do you want me to do?"

"I don't know," Beth said. "You could arrest me."

"Fucking junkie," said the social worker, though the neighbor, who knew a junkie when she saw one and was surprised that the social worker could be that naive, said that before the case went to the courts, she'd just as soon do a little personal investigation and see if she couldn't find a way to make this problem disappear.

The neighbor left Beth sitting there, and opened the refrigerator. The stench was overwhelming. She said to little Tamara, "Honey, what have you been living on?"

Tamara told the lady that there had been crackers in the cupboard, but they were all gone, which was why she was in the hallway, to see if somebody had more. She would also tell her about Grandma Risa.

As for Beth, she let herself be carried on the cogs of that particular machine, just as, she knew, she had always let herself be carried, just as Larry had been carried to an end implied in its beginning. There was always going to be the journey. Then there would be death. What else was there to consider? That was the end of the conversation.

In ART THERAPY, BETH DIDN'T want to work with clay or beads. The loom, which was sought after by most patients, didn't interest her. She did participate in a session on artificial flowers. The wire was pre-cut and shaped to make sure there would be no sharp edges. The patients got strips of sticky green cloth to wrap around the stems, and the petals were dipped in liquid plastic that dried under a heat-lamp into a translucent glassy film of pink or blue. Beth made three of those flowers and put them in a plastic cup on the table by her window. Everyone agreed it was a breakthrough, the first time she'd shown any interest in her environment. Still, given her family history, the psychiatrist had his suspicions. In anticipation of a manic episode, he started her on lithium.

When Laurel visited her that Wednesday, she said, "The flowers are so pretty. Did someone give them to you?"

Beth was in the throes of tranquilizers, and she nodded, hoping that would be enough of a response to get by.

"Who?"

"My mother," Beth said. Then, she wanted to knock her head hard, because that wasn't what she'd meant to say at all. They'd think she was hallucinating again and they'd increase the Thorazine. "No, no," she said thickly. "What I meant is I gave them to me."

"Honey, Bethy," Laurel said, "You know, I wish they'd let you visit me, just for a weekend. Judy and I have the sweetest little house in Philadelphia. And we got a dog. You know what I named that dog? You'll never guess."

Beth's head hurt, just from keeping track of all those words and watching Laurel's short hair flip around her head. Did everybody's head move that much when they were talking?

"I named him Po!"

Beth knocked the cup of flowers off the table, and she raised the table high and would have knocked Laurel's head off too, but Laurel gave a hard whisper.

"Beth—no! They'll do something to you if you hurt me. Oh God, don't, please!"

Laurel's hand gripped the table. She was crying. Tears streaked down her smooth, flushed face. Beth took a few breaths, and then let Laurel guide the table back to the floor. "Maybe you shouldn't come here anymore," Beth said.

"But you're getting better, aren't you?"

"I'm not going to get better," said Beth.

Laurel put her arms around Beth and said, "Bethy, I wish you'd just know how many of us love you. I wish you'd let us help you."

"Hey, Laurel, it's okay. Don't cry, all right?" Beth detached herself. She didn't like people touching her. She'd gained a lot of weight, and it made her own body unfamiliar. "Listen," said Beth, "you can take those flowers if you want." They were in pieces, but she reached down to gather them. That took some effort. By the time she'd finished, the room was dark, and Laurel was long gone.

M AX FINE CAME BY ON Sundays. Those visits were carefully monitored by the staff, as everyone agreed that Beth had the potential to be violent. Still, this was the Princeton Institute, not Bedlam. She was permitted to walk the grounds in his company. Max Fine was not a man who seemed at home outdoors. In winter, he wore a dark blue stocking cap, buttoned his overcoat all the way up his chin, covered his mouth and nose with a scarf and looked, for all the world, like one of the inmates. Beth wore a parka he'd brought her, one she hadn't worn since she had been sixteen. It was far too tight now. She had some trouble walking. In spring, when they'd reduced the Thorazine and tried more Lithium, Beth had an easier time negotiating her way around, and she stripped off the coat and seemed relieved to stuff it in the back of her closet. Max said, "Aren't you cold?"

"What did you ask me?" Beth said. She was thinking about something else.

"I wondered," Max said, "if I ought to get you another coat."

"No, no," Beth said. "I can't fit into anything now. Besides, you wouldn't know where to get one."

"I could ask your Aunt Beatrice."

Beth stopped in her tracks and turned to look at her father. "Does she know I'm here?"

"Of course she does. It's not a secret."

"How come she's never been to see me?" Beth asked him, and she realized she was accusing him of something.

Max found a bench and sat there. His hands were on his knees, and that thick, closed coat made his movements stiff. "Bitsy," he said, "your aunt can come to see you any time she chooses. She has chosen not to. That's all I can say."

Then, Beth broke in with a question she'd had since she arrived. "Dad, is this where mom was?"

Max looked startled. He said, "No. No. She was never here. She should have been. That's what your aunt Beatrice says. She blames me for not addressing the matter. She always said I was in—what is it those head-shrinkers say now? That I was in denial."

"Oh, come on, dad. You gave the woman a fucking lobotomy," Beth said. Although the words were flippant, her heart was pounding. Max Fine answered in a voice that made the hair on the back of her neck rise.

"I did *not*. I did not touch that woman. I loved your mother and I did not harm a hair on her head!"

"Somebody hurt her," Beth said. "If it wasn't you, who was it?"

"I don't know who hurt your mother," Max said, "but whoever did managed to do it pretty thoroughly before I came into the picture. *I loved her*. But it wasn't enough. And you can go ahead and say I was the one who killed her. You won't be the first."

The staff members who kept watch heard the raised voices and approached the bench, but they stopped short, because Max Fine had lowered his head into his hands, and he was weeping. Beth shivered, raised a hand to touch him, lowered it again, and took a piece of tissue out of her trouser pocket. The tissue had gone through the wash with the trousers, and it was in shreds. She handed it to her father, and he took it without looking up and blew his nose into it. They sat there until visiting hours ended.

"WHY WOULD A WOMAN HAVE her head shaved?" Beth asked her psychoanalyst. It was the first thing she asked him when they had their session after her father visited.

"Why do you think she would?" the analyst asked.

"Well," said Beth, sitting on the edge of the couch, "I've been thinking a lot about saints lately, the way they choose what other people don't
choose. I mean, there's that French woman who starved to death because
she didn't want to eat more than prisoners of war. What's her name again?"

"Simone Weil," said the analyst.

"Well, maybe a woman shaves her head because she becomes a Buddhist," said Beth. "Maybe she becomes one of those Orthodox Jewish ladies who wear wigs."

"Does religion interest you?" the analyst asked her.

"Not really," said Beth. "Wigs interest me. Why would somebody
wear one?"

"Perhaps," said the analyst, "they have something to hide."

Beth was running out of patience. She said, "Listen, I want some
straight answers. Suppose someone lived pretty close to a lot of atomic ex-
plosions. When did they start using chemotherapy to treat cancer?"

The analyst took a deep breath. "Beth, your mother didn't have cancer. She was manic-depressive. She didn't choose to shave her head. It was
shaved to administer early shock treatments—still experimental at that
stage. But the sequence of treatments was never completed and she took
her own life. The methods have been refined over the years, and now shav-
ing is unnecessary. I'm telling you this because we are considering this
form of treatment for you."

"But I'm getting better," Beth said

"They won't hurt, Beth," said the analyst. "You won't even remember
them afterwards."

"I thought you didn't do that kind of thing here. I thought that if I
talked to you—and aren't I talking to you?—that I wouldn't have to take
all the shit you've been giving me. What am I supposed to do? Who am I
supposed to become?"

"Beth, you must be careful not to be impatient. Consider your
mother—"

"Why do you keep talking about my mother? What my mother chose
to do is none of your fucking business!" Beth was on her feet now, and she
started for the door, but the analyst called over her:

"It won't be done without your consent, but it has helped thousands of
people who were where you are now, at your stage of recovery."

"And it could have saved my mother's life?" Beth cried out, and it was
a cry of pain. "Well I don't want someone else's life! I want my own!"

She left the analyst's office and tried to contain her anger as she walked
back to the ward. She was allowed to walk alone now. The plate-glass win-

dows in the hall between the wings let in so much sunlight that it was like walking through a column of flame. Breathless, she sat on the bed, and opened her window a crack. She had been in the institute for two years.

AFTER THAT SESSION, SHE WAITED for the shock treatments to begin, and as each day was one on which they did not occur, those days achieved a sort of sameness—wake up, pills, television, magazine, television, pills, group therapy, pills. One day, she was told that Freddie Burgess wanted to visit, and she said, "Isn't it Claire Burgess?" and sheer curiosity made her say she'd like to see her.

Freddie was underdressed. It was, she admitted, her first trip north, but she should have known better than to think she wouldn't need a jacket in October. She looked older, carefully put together, with small hoop earrings and a matching sweater set, but not really far from the surface was the teenager she'd been in Melody. They sat in a room full of healthy ferns and faced each other in two wicker chairs; it was called the Sun Room, but the sky was overcast that day. Freddie, as it turned out, was on her way to a Black Business Owners' conference in New York. She was so nervous in Beth's presence that Beth found herself speaking in a whisper. "It was nice of you to come."

"We're all praying for you," Freddie said.

"Even George?"

That made Freddie laugh, and she was relieved to laugh. "My heathen husband," she said. "He's still making up his mind if he's a Methodist or Baptist, but he's leaning towards Methodist 'cause he doesn't want our little Claire in that pond with all the snakes. But you know, George worshipped your Ron."

"Total immersion," Beth said.

"Is it alright to mention him? I mean, I guess I did already," Freddie said.

"Perfectly alright," said Beth. "So is he, I guess, where ever he is. And I'm all right that he's all right. We're all just fine."

"Well, you look fine," Freddie said. "Really, this is such a beautiful place, it almost makes me want to—"

"Want to what?" Beth asked.

Freddie said nothing then. She dug into her purse and pulled out a box of pralines. "These are from Cy and Sherrie." Hesitating first, she said, "You're pretty thin."

"I used to be fat before they switched the medication. Now, they keep trying to feed me," Beth said. "But I'm like Simone Weil. I figure, if I eat as much as a Mississippi sharecropper, that's as much as God wants me to eat."

"Well, eat these," said Freddie. "Cy'll kill me if he hears you don't."

"Oh, Cy won't kill you," Beth said. "You should know that by now." She heard her voice break, and she wished she could take a needle and thread and repair it, make it whole again, because she couldn't bear what she was doing to Freddie, strong, wise, Freddie, who, just by looking at her, seemed to turn into a miserable girl.

"Lord, Beth," she said. "You've got to get out of here."

"Why?" Beth asked her. She couldn't help it. She had to ask.

"It's a waste," said Freddie. "That's why. It's like throwing something good away."

"Larry was thrown away," Beth said.

"What does that have to do with anything?" Freddie asked her. "I don't understand. It's like an excuse or something—pardon me for saying so. Like you've jumped ship."

Beth said, "There is no ship." But she said it so softly that she wasn't sure if Freddie heard her.

SHE KNEW SHE COULDN'T KEEP it up forever. That much had changed. When she came to the Institute, she couldn't imagine herself leaving, and now she knew that she would eventually have to go. They never mentioned the shock treatments again, but they threatened an intravenous if she didn't eat her meals. They—this generalized they, this conspiracy, this group of normal people who decided what constituted normalcy—they thought she ought to call her daughter. They said it would be an important step. They also thought she should consider a weekend visit with her father. Beth refused both requests, in part to prove she had the power to do so, and in part because accepting them would mean that she was on a particular path, the path they'd chosen.

Her weight had stabilized at just over one hundred and ten pounds. Her hair had thinned out to a kind of transparent, pink floss, and she surprised herself one morning by trying to braid it and discovering that it was almost as long as it had been in 1964, though considerably more brittle. She seemed to have been turned into another version of who she had been then, skinny, bug-eyed, only once she had been in sharp focus and now she looked as though someone had run an eraser over her.

She took to looking in the mirror. They told her father this was quite promising. He was visiting less frequently now, and when he saw her, she could tell he was suppressing something between grief and revulsion, but she didn't call him on it. She'd learned that much. In fact, she heard herself say, as from a distance, "Thank you. Thank you for saving my life." He didn't look pleased. In fact, he looked suspicious. Max Fine was no fool.

When the inevitable would come, when she would be out on the street, she knew how she would be expected to behave. It struck her that at no point in her life before did she have that knowledge. She had always improvised. Now she had rules. The rules would do her living for her. If you don't live by rules, they're waiting for you, like a pickpocket in an alleyway, like a gun in the dark, like a bomb in a car.

She asked Laurel, "Do you and Judy want a roommate?"

When Laurel hesitated, Beth shrugged.

"I understand. You figure I won't get along with your dog."

"It's only," Laurel said, "I think it's too soon to talk about that. One day at a time."

Beth kept her sardonic comments to herself, because she knew how desperately she needed Laurel to take her in. If not, she would undoubtedly end up living in some halfway house, or with her father. After Laurel left, she circled the grounds, hands thrust in the pockets of an old sweatshirt, hair pulled back hard, burning off nervous energy and wondering if she could do something wrong, anything wrong—kick over a table, climb the fence, run into the street, shout "Fuck you, nigger!" at the only black psychiatrist at the Institute—so they'd shoot electricity through her brain and burn away whatever drove her on. She walked for hours and tried to summon up the force that did when the spirit said do, but it eluded her, and the wide circles of her walk contracted until she was circling her own bed.

She laid herself down. She was spent. And she had gotten nowhere.

"FINE, GET UP."

Before she even opened her eyes, Beth knew the voice, but she thought she was dreaming.

"What are you doing, pretending to sleep? I need to talk to you, and I only have ten minutes."

"Sue?" Beth sat up. In her room, sitting in a chair by the window, was Sue Francis Walsh. She wore a loose, purple gown and a turban, and she had woken Beth up by shoving her hard, something Beth only realized when she felt the ache in her shoulder.

"You must sleep all day," Sue Francis said, "from the looks of it."

"What are you doing here? Am I dreaming?"

"I don't know," said Sue Francis. "What you dream is not my business." Her posture was erect as ever, and even after Beth sat up, she towered over her. "I can only stay for ten minutes," she said again, and to press the point, she lifted her slim arm and showed Beth her watch. It was seven in the morning.

"How'd you get here? It's not visiting hours."

"I'm not a visitor," said Sue Francis. "I've come from D.C. Interview for a fellowship at Princeton. I got a ride waiting. Knew you were here though."

"I am dreaming," said Beth. Then, the way someone would pinch herself to test the theory, she said, "Take off your turban."

"Suit yourself," said Sue Francis, and then Beth knew it had to be a dream because Sue Francis's head was shaven. It must have been done recently because it was quite smooth, the color of taffy. She put the turban on her knee and said, "I just want to know what you think you're doing."

"I'm sleeping," said Beth.

"No—what you're *doing*," Sue Francis said. "For years that's all I hear. Beth Fine was so affected by his death. She went crazy. Couldn't take it. Couldn't bear to lose him. Listen, he was my husband."

"Sue, I know—"

"No, you don't know. He was my husband. What was he to you?"

Beth was fully awake now, and this bald, stern, woman knew it; she would be responsible for what she said. She answered, "He taught me things."

"That's nice," said Sue Francis. "So what did he teach you? To fuck around in this country club?"

Beth opened her mouth and was about to tell Sue Francis what she had told Laurel and Freddie and anyone else who could follow what had felt like logic, about where life would ultimately lead them and how there was no boat and every other metaphor she'd polished through these three years since Larry died. However, she knew. That wasn't what he'd taught her, not at all. And Sue Francis would have none of it. She'd chew it up and spit it out.

In fact, Sue Francis did spit, just the way she had when she was eighteen. "You pull yourself together. You've got a child. You should be ashamed of yourself."

"I am ashamed," Beth said, though she knew that wouldn't help.

"And you stop acting like the widow. I'm the widow," Sue Francis said. She checked her watch. "Okay. I'm done here. You heard what I said?"

"You said you're the widow," Beth repeated.

"Then I've said what I came to say." Sue Francis rose and gave a final sniff. "What would it take for you to let in some air, Fine? It smells like a wet dog in here." She yanked the window open hard, and it snapped up and reverberated. "Cheap piece of shit."

She put her turban back on her head and marched past orderlies who, as it turned out, had assumed she was a doctor. It was only later that Beth would confirm they'd seen her, and so could be certain that it hadn't been a dream. There also was the open window. It let in fresh, cold air. That was real too.

Epilogue: 1986

ONCE THERE WAS A GIRL who did everything wrong. For instance, there was the time she tried to reconcile with her daughter's father. Ron had come in for Tamara's graduation, and after a number of phone calls, Beth convinced him that the three of them should visit Mississippi.

"She hasn't seen your aunt since she started spending summers with you," said Beth.

"Whose fault is that?" Ron asked. Since Tamara left for college, Ron had kept up his old habit of the weekly phone calls, only now he called Beth. The official reason was to check up on Tamara who, he claimed, was basically unreachable at school. The unofficial reason, Beth suspected, was that according to Tamara, Josephine had left him for a younger man, and he had nothing better to do with his time on a Saturday than pick a fight with Beth. It struck Beth as typical that the expensive connection from Tanzania would be used for this sort of bickering. This was the way he flirted. It always had been.

"Well no one's blaming anybody here," Beth said. "Frankly, she never showed much interest in going down to Mississippi until she met Sue Francis. You know what she said to me? She actually said 'I always thought it was just white girl's business.'"

"Oh man, baby, what did you do to that poor girl?"

"Well, me and Laurel get to talking, you know, and she starts thinking it's going to be a lot of self-congratulation. You know what Laurel's like."

"Yeah, I know. But do *you* know?"

Beth tried not to enjoy these conversations too much. They were unhealthy. Ever since Tamara had left home for Stanford, in spite of students, colleagues, and a handful of good friends, Beth had been lonely. Although she could now stay out as late as she pleased, she still found herself in bed by ten with the radio on to keep her company. For a while, she'd feared that once she was alone again, she'd start to slip, and it was a relief to find that her unhappiness was quite ordinary. Still, was it mentally hygienic, as it were, to turn down an invitation by a handsome law professor to hike on Hawk Mountain because she was expecting a call from her daughter's father?

What was worse, her airplane arrived an hour before Ron's was due, and she spent forty-five minutes in the ladies' room, opening her carry-on bag and trying on three different combinations of skirts and blouses. Her hair had been colored recently and expensively at a salon that she had only dared to enter when the woman behind the reception desk saw her gazing through the window and opened the door.

She spotted Ron immediately. She had though he'd be wearing some sort of African robe, but instead, he had on a light linen shirt and khakis, and as he'd warned her, he had grown a beard and now wore horn-rimmed glasses. Even though he was over forty, the effect was, frankly, like a little boy posing as a professor.

She could tell he was looking her over too. He tried to hide behind a yawn. "The flight here's deadly. No wonder I haven't been back for a visit."

"Well," said Beth, "there was the little matter of prison for draft evasion."

After the easy banter on the phone, Beth knew she sounded odd and artificial. She was glad that they both had luggage to claim and bags to carry so they wouldn't have to figure out what to do next, and when they took a cab to the hotel near campus, they checked into separate rooms. Then, maybe five minutes later, Ron knocked on Beth's door and they sat a distance apart on the bed, and shared a tiny bottle of Cabernet which cost, Beth speculated out loud, about as much as a laborer in Tanzania earns in a week.

"That's about right," said Ron. "That's pretty good." He moved in closer.

"Hold on," Beth said, though she could hardly control her own voice. She sat back on her hands.

"Hold on what?" Ron asked.

"Just hold on, okay? I'm just not sure."

"Baby, we're going on a long vacation. Shouldn't we figure it out early so we can just relax?"

"You've got to let me take my time," Beth said. "Go take your glass of wine to your room before you spill it all over yourself."

After Ron left, Beth wondered why she'd made him go. It felt absurd, because after all, he was right. They might as well get on with it rather than drawing it out to the point where it would start to feel significant. Yet of course, Beth wanted it to feel significant, wanted it badly. She opened another bottle and drank it all by herself.

IF TAMARA NOTICED ANYTHING STRANGE about her parents, she didn't show it. She led them around the campus, introduced them to her biology instructor, a Japanese man who seemed, to both Ron and Beth, to be suspiciously young—"You think there's something funny going on there?" Ron whispered to Beth, and Beth replied, "He's not her type"—and finally the three shared a pre-graduation dinner at a restaurant that served what Tamara called "Asian French."

"What's up with you and the Japanese guy?" Ron asked her.

"Dad, come on. I told you. He just went to the med school I'm going to go to."

"So if he's a doctor, what's he doing here?"

"He's an MD-PhD," said Tamara. "I know what you're going to say. It's a lot of letters of the alphabet. Don't even start with me." She treated Ron with an edgy indulgence that Beth envied and respected. That night, they heard her sing in the college choir. Both Ron and Beth were able to pick her voice out, like a bell in a meadow. The next day was graduation, and Beth asked her what time they should come. She said it depended on whether they wanted to go with her to synagogue.

"What the hell," said Ron, "are you talking about?"

"Oh," said Tamara. "I guess I just meant mom."

Beth said, "Okay. What the hell are you talking about?"

"I go on Saturdays," said Tamara. "It's just something I started doing. Don't worry. It's not like I joined the Moonies or anything. I mean, I'm already Jewish. If mom's Jewish, then I have Jewish blood."

"Jewish blood?" Beth shook her head. "Come on kid. You're a scientist. You know there's only one kind of blood."

Tamara's pretty, snub-nosed, flexible face screwed up tight, and she finally asked, "Why do you always do that?"

"Do what? What's she doing now?" Ron asked.

"She pretends there aren't distinctions, Dad. You know that," Tamara said, "But it's all about distinctions, and if I want to reclaim my Jewish self—"

"Oh baby," Ron began.

"I think we'd better call it a night," said Beth. She let Ron pay the check. After they dropped Tamara off, they both gave a gasp, looked at each other, and started laughing.

IT WAS, HOWEVER, NOT A laughing matter. Tamara told her parents that she would need to keep the Sabbath on her trip, which would involve some hours in a synagogue. "I know they have them in

Mississippi," said Tamara. "I did some research." She presented them with a list of towns and addresses, and when Ron asked her what she thought they'd make of a black girl coming in to pray, she just shrugged. "What do I care what they think? That's their business, not mine."

"Sweetie, what does keeping the Sabbath mean exactly?" Beth asked. "I hope you don't expect us to not turn on lights and not drive."

"I don't expect you to do anything much," Tamara said. Then she added, "I guess we might have to do some driving."

"So you're, say, sort of a California Jew?" Beth said.

"Cut it out," said Ron.

"You like this idea?"

"Yes," said Ron, looking pedantic in his horn-rimmed glasses as he read over the list. "I like it. Kind of like a Freedom Ride."

Tamara said, "You get it dad. You get the picture."

Beth shook her head, and as she helped her daughter pack up her apartment for storage, she couldn't help wondering what Grandma Risa and Grandpa Walter would make of this turn of events.

AFTER A FEW DAYS IN San Francisco, they flew to Memphis. The plan was to drive down to Tutwiler, go to synagogue in Greenwood, pass through Melody, and then make their way down to the Gulf Coast where they would leave their car in New Orleans before each of them flew home. Ron's return ticket was open. It was his first trip home in almost twenty years, and he wanted to be, as he put it, flexible. He made them rent a Cadillac. "Believe me, on a long trip like this, we won't regret it." He did the initial stretch of driving. Beth adjusted the radio and Tamara stretched out on the spacious back seat.

"Don't you want to look out the window?" Beth asked her.

"Mom, relax. I've got two weeks to appreciate Mississippi," Tamara said. "What I'm appreciating now is this back seat."

Beth turned the radio tuner, and they argued about the station in a way that was guaranteed to put Tamara to sleep. Then, Ron asked, "You got a cigarette?"

"You're in America now. We don't smoke here."

"Just one?"

Beth smiled. "If I had one, I would give it to you. But I gave you the last one in 1964."

Ron should have been keeping his eyes on the road, but he laid his arm across the seat, and looked right at her. "Now?"

"You're driving," said Beth.

"I could pull over."

"Tamara's back there. You've got to be kidding."

"Our child. She's our child, back there sleeping. She won't mind."

Beth wasn't sure if how long she could keep this up, but she didn't fight the way those fingers felt against the back of her neck. She leaned into them and let them do their work. She closed her eyes.

IT LASTED UNTIL THAT NIGHT. Grandma Risa and Grandpa Walter, white-haired and none-too-steady, hobbled out to greet them, and Tamara yelped like a little girl and tried to jump up on Grandma Risa, who held up a hand in warning and said, "Tamara, don't. I'm not a jungle gym."

"You are!" Tamara said. "You're my own personal jungle gym. I remember."

Ron shook his uncle's hand and kissed his aunt, and Beth was surprised and delighted to be led into the kitchen.

"You know how to make Green Goddess dressing?" Grandma Risa asked her. "I tried to remember the recipe, because it was Ronny's favorite, and I got most of the ingredients here." On the counter was a tin of anchovies, a tub of sour cream, some corn oil, and what looked like rehydrated parsley. "Of course, Mr. Chen had to special order the anchovies."

"Mr. Chen still owns the store?"

"Mr. Chen passed it on to his son, so now he's Mr. Chen," said Risa. She took a head of lettuce out of the icebox. Beth could see it was hard for her to bend. "Now, I made the pork already, but I was hoping you could make the salad."

Beth wasn't about to tell Grandma Risa that she wasn't sure what was in Green Goddess dressing any more than she could tell her that Tamara wouldn't eat pork. In the end, Tamara ate everything on her plate and wiped the gravy up with bread. Then, she settled on the porch to talk to Grandma Risa, and that was when Grandpa Walter pointedly directed Ron and Beth to their bed.

"You two probably won't get much in the way of privacy for a while," he said. "If I were you, I'd take advantage."

So what could Beth do? She took advantage.

AS THEY DROVE TO GREENWOOD the next morning, Tamara said she didn't want to be disrespectful to her grandparents, and that was why she ate the pork and also why she didn't leave for Friday night services right after dinner. "Honoring your family overrides everything," she said. "I read this book by Rabbi Marty Weinglass called *Body and Soul*. It talks about how following Jewish law is just a way to live an authentic life, like, with compassion."

Beth said to Ron, "Aren't you sorry you didn't baptize the girl when you had the chance?"

Ron reached behind him to touch Tamara's leg, the sort of gesture a father would make while he was in the front seat and wanted to remind his daughter that he knew that she was there. Beth was at the wheel now, driving the brief stretch of state highway to Greenwood. Tamara told them that morning services generally started at ten. It was hard to get away from William and Theresa's home before breakfast.

"I ate the bacon to honor them too, in case you were wondering," said Tamara.

"I love you," said Beth, "in case you were wondering."

"I wasn't. Thanks, I guess. And baptism was originally a Jewish practice, for your information." She looked out the window at the Mississippi Delta, hypnotic and shimmering, raked and flecked with green. A crop-duster passed overhead and the hood of the car was powdered with insecticide. Tamara closed the window.

They reached Greenwood by eleven, and as they approached the synagogue, Beth noticed that Ron had removed his arm from her back, and he was sitting half-hunched over.

Tamara said, "You were in Greenwood before—both of you—right? You must have seen this place."

"I was—we were—never in this part of town, cutie," said Ron. They were driving through the business district, past darkened storefronts, and an overwrought Chinese restaurant. None of the shops seemed open and it struck Beth that in the years since she had been in Mississippi, Greenwood had become a ghost town. Where were all the white people? There were a few dusty cars parked sideways, in a lot near the river, and in her rearview mirror, Beth could see the courthouse.

"Look. That's where your dad nearly got killed," said Beth. "You want to park and take a look?"

"We can do it later," Tamara said. "Besides, I don't think Dad wants to make a detour. He looks sick."

"I'm fine," said Ron. "I just think maybe I ought to get in back with Tamara. I get carsick up here if I'm not driving."

"You can drive if you want to," said Beth.

"We're almost there," said Tamara. She read off the address. "That's it. But it looks closed."

The synagogue was a handsome building with a brick front and stained glass windows, and Tamara got out of the car to try to open the door. Then, she knocked. Beth kept the motor running, and she said to Ron, "Really, you can drive."

"No," Ron said sharply. Then he added, "I'll take the long stretch when we go down to the Gulf."

"You don't have to prove anything."

Ron gave her a look. "Don't I?"

Then, Tamara was rapping at the car window. Beth lowered it and she said, "They only have services on Friday nights, I guess. I wonder what they do on Saturdays."

"Sweetie, they work," said Beth, and then she remembered Cy Cohen and she took a chance and said, "I promise you a synagogue in Mississippi. And a Mississippi Jew."

"I'm a Mississippi Jew," said Tamara.

Ron interrupted. "Get in the car." He looked grim. When she got in, he said, "I don't like you all bent over knocking at a window like that. It gives people the wrong impression."

"What impression is that?" Tamara asked him.

Ron didn't answer. They drove out of town, across the tracks, and Beth could see Ron's shoulders loosen as they entered the black neighborhood. He pointed out the restaurant where Movement people ate, the site of one of the SNCC offices—"We'd set them up, they'd burn them down"—and the playground close to Broad Street High where Stokely Carmichael started the people chanting "Black Power."

Tamara asked Ron, "Were you there the time SNCC threw out all the white people?"

"Man, where'd you hear a thing like that?" Ron asked her. "From that Laurel?"

Beth said, "Well, isn't it true?"

"Girl, you know yourself that times just changed," Ron said. "Of course, there were some tough cases. Remember Frank Court? We'd been up all night hashing out a position about whether Frank's anti-Vietnam work was SNCC business, and we were all tired and funky the way we got, and Frank broke away and just walked off to bed. Told me that he'd heard that when SNCC started back in 1960, they'd figured they'd last maybe about five years."

Beth said, "That was about right."

"You two are depressing me," said Tamara.

"Well talk about depressing. That used to be the garage where we kept my fleet," Ron said. It was a vacant lot now. As they turned back towards the highway, Beth slammed the brake.

"It can't be," she said.

It was: Bluebell herself, the '62 Corvair, parked in front of a Laundromat, scraped down and colorless but knocked back into the shape of a car. Its owner was piling laundry into the trunk. Ron gave a hoot and started pounding on the dashboard, and he rolled his window down and called out: "Baby, that is a lemon! You hear me? Unsafe at any speed!"

RON DROVE THE NEXT STRETCH, which meant that it took less than two hours to get to Melody. Tamara was insistent about stopping at a crossroads shack, and he consented to pull over long enough for her to try a fried pickle. Then, it was a straight run, and the Delta turned to hills, the names of towns had fewer syllables, and, as Beth said to Tamara, who was barely listening, they had passed out of what Movement people called the difficult counties to the easy ones.

"But this is where you shot the guy," Tamara said.

"I didn't shoot him," said Beth.

"You just won't admit it. That's why you haven't formed a lasting relationship, because you repressed it."

"What's this about?" Ron asked.

"Oh, Tamara has a theory," said Beth. "She took a psychology course when she was a freshman and decided that I suffer from some syndrome."

"Then I'm glad I'm driving," Ron said. Beth gave him a smack. She was, however, glad that he was driving too. She had been impressed with how calmly Ron had taken all of the changes that had marked his part of Greenwood, and as they approached Melody, she was pretty certain that she would lose her cool. Already, she noticed the new ranch houses tucked into the hills.

"You're sure there's a synagogue in this town?" Tamara asked. "It wasn't on my list."

Beth was grateful for the distraction. "It might be too small. But it was there when Laurel and I were here. I knew a guy who had a key to the place, and there was a black caretaker."

"You mean a *Gabbai*," said Tamara.

"Okay. A *Gabbai*. He was a SNCC person. And he married Freddie. She's a SNCC person too."

"Did all you people marry each other?" Tamara asked.

"Yes, and then just about all of us divorced each other. Good thing your father and I never got married."

They were turning into the road by the tracks. Ron gave Beth's shoulder a squeeze. "You want to go into town and look around some more," he asked her, "or just head straight to this guy's store?"

"We've got some Torah to read," said Beth. She didn't need to direct him to the shops between the tracks, nor was it hard to find a parking place. She recognized, with wonder, Cy Cohen's old Packard. "My God," she said, "Ron, how do you people down here keep those cars running?"

"Prayer," said Ron. He turned off the engine and said to Tamara, "Come on, Gideon. Lead the way."

Beth was relieved to find the storefront essentially unchanged. There was still the sign: COHEN'S DRY GOODS, a little more weathered, hanging a little lower on its hinge. The door, as far as she could tell, had the same piece of tape on the crack in the glass that it had in 1964. The bell still rang. There was a black teenaged girl behind the counter. She was reading a comic book.

"Hi. We're looking for Cy Cohen," Beth said. Tamara immediately broke away and started sifting through a rack of work clothes which, as far as Beth could tell, were still the same assortment that Cy had in 1964, and which had, apparently, come back into fashion.

"He's at the other store," said the girl.

Then, Beth took a chance. "Are you Claire Burgess?"

"Yeah," she said. "Why?"

Beth said, "I guess you wouldn't know me. I mean, I never met you. But I know your family pretty well. I stayed with your great aunt in 1964."

Claire's interest piqued, and she put the comic book down and said, "Were you the one with the guitar, or the one who shot a man?"

"What did I tell you!" Tamara called over. She had a jeans jacket on, and she asked, "Mom, can I buy this after Shabbat?"

Ron looked at his watch. "What time is Shabbat over? Because you've had your fried pickle, but I need my lunch."

Claire didn't seem confused by the conversation. "Shabbat's not over until late tonight—almost ten," she said. "You've got plenty of time. You want my dad to open the Temple?"

"George has the key?" Beth asked.

"Mr. Cohen has one key and my dad has the other. Now they got a *minyan* on Friday night, but it might be hard to get one together on Saturday because Saturday's the big shopping day, you know, and they got businesses to run." Claire took out a bag of pork-rinds and she said, "You want some, or are you kosher?"

"It's okay," Tamara said. "I'm not very kosher."

Beth tried to keep her head from spinning, and in the end, she balanced herself on the edge of a table where heavy T-shirts were displayed and said, "I think we ought to see if Cy Cohen can help us."

"Sure thing," said Claire. "You ought to know though that for him, women don't count when it comes to *minyan*. He says it's cause he's orthodox." She laughed. "Me, I think it's because he married a fool."

As it turned out, Cy Cohen's other shop was on Two Street, and it sold far flimsier goods, low-slung jeans, halter-tops, high boots, and tiny jackets with rhinestone buttons. They would also discover that Freddie had opened a department store of her own on Melody's main street, next to Meltzer's Shoes. Cy was often there as well. He moved from store to store, restless and increasingly cranky, and he'd grown a beard, like Ron, and wore a Texas-style string tie. Cy wept when he saw Beth, and fifteen years after the fact, she finally said, "Thank you for the pralines."

"You look terrific. I mean it." Then he said to Ron, "You're a lucky man."

Tamara was restless. "Couldn't you guys catch up after *Havdalah*?"

Cy looked downcast. "Honey, I'm sorry, but everybody works today. That's why we worship on Fridays."

"They can't get away for an hour or two?" Beth asked him. She gave Cy a long look, one with which he was familiar. He shrugged.

"You always get me into hot water, honey, you know that? Every goddamned time. I can't make any promises, but maybe I'll go around and see what I can do."

"I'll help you," said Tamara. "But I've got to count."

"One thing at a time," said Cy. "I'd gladly be the second synagogue in Mississippi to accept women in *minyans*, but I won't be the first." He shook his head again and again and said to Beth, "The girl's beautiful. I tell you, absolutely gorgeous."

"What did you think she'd be?" Beth asked, and the question stopped her short. She knew what Cy thought Tamara would be.

In THE END, THEY FOUND out that Po lived in a group home in Gulfport called the Christian Rehabilitation Center. After his mother died, friends and family had pooled their resources to send him there, and in fact, the fee was high, but it was a good place for him, they were told, and he had made a few friends and even started talking a little. As it was on the way to New Orleans, Beth convinced Ron and Tamara that they should stop and see him.

It wasn't easy. As they drove south, they argued about whether to spend the night in Jackson or to find a hotel closer to Gulfport, and Beth insisted on heading straight there. Tamara said, "If we go that far, we might as well go all the way to New Orleans."

"She's right," said Ron. "I know you feel some kind of obligation—"

"I don't feel an obligation," Beth said. "It's something I want to do." She was driving now, and she could tell that Ron wanted to get behind the wheel. He looked restless in a way that made her feel restless too. Beth said, "He's an old friend."

"Friend?" Ron turned to Tamara and asked, "Does your mother have many friends back home?"

He seemed to be joking, but Beth felt stung, especially when Tamara started to laugh knowingly. She felt her foot press on the gas a little harder, as though she could outpace her circumstances. "Look," she said, "if I know where he is, I can't just leave without seeing him. It wouldn't be right."

But when they stopped for lunch, Beth put in a call to the receptionist who said that visitors needed to register a week in advance, or there was a ten-dollar charge.

"What's that about?" Ron asked when Beth told him. "They think we're coming there to see a freak show?"

"Who knows," said Beth. "It's ten dollars. I've got it."

"That's not the point." Ron was genuinely angry. "This is—I have the word now—this is self-indulgent. We have maybe forty-eight hours left here. Is this how you want to spend it?"

Tamara said, "Stop it, both of you. Why do we even need to go there? Mom, from what you tell me, he won't even know who you are."

"That doesn't matter," said Beth. "I know who I am."

"What's that supposed to mean?" Ron asked.

"What it means," said Beth. Their platters—all three had ordered catfish sandwiches with sides of coleslaw—sat untouched. Beth wanted to say something about life, and how she saw it as a chain of actions and their consequences, but it was very much the sort of thing she would have said when she was twenty, and she couldn't use that language anymore. It wasn't so much that she had outgrown it as that she'd lost her faith in abstraction. She had more faith in people now. At least she hoped that was the case. She looked up at Ron, then, but he didn't meet her eyes.

THE FACILITY WAS A RAMSHACKLE building some miles from the beach, with a strip of highway on one side and a railroad track on the other. As it turned out, they never had to pay the fee. Po was sitting on the front porch with two other black men. One of them had an enormous forehead which made one eyebrow so high it seemed as though his face had been twisted like Silly Putty.

"I don't like this place," said Tamara.

Beth approached Po. "Hey," she said.

Po looked up. He'd gone gray, and he had another chin, but aside from that, he hadn't changed much. He was wearing a freshly laundered shirt, half-unbuttoned. Beth hadn't remembered so much hair on his chest. He nodded at Beth and said, "Yeah."

"You want to go to the beach?"

"Yeah," said Po. He looked back and forth at his two companions, and almost apologetically, rose and started down the porch. There were no guards, no groundskeepers, no one to stop him. He seemed to know where to go, as though he recognized the Cadillac. It struck Beth that anyone could have done what she did, taken him away, and killed him, left his body in a river or under a wharf. The power she held, the trust he gave her, moved her beyond comprehension.

Tamara, however, wasn't happy about sharing the back seat with Po, and Ron wasn't happy about making her do it. Everything in his manner showed his impatience and his disappointment, which Beth knew was part of a deeper disappointment. This was the last leg of the trip. The next day, the three of them would be in New Orleans, and they would get into their respective airplanes, or they wouldn't. To add another complication, to take Po to the beach during their last, few hours together, felt like a provocation.

Let it be a provocation. Beth was driving now; that Gulf road was so beautiful she might have driven on forever. On one side were those live oak trees, and on the far side was the sea. The wharves stretched out like long black fingers, and straight on ahead was Waveland, where they'd raised so many questions, and maybe it was a little like raising the dead, what she was doing. They would return Po afterwards, with his shoes in his hand and his sandy bare feet tracking up the porch, and a strand of seaweed clinging to his calf. Then, they would go on, and stay the night in that hotel in Gulfport, and the next day, she knew that she and Ron would not get on the same airplane, but she couldn't help herself. This was just who she was, and if she kept it up, she would ruin everything.

THE AUTHOR WOULD LIKE TO thank *Waveland*'s many initial readers, particularly Gail Hochman, Rebecca Tannenbaum, Dayle Zelitch, John Rufus Caleb, and Julie Odell, as well as my supremely patient husband, Doug Buchholz. I also owe a debt to David Factor whose fascination with cars of the '60s informed the direction of this novel. Sometimes, help came from unexpected places. On a road trip through Mississippi, I encountered a talkative Greenwood shopkeeper named Murray Kornfeld, and the business card from his dry goods store remains in my wallet. At a conference, I met James Kates, of Zephyr Press, a Freedom Summer volunteer who graciously and ruthlessly vetted my book for accuracy; more recently, *Waveland* got a second vetting from SNCC veteran Masaru Edmund Nakawatase who caught—among other glitches—the wrong route number on a New Jersey state highway. Any remaining errors are my fault. Of course, I am ever-grateful to Nic Esposito, Linda Gallant, Claire Margheim, Lisa McHenry Bendel and the rest of the staff at The Head & the Hand for their care, creativity, and enthusiasm.

Readers who would like to learn more about the Student Nonviolent Coordinating Committee should certainly begin with Clayborn Carson's *In Struggle,* a clear-headed, inspiriting and heartbreaking account of SNCC's origins and its multiple transformations. There are some wonderful accounts of Movement work in Mississippi, including John Dittmer's *Local People* and Charles Payne's *I've Got the Light of Freedom.* Those interested in the 1964 Summer Project will find a disproportionate number of books—precisely what SNCC staff both feared and intended when they invited close to a thousand white students to join a Black-led movement. I suggest beginning with Elizabeth Martinez's collection, *Letters from Freedom Summer,* where the volunteers speak for themselves.

EARLY SUPPORTERS:

Jean Brody
Alan Chelak
Harold and Natalie Gorvine
Rachel Kamel
Rhena Kelsen
Lance Laver
Margaret Lenzi
Eileen Levinson
Mark Roth
Jaqueline Scwartz
Carol Towarnicky
Susan Yanovski
Steven Zelitch

Simone Zelitch is the author of three novels, *The Confession of Jack Straw, Moses in Sinai,* and *Louisa,* which received starred reviews from *Library Journal, Kirkus,* and *Publishers Weekly.* Her work has appeared in the *Lost Tribe* anthology and has been read by Susan Stamberg on National Public Radio's *Hannukah Lights.* She recently discovered, to her delight, that *Moses in Sinai* is taught at the University of Miami, as part of a Freshmen seminar called "Bad Jews." She teaches at the Community College of Philadelphia.

As Beth Fine would tell her daughter years after Freedom Summer, back in 1964, she was the girl who did everything wrong. She takes part in a wade-in to desegregate a public pool, and almost drowns. When she joins Northern volunteers to staff Freedom Schools and register voters in Mississippi, she speeds down a highway, hits a cow, and ends up in jail for prostitution. Beth believes in questioning authority, and her courage and commitment to social justice both define her and lead to her undoing. Alienated from her family, she still finds herself as an outsider in a movement that exposes the limitations of her good intentions. As she strives to transcend these limitations, her commitment deepens, her questions change, and the nature of authority and justice become harder to determine.

"*Waveland* captures what it was like in 1964, to want to live for freedom and be willing even to die for freedom. It captures what it was like for young Northern volunteers to travel South to be part of a movement to make this society better. It captures the vibrant commitment of SNCC and the organizing that helped to change this country. It captures what it is like to try to live your values, try to change the world through trusting in local people and organizing, and finding perhaps you change yourself most of all."

– Heather Booth, Freedom Summer veteran and former
Executive Director of the NAACP National Voter Fund

PRAISE FOR PREVIOUS WORK

For *Louisa*:
"Haunting...a provocative depiction of the enduring mysteries of human relationships."
  – *Publishers Weekly* (starred review)

"A wonderfully bittersweet work that broods loss even as it affirms human resilience, connec and faith in providence."
  – The *New York Times Book Review*

ABOUT THE AUTHOR

theheadandthehand.com

Simone Zelitch is the author of three novels, *The Confession of Jack Straw, Moses in Sinai*, and *Louisa*. which received starred reviews from *Library Journal, Kirkus*, and *Publishers Weekly*. Her work has appeared in the *Lost Tribe* anthology and has been read by Susan Stamberg on National Public Radio's *Hannukah Lights*. She teaches at the Community College of Philadelphia.

$18

ISBN 978-0-9893125
90
9 780989 312585